Masquerades and Murder

Rachel Lynne

Seven Oaks Press

Copyright ©2022 by Rachel Lynne

All rights reserved.

No portion of this book may be reproduced in any form without written permission from the publisher or author, except as permitted by U.S. copyright law.

<u>**The Holly Daye Mystery Series**</u>

Hounds and Heists

Masquerades and Murder

Carolers and Corpses

Priests and Poison

Plantations and Allegations

Scarecrows and Scandals

<u>**The Cosmic Café Mystery Series**</u>

Ring of Lies

Holly Jolly Jabbed

Broken Chords

Contents

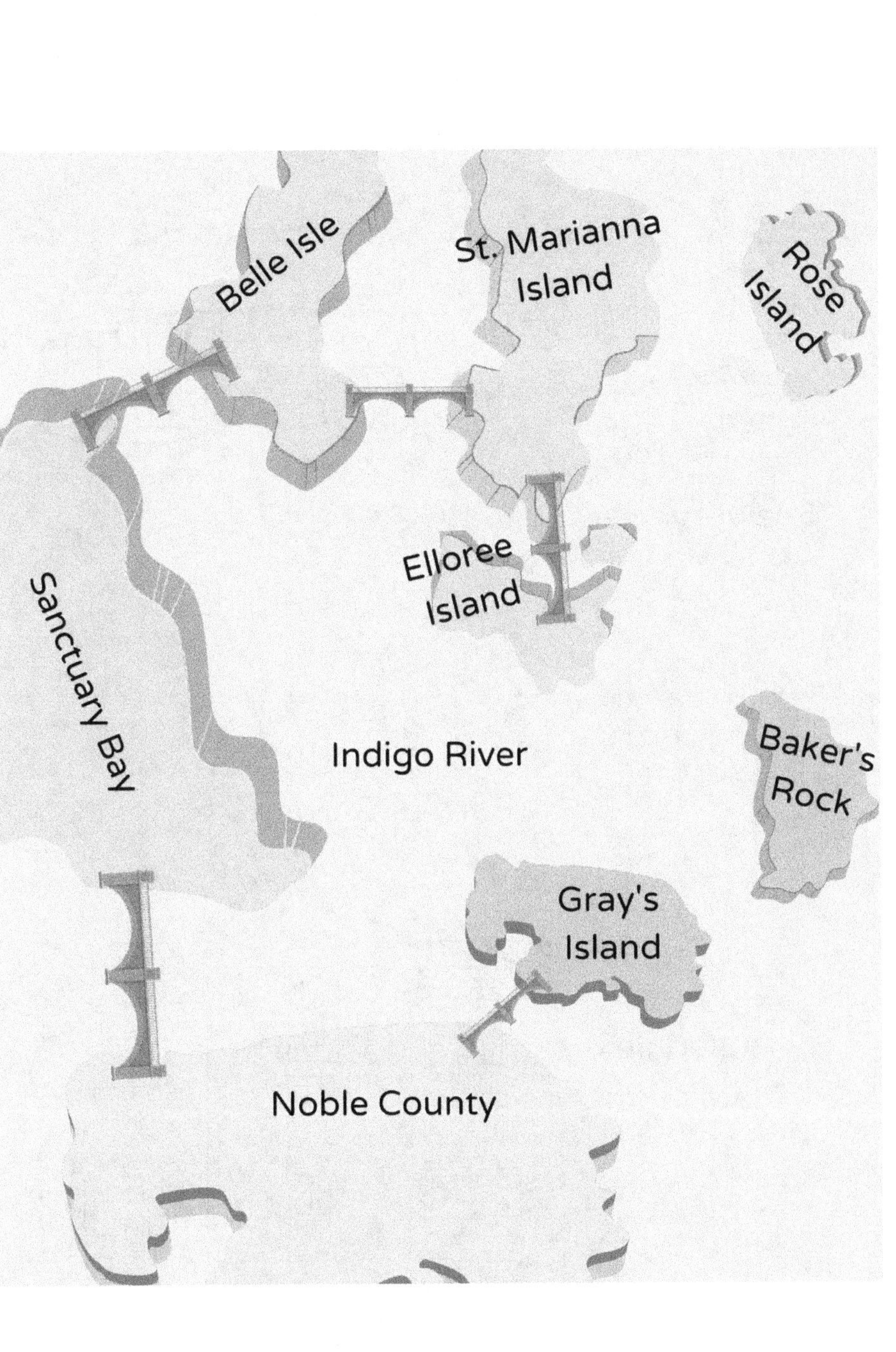

Belle Isle
St. Marianna Island
Rose Island
Elloree Island
Sanctuary Bay
Indigo River
Baker's Rock
Gray's Island
Noble County

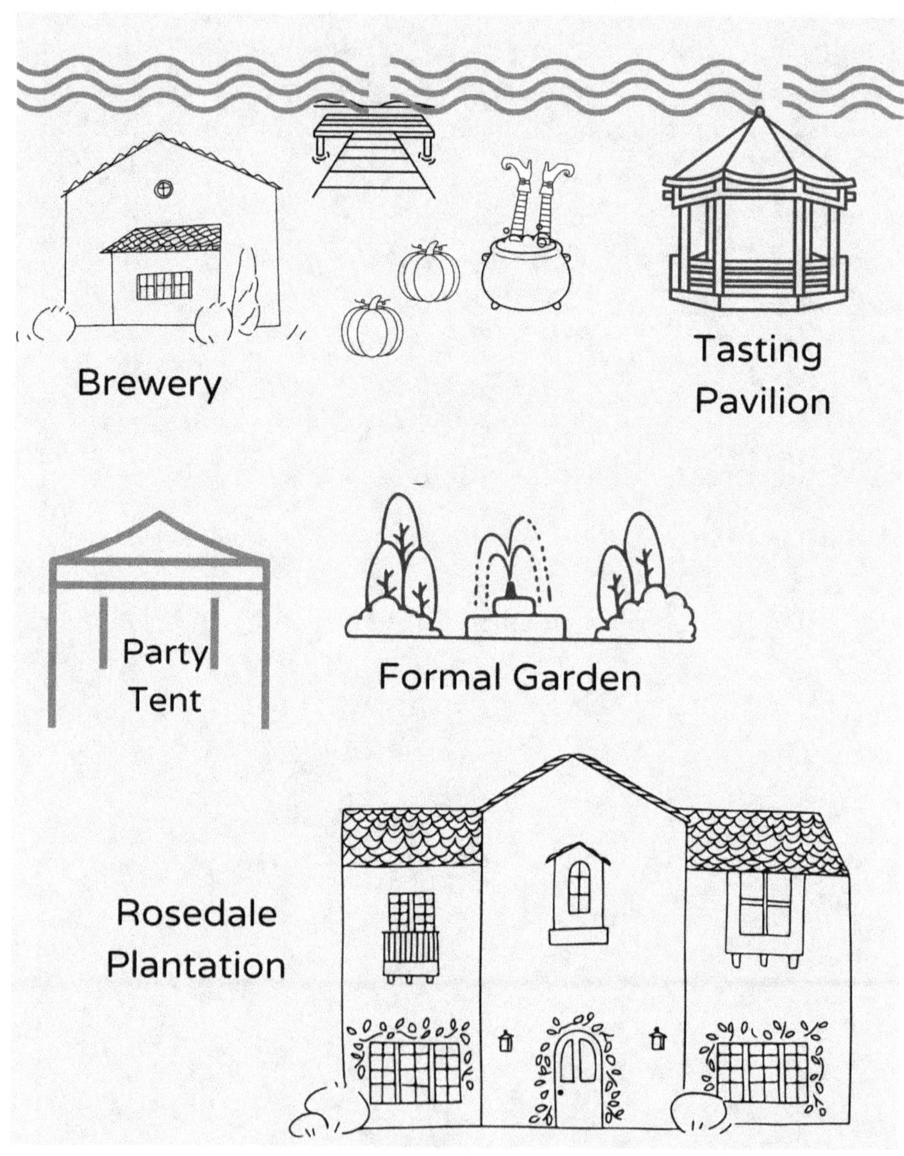

Brewery
Tasting
Pavilion
Party
Tent
Formal Garden
Rosedale
Plantation

Cast of Characters

Holly Daye

A retired deputy sheriff turned events decorator; she's never met a mystery she didn't like.

The Colonel

A brindle English bulldog. He provides emotional support for Holly, has been known to dig up a clue or three, and sometimes saves the day!

Dewey Barker

Holly Daye's younger brother. A nice guy that just needs to find a good woman to keep him on the straight and narrow; or so his mama insists.

Euphemia *Effie* Barker.

Holly Daye and Dewey Barker's doting mama. Ms. Effie is the queen of her front porch and knows everything that happens in Sanctuary Bay; if she doesn't, then it didn't happen.

Megan Hearn

A journalist turned podcaster looking to make a name for herself, by any means necessary.

Mark Timmons

Part owner of River Rat Brewery. A native of Sanctuary Bay, he longs to swim with the big fish without becoming dinner.

Glenda Timmons

Recently returned home to Sanctuary Bay, she's worked her way to the top and the brass ring is in sight; nothing will be allowed to derail her plans.

Dale Scruggs

Part owner of River Rat Brewery. A disgraced jock and failed entrepreneur, this is his last chance for glory, and nothing will keep him from scoring.

Edison Marlow

A mystery writer and toast of Sanctuary Bay society, his sparkling wit and easy charm hide shame and a longing to atone.

Jody *Griff* Reid

Prominent attorney turned congressional candidate. Losing is not an option.

Rae Ella Reid

Former Miss South Carolina, she's played the dutiful wife and mother, but the act only goes so far.

Chapter One

A soft tug on the leash and a click of my tongue were all it took to set The Colonel in motion. He snuffled among the shrubs lining the gravel path, marked a few spots, and then looked up at me with his typical bulldog grin.

"All done, boy?" The full-body wiggle reply lightened my mood and put a smile on my face; my furry friend never failed to lift me out of the dumps, though the relief was fleeting in this case.

I blew out my breath and started walking back towards the white party tent, careful to brace my cane before trusting it with my weight. The gravel paths that connected the boathouse and gardens of Rosedale Plantation had caused me considerable trouble all afternoon but, with my brother's help, I'd managed to decorate the tent and grounds in less time than I'd estimated, though not without confrontation.

I gritted my teeth. My brother had packed up the truck and left hours ago, but I was still irritated with him. Dewey had been a magnet for trouble since we were kids, and I should never have listened to Mama and hired him.

However, my injuries had left me with no choice. I couldn't climb a ladder, and using the cane meant I couldn't even carry much. Those facts didn't ease my temper. Dewey, as usual, had managed to get into a scrape, and of all people, he'd chosen to anger Megan Hearn; it'd be all over the county before morning!

The incident with the local podcaster and all-around arrogant little madame was fresh in my mind. It seemed like she went out of her way to set people's backs up- speaking of ... I frowned and peered into the shadows as angry voices rang out. Someone was pitchin' a fit.

"I don't have it!"

"Find it, or else …"

"… the beach …"

The reply was muffled, and I couldn't tell if it was a man or a woman but whoever they were, they were very angry and that set off my cop radar. Even retired, the training never went away.

I snapped the leash and directed The Colonel to change directions. We were moving towards the entrance to the gardens and the source of the argument when Megan Hearn stomped out.

I snorted. Now, why wasn't I surprised? I was ten feet away and darkness was closing in, but I could see that her lips were pursed, and her jaw was clenched. She stalked towards the tent, glaring at her phone and muttering under her breath. She looked up and met my gaze as she passed. Whew, if looks could kill!

I wondered whose cage she was rattlin' now. My eyes widened as Edison Marlow stepped through the garden gate. He stopped to adjust his houndstooth cape and straighten his deerstalker cap before slipping his pipe between his lips and heading back to the party.

The mystery author and I had met earlier in the evening, I'd complimented him on choosing the Sherlock Holmes costume. While only a brief conversation, I'd found him witty and urbane. He'd have been the last person I'd expect to find embroiled in an altercation, especially in a public place but then Megan Hearn could start an argument in an empty house.

Her behavior earlier in the day still astonished me. Though Glenda Timmons had arrived in time to calm the situation before more than a handful of people could rubber neck, just thinking about her temper tantrum and shouting match with my brother made me cringe.

It had been unprofessional, and my mind kept dwelling on it, wondering if I could have done something different …

"Dewey, if you could just climb up there and straighten the fourth pumpkin from the left I think we can consider it done."

The jack-o-lantern arch at the entrance to the brewery had been a great idea on paper, but I'd underestimated how many craft pumpkins we'd needed. That had led to sending Dewey to the store, and to Jed Prine's house to borrow his Dremel tool so I could carve two dozen silly faces in under an hour.

While he was gone, I'd rushed to begin assembling the witch's circle and cauldron display on the stage where the brewery owners would launch the new line but there were still little things to be done and guests were arriving!

I blew out a breath and tried to calm my rising panic. I'd seen the caterers getting ready and the sounds of a string quartet tuning up drifted on the breeze.

"Ah Holly, it looks fine, let's just-"

"Ahh!"

A woman's scream jolted me. Halfway up the ladder, Dewey's wide-eyed gaze met mine for a split second before he leaped off and raced up the path in the direction of the sound with The Colonel hot on his heels. I hobbled after them, as fast as a stiff leg and a cane would allow.

A hedge of camellias framed a formal garden designed in a grid pattern. Geometrically shaped beds were filled with flowers and fanciful topiaries enticing visitors to explore. The four main paths met at a bubbling fountain framed by lush potted Sago palms.

Raised voices, one clearly belonging to my brother, led me to the fountain, where I found a bevy of brightly costumed guests staring in scandalized fascination as local podcaster, and legend in her own mind, Megan Hearn berated Dewey while The Colonel barked, growled, and pawed at their legs.

Winded, I leaned on my cane and caught my breath while I tried to piece together the problem. Megan, dressed as a 1950's girl in cherry red pedal pushers and a white shirt, was dusting herself off and rubbing her bottom as she screeched at Dewey and pointed at the path.

"You're a menace!" Her blond hair was styled in a high ponytail with a red and white polka-dotted scarf tied as a bow bouncing as she tossed her head. Bright red lipstick and a cat-eyed mask completed her look. The only anachronisms to her costume were her dangling emerald and diamond earrings and a pair of red-soled black stiletto heels.

Oooh, those had set her back a pretty penny! They were also her problem. Who wore four-inch pointy heels to an event held on the lawn? And those earrings were more suited to a glitzy ball than an outdoor masquerade party.

"Lady, I was just helping you up!" Dewey pressed his palm to his cheek and scowled at her.

What-my eyes widened as Dewey moved his hand. Three long red scratches marred his face. She'd scratched him? I was about to step in when Dewey shushed The Colonel and then turned back to Megan.

"Look, are you all right? 'Cause I gotta get back to work-"

"You left that cord there!" Megan hissed at Dewey. "I could have been killed! What kind of idiot runs an extension cord across a sidewalk? I'll have you fired-"

"Ma'am, I didn't-"

"Yes you did, and I am going to tell Mark to ..." Megan's hissy fit continued for several minutes, with Dewey trying to pacify her and The Colonel adding to the mayhem with his vocal antics.

I called Dewey's name under my breath as I kept a tight smile on my face. The longer Megan fussed the more the crowd grew. I recognized Edison Marlow, his book was being turned into the TV show they'd been filming on Bay Street, along with Sanctuary Bay's mayor, Councilman Vanderhall, and Glenda, the wife of one of the owners of River Rat Brewery. Just what I needed.

My smile morphed into a grimace as I made eye contact with Rae Ella Reid. Lovely. If Rae Ella was there then her husband Griff wasn't far behind and dollars to donuts, my ex-husband and his latest toy were also somewhere close by; Griff Reid being Brooks' law partner and a seated congressman *if* he won the upcoming election.

This was why I'd planned to be long gone before the party started! I whistled for The Colonel and called Dewey's name again but both males were committed to their battle of wits with the unarmed woman.

I was debating the best way to avoid more of a scene while praying Megan would run out of steam when she lifted her stiletto-clad foot and attempted to kick The Colonel.

It all happened so fast ...

"And shut that stupid mutt up-"

Megan's sharp heel was poised to connect with my buddy's fat belly and Dewey rushed to his rescue.

"Lady, you touch that dog and it'll be the last thing you do!"

My eyes about popped from their sockets as Dewey stepped between Megan and The Colonel. Her foot hit Dewey's shin, he jerked away, and the mouthy podcaster once more found her butt meeting gravel.

The telenovela-level hysterics had been my cue to act. Over the course of my twenty-five years as a sheriff's deputy, I'd perfected my *cop* tone. I stepped between the two but before I could say anything, Glenda Timmons rushed over and took charge.

"Ms. Hearn, are you all right?" Glenda met my gaze and flashed a tight smile. "I'll take it from here, Ms. Daye. Please continue with your work."

Gladly. I motioned for Dewey to skedaddle and turned to follow him, but an inelegant snort from Megan drew my attention. I turned my head in time to see her smirking at Glenda while fingering one of her gaudy earrings.

Megan's actions were odd, but even more puzzling was Glenda's reaction. The older woman had turned white as a sheet and her throat moved convulsively. She brought a trembling hand to her mouth, stifling a cry. I'd started toward the women when Glenda spun on her heel and raced out of the garden.

The podcaster watched Glenda run away with a smile twisting her lips. Her scornful expression made the hair raise on the back of my neck. The woman seemed to thrive on provoking others.

Megan was bad news and, thankfully, not my problem. From the sounds of her quarrel with Edison, she was dedicated to ticking off everyone within a quarter-mile radius. I shook my head and moved to rejoin the party.

Completing the event decorations ahead of schedule should have meant I was relaxing with a good book while soaking my leg in the hot tub but, due to my inability to say no ... I sighed and pulled at the mask covering my eyes. This is what came from having well-meaning friends. *You need to get out. You need to socialize.* Or my favorite. *Get back on the horse, Holly!*

If that meant dating then no thanks, after a nasty divorce, I had no interest in bringing a man into my life any time soon. I snorted and pushed past merry revelers, intent on finding my table and parking myself in a chair for the evening, but the universe had other plans.

"Holly! There you are. Come and meet some friends of mine."

I pinned a smile on my face and allowed Louise *'Lou Lou'* Tomlin to halt my progress.

Ms. Lou Lou was the current mayor of Sanctuary Bay, but that wasn't the reason I'd let her derail my plans. She was one of Mama's oldest friends, and she'd taught my Sunday School class.

I shifted my cane to my other hand and gave the tiny woman a one-armed hug. "Hey Ms. Lou Lou , how are you?"

Careful not to smear her lipstick, she air kissed my cheek. "I'm doing well, Holly Marie." She patted my arm and turned to a couple standing across from us. "Holly, I'd like you to meet Tim and Heather Rudd. They've just moved down from Connecticut."

My eyes widened behind the mask, another family coming from the north. The Lowcountry had seen an unprecedented influx of people moving from the colder regions lately; If we weren't careful, they'd start mistaking us for Florida!

I smiled and offered my hand. "Holly Daye, nice to meet you. What brought y'all down this way?"

Lou Lou jumped in before either of the Rudds could reply.

"Tim and Heather bought a home in Bayview Estates." She cocked her head and looked at Heather. "The Adams place and Tim is going to be working with Ed Whitten. Won't that be nice?"

"Mmmm, yes." My smile was forced. Northerners buying up our founding families' homes and working for Royal Ventures; Nice wasn't the word I would have used. Ed Whitten was a hot-shot investment banker, and his firm was responsible for the development of several new golf communities in our area.

Too much of our natural landscape was being gobbled up by developers and our roads were clogged with the added traffic. Thank God the hurricane that had come up the coast a few weeks ago had stayed offshore enough that damage was negligible and limited to the barrier islands.

We wouldn't remain that lucky though, and with the rapid population increase evacuation would be a nightmare. Still, Lou Lou loved all of the growth, as did most of the businesses in town.

As a former deputy, I saw the influx as a mixed blessing. More services as the tax base increased, but that also meant more crime, not that it was my problem anymore.

I shook off my pessimistic thoughts as Heather addressed me. "Ms. Daye, the mayor says that you are responsible for the party décor?"

I nodded and braced myself for criticism. I should never have let my friend Connie talk me into accepting the job. She was the one that had gone to college and then opened the Glitter and Garland craft store.

The brewery had wanted her to design their event, not me. A conflict in her schedule should have sent them elsewhere but Connie had recommended me instead.

What did I know about decorating? Yes, I did Mama's porch up for every holiday and yes, Connie and I had been in charge of proms and the like in high school, but I had no formal training; I'd dropped out of art school, and being crafty wasn't enough-

"I'm sorry?" I shook my head and focused on what Heather was saying.

She smiled. "I was just saying how much Tim and I love what you've done in here." She glanced around the tent, pointing at the round tables covered in black cloths and lace toppers. "It's very Edgar Allen Poe and those centerpieces are divine! Did you design those?"

A genuine smile lit my face as I realized she wasn't going to complain. Connie and I had chosen to do a Victorian gothic theme for the party tent, leaving the traditional Halloween kitsch for the brewery areas down by the boathouse. I'd found some stuffed ravens and that had set Connie's mind working.

In the end, we designed floral pieces with curly twigs and Spanish Moss to house the birds. Blood red roses and seeded eucalyptus made up the base and we'd added candles and natural curiosities among the flowers.

"The mayor tells me we're neighbors, too! I love what you did with your porches!"

I smiled and shifted so my weight wasn't on my bad leg. I bit my lip and wondered how to get out of the conversation. They were nice and all, but I needed to sit down. "Um, thanks. Uh, it was nice to meet y'all, I need to-"

"We won't keep you; only would you have time to come by the house and give us a quote on decorating for Thanksgiving and maybe for Christmas, too? Tim's family is coming down for the holidays and I'd love to show the new house off ..."

My eyes widened. She wanted to hire me? To decorate her house for a holiday? "Uh, sure, I guess. I mean, you know I'm not a professional -"

"Holly will get with you early next week, Heather. Excuse us, won't you?" Ms. Lou Lou took my arm and guided me away.

"I'll get you her number, Holly Marie, and don't you dare not call!" She steered me toward my table, a smile on her face as she scolded me through her teeth. "Tellin' folks you aren't a decorator! Here I am getting you business and you go-"

"Ms. Lou Lou , I'm just being honest! I don't want to lead people on or-"

"Sit yourself down, I noticed you rubbing that leg." She perched on the edge of the chair beside me. "I talked with Effie just yesterday and she says you've been trying to get out of this brewery job for weeks-no, and I don't want to hear any of your excuses!"

She huffed. "You don't need a college degree to decorate, young lady!" She patted my arm and rose. "You listen to me, you're gifted. This tent is fine as feathers, no fancy decorating company from Charleston could have done better. Lots of people are talking about how good it all looks and I'm telling them to get in touch with you," she wagged a finger at me. "So don't you go talking them out of hiring you!"

She stared at me until I squirmed and muttered. "Yes ma'am."

Lou Lou nodded. "That's all right then. You rest and I'll check in with you at the end of next week. The chamber of commerce is talking about a Christmas village in Goodwin Park, and I think they should consider you for the job-ah ah, don't argue."

She flitted off before I could protest, leaving me to roll my eyes and wonder what I'd done to deserve a town full of managing females on my case; the answer was being the child of Euphemia Sinclair Barker.

A muffled laugh from behind me had me twisting in my seat. Edison Marlow grinned at me and tipped his glass in a silent salute.

"You handled that with aplomb. Busy bodies," He shook his head. "I'd have lost my temper."

I smiled. "Nah, I'm used to it. She didn't mean any harm."

He shrugged. "Maybe not, but this town ..." He gave a mock shutter. "I've been back less than a month and I'm ready to climb the walls."

I nodded. "Not much to do compared to- where were you living?"

"California, and yes, Sanctuary Bay is lacking in night-clubs, museums, concerts ..., but I could deal with that. It's the nosiness I find intolerable."

My lips twisted into what I hoped was a smile reflecting sympathy, though I had no reply to his statement. I'd grown up knowing most of the town was watching my every move; it'd kept me on the straight and narrow, though it had made my brother sneaky. I frowned. Edison was also a native son. I said as much and was rewarded with a laugh.

"Oh yeah, I had the dubious honor of being born here, but I ran off to college not long after I graduated."

"Oh, I must have misread the article."

He cocked an eyebrow in question.

"The paper ran a feature on you a few weeks back. Announced the filming of your TV series, congratulations, by the way."

"Thanks, it's pretty wild. A lot to get used to in addition to being back here." He chuckled. "Heard I missed the hurricane.

Can't say I'm sad about that! Not sure which is worse, Cali's earthquakes and wildfires or our storms."

"Oh, earthquakes no contest, we have lots of warning before a hurricane blows in."

He nodded. "True. But I still don't plan on riding a hurricane out. Was there much damage with this last one?"

I shrugged. "Eh, not bad in Sanctuary Bay. Most of the storm stayed offshore but a few bands caught Rose Island ... oh, and the storm surge destroyed an old hunting cabin out on Shell Point. You heard about what they found during clean-up?"

Edison licked his lips and looked everywhere but at me as he shifted in his chair. "Shell Point? I don't think I know where that is ... but either way, I've been busy since I got back."

"I'm sure." I laughed. "tell me where you hide though because the whole town is buzzing over the news, and you were a teenager in Noble County and never went to Shell Point? It was *the* hangout in my day!"

His smile waned and he fiddled with his pipe. "Ha, guess it wasn't trendy by the time I was of age and, as to hiding ..." He chuckled and shook his head. "Sorry, no safe space, just lots of writing and meetings with the producers." He propped his elbows on the table and rested his chin on his palm. "So, what has the whole town talking, I thought the news of the month was the filming of my book."

"Oh, that's also a hot topic but the gossip mill is having a field day speculating on the identity of the remains they found at Shell Point- you all right Edison?" The author suddenly looked like he was going to toss up his dinner.

Was it something I said, or something he ate? I touched his arm, and he jolted back like he'd been struck by lightning. "You don't look so good; can I get you some water?"

He gulped and directed a wide-eyed and slightly glassy stare over my shoulder. "No, um, I'm fine, will you excuse me? I need to uh, get some air."

"Sure, nice talking to you ..." He was gone before I finished my sentence. I watched him exit the tent, brushing off several people's attempts to stop and talk. One minute he'd been fine and then like flipping a light switch- I was thinking back over our conversation when The Colonel whined.

"Hey buddy, you tired of that old hard floor?" He wiggled and hit my leg with his big foot. I assumed I'd guessed correctly and pulled a chair closer. I helped him into the seat, and he snuffled at my hand, did an awkward turn, and then settled with a huff.

A glance at my phone suggested something other than sitting on the floor was bothering him. "Sorry buddy, we'll go just as soon as I can politely escape." I laughed and patted his head. "Feeding you will be my excuse!"

The Colonel, unimpressed with my strategy, merely sighed and closed his eyes, leaving me to entertain myself. I adjusted my mask and propped my chin in my hand. The dinner portion of the party was limited to a handful of dignitaries and local influencers. Why I'd been included as a guest was beyond me and, if not for well-meaning friends, I'd have ignored the invitation.

I had to hand it to the River Rat Brewery. Holding a masked ball on Halloween to celebrate the launch of their newest ale was a hit with the locals. Whether that translated to high sales for their Witch's Brew remained to be seen.

My gaze landed on the cluster of friends responsible for my attending the event instead of just decorating it. I snorted. Scooby-Doo and the Gang.

Craig Everette, one of my oldest friends and my former boss was dressed as Fred which went perfectly with his current girlfriend's auburn hair. My intrepid journalist friend Jessica Ziggler was perfect as the uber-smart Velma, which left me ... and The Colonel.

I shook my head. The Shaggy costume of brown corduroy pants and an oversized green shirt was certainly the most comfortable I'd ever donned, but my English bulldog was a far cry from a Great Dane!

Correction, he was dopey enough to easily be in character. Not that I'd admit it to Jessica, but her idea had been a clever workaround to my needing a support animal.

That I needed emotional comfort for my continuing anxiety was a sore spot with me; I should have been stronger, should have been able to bounce back, regardless of the shrink saying it was normal after the trauma I'd suffered.

I rolled my eyes and sat back in my chair. Was being shot during a routine summons delivery *really* traumatic? People had suffered far worse than me and not become a basket case. I despised my inability to move on even as I was powerless to stop my mind from replaying what little I recalled of the shooting on an endless loop. Just thinking about it made my mouth go dry and my hands tremble.

The clearing was dark except for the headlights on the truck. Where have they gone? I know I saw people- a flash, searing pain, darkness- I gulped a glass of water and shook my head, pushing away all thoughts of that night. I was not about to have a full-on anxiety attack in public!

I needed a distraction. I let my gaze roam around the tent as I massaged my thigh and fought to control my breathing. I concentrated on stroking The Colonel's wiry coat, feeling his warmth embrace my shaking hand ...

I exhaled slowly. The tension eased from my muscles, and I leaned back in my chair. Huh, it'd worked! A mental high five to the shrink. I drew a few more deep breaths and let my gaze wander. The brewery's choice of dinner guests puzzled me.

Inviting the mayor, councilman, and a congressional candidate made sense if you were trying to get noticed in Sanctuary Bay, as were the invitations to lead reporter Jessica and wealthy socialite Marla Cassidy; Craig was here as Marla's guest.

It was likely the Rudds had been sent to represent Royal Ventures since Ed Whitten hadn't put in an appearance. I frowned as my gaze landed on Edison Marlow. The color had returned to his face, and he seemed relaxed and focused on having a good time. He was laughing at something a man in a gladiator costume was saying.

Mayor Lou Lou was talking with Councilman Vandershall, Craig and Marla were at the bar, Jessica was slightly farther away and seemed to be part of a crowd surrounding Griff Reid and ... I squinted, though how that was going to help me see through people was beyond me.

Dale Scruggs was playing the good host, but his business partner was absent. I glanced around, looking for the Greek goddess costume Glenda was wearing but she was nowhere to be seen.

Dale Scruggs. He'd certainly come out smelling like a rose after the disaster of his last business venture not to mention the scandal in his high school days. I wondered if Mark knew how Dale had lost the three gyms he'd run in the Lowcountry.

Perhaps he'd changed. My inner skeptic snorted at the idea. I told her to pipe down. It was possible. People grew up and learned from their mistakes-regardless, it was none of my business.

To my shock, my ex-husband wasn't present, whether because he hadn't been invited or had other plans I could only guess. Either way, I was grateful because I wasn't sure I could have been civil.

I'd known Brooks Daye since high school. We'd dated, I'd become pregnant, we'd married. End of story, until I'd gotten myself shot and Brooks decided my injuries and then recovery were too boring and exhausting.

He'd gone and found himself a girl younger than our son and Jessica had told me yesterday that a rumor was running through the country club; Brooks was gonna be a daddy again.

I huffed and pushed thoughts of Brooks away, I had enough on my plate without worrying about him. My leg was starting to throb. I kneaded the muscles and looked for more to occupy myself.

A round of curses rang out, drawing all eyes to the cluster of people standing by the bar. Craig and Marla had turned toward the commotion and Councilman Vandershall was shaking his head and backing away.

I frowned. What was going on? I started to stand for a better look but a flash of red, followed by another burst of profanity and then a parting in the crowd told me all I needed to know.

Megan Hearn. Could that woman go an hour without causing a commotion? She turned and said something to Griff Reid before stalking out of the tent. Always drama with that one.

I shook my head and turned my attention to what remained of our dinner. If they didn't get a move on and start the product launch I was gonna have to beg a ride because the only suitable treat for The Colonel was a bit of yeast roll and he wasn't gonna be a happy camper with that offering.

Lack of red meat notwithstanding, the menu had been delicious. A spotlight on local delicacies. She-crab soup, grilled shrimp, Carolina Gold rice ... I was as full as a tick and had no desire to participate in the next portion of the evening, though I couldn't deny that I was looking forward to everyone's reaction to the scene I'd assembled at the tasting pavilion.

The new brew's name had inspired me to assemble a witch's circle and cauldron, complete with dry ice and green lights. At the last minute, I'd put a pair of witch's legs upside down in the cauldron and the overall effect was classic, funny Halloween, or at least I thought so. Dewey had grumbled that it was cheesy but what did he know-my phone rang, and I sighed. Speak of the devil ...

"Hey Dewey, what's up?" I braced myself because my brother wasn't ever going to call me *just to chat*. He either needed something, had *done* something, or there was a problem with Mama.

"Hey Holly, just wanted to tell ya I gotta come back to Rosedale."

I frowned. "What? Why? Are you here now?" I could hear road noises in the background, but I wasn't sure if he was coming or going.

Dewey huffed. "I got home and cleaned out your truck, but I couldn't find the Dremel kit, and I promised Jed I'd drop it off tonight; he's got some project he needs to finish this weekend."

My eyes widened. I hadn't wanted to borrow tools from Jed for just this reason! Daggum irresponsible Dewey! Now I'd have to buy Jed a new-

"Holly? You there?"

"Yeah."

Dewey huffed. "No need to get snippy ..." He continued to ramble on about the toolbox, how he'd left it behind, and something about Megan Hearn but I tuned him out and concentrated on getting to my feet. The need to shout was rising in me and I'd prefer to do that without an audience.

I rustled The Colonel from slumber and limped out of the tent, plastering a smile on my face as I encountered Griff Reid and Rae Ella at the tent entrance. They were coming back in but stepped aside to let me and my dog pass.

I nodded and kept moving, pantomiming taking a call so I wouldn't have to stop and chat. Not that they looked as if they'd welcome conversation. Griff's jaw was tight, and his lips were pursed while Rae Ella's lower lip trembled, and the tip of her nose was red. A major faux pas for a former beauty queen.

She looked as if she'd been crying. I shook my head. Seemed more people than just Megan Hearn were incapable of having a pleasant and peaceful evening. I was beginning to wonder if it was something in the water.

I wandered down the main path a ways and then plopped down on a stone bench while Dewey continued to burn my ear. A pause in the conversation let me get a word in edgewise.

"Are you sure you know where you left the toolbox?" I rolled my eyes as Dewey again took me step by step through his movements when he'd last had the kit. "That's fine, Dewey. Look, I'm gonna- hold on, Dewey."

A man's voice reached my ears. Sounded like someone was making an announcement. I frowned and tilted my head, though why I thought that'd let me hear any better ... Movement at the tent entrance followed by laughing guests exiting drew me to my feet.

It looked like we were finally going to head to the brewery. A band was scheduled to perform after the launch, but I had no intention of staying. For once, Dewey's mistake was gonna be of benefit to me; I wouldn't have to beg for a ride home.

"Hey Dewey, I'm gonna head down and pick the toolbox up-oh, you're in the parking lot? Well, wait for me, I'm gonna catch a ride home." I hung up and clicked my tongue. The Colonel snuffled and grunted a few times and then reluctantly got to his feet.

I stifled a laugh. He was at the end of his tolerance for people, walking, and an empty belly. Any minute *stubbornitis* was gonna set in and someone would have to carry him to the truck.

"Come on boy, Dewey's waiting." That seemed to perk him up, whether because he liked my brother or just associated him with food was anyone's guess; Dewey had a habit of slipping the dog treats.

The guests were meandering through the gardens, so I took the direct route across the lawn and in minutes I was in front of the boathouse. Voices sounded from behind me as the other guests drew closer. I picked up my pace and headed down the path to the tasting pavilion.

The boathouse resembled a two-story bungalow. Clad in cedar shake, it had arched windows and a porch running the full width of the ground floor. They'd converted it to a micro-brewery, but it'd been too small for a tasting area so a pergola, complete with a small stage and tables had been erected along the banks of the river.

We'd decorated the porch with the pumpkin arch and framed the door with bundles of corn stalks but most of our décor had been reserved for the launch area. I moved down the path as fast as my cane enabled; I wanted some evening pictures of my decorations before everyone crowded around.

I was halfway to the pavilion when my cane lost purchase on the path. I wobbled but was able to steady myself by grabbing hold of the shrubs that lined the walk; I saved myself a face plant but now I reeked of rosemary.

A glance at the concrete showed nothing but a scattering of soil. My brow furrowed. A bit of dirt would cause my cane to slip? I gritted my teeth. From the beginning I'd chafed at my injuries and the limitations they brought but, ten months later I wanted an end to it all. I started physical therapy next week and, for once I was excited to go to the doctor; rehabilitation couldn't come soon enough.

I wiped the rubber tip of my cane on the grass and continued walking. I'd taken no more than four steps when a rustling came from the hedge. Before I could stop him, The Colonel started barking and lunging.

"Colonel, that's enough!" I'd tried to hold him back, but he was on the scent of something and before I knew it, he'd jerked the leash from my hand and taken off. He was closing in on the shrub line, barking and growling for all he was worth when someone shot out of the hedgerow and ran back into the garden.

It'd been too dark to see who'd been hiding, a flash of light clothing was all I'd really noticed plus, I was too concerned with getting my dog back to worry over much, probably a guy using the bathroom. "Boy, come here!" I whistled and he stopped, though he was primed to race off again.

I patted my leg and pitched my voice to sound happy and relaxed. "Colonel, come on, hurry, hurry ..." His tongue lolled from his gaping mouth and every part of his pudgy body was wiggling and twitching.

I knew that look, any minute he'd dart off in hopes we would play his favorite game of, *I'm gonna getcha.* I sighed and used my entreaty of last resort. "Colonel ... you wanna treat?"

His ears twitched and he tipped his head. "Yeah? Treat? You gotta come here, come on!" He rushed toward me, and I was able to grab the leash. It never failed but now I was gonna have to reward him.

"Come on you little rascal, we'll find Dewey and he'll get you a treat from the truck." I continued down the path, yammering with my dog and listening to the chatter coming from the garden; the rest of the guests would catch up with me in a few minutes.

I rounded the bend and slowed as the courtyard came into view; something wasn't right. The pavilion was much darker than I remembered from previous visits. The pergola was equipped with lighting, and I'd added more to highlight the decorations so why was the stage area so dark? I squinted and looked toward the stage.

My witch's circle and the eerie green smoke rising from their cauldron were just visible in the glow of the faux fire light. I could see the outline of legs amidst the fog-I frowned, why did the green and white striped stockings have a red cast?

I jumped as something moved in the shadows next to the pot. "Dewey?"

A grunted reply raised gooseflesh. I moved closer. "Dewey? Is that you?" I could now see the outline of the witches as well as the figure of a man- I scowled. "Dewey Barker, why didn't you answer me?"

I shook my head and hobbled over to the post that held the switch for stage lights. Enough messing around. A crunch of gravel and laughter announced the arrival of the other guests. They'd start the presentation any minute and I still hadn't gotten my pictures ...

I flipped the switch. Light flooded the stage, a woman shrieked, and all hell broke loose.

I twisted around and gulped. Dewey was standing on the edge of the stage. His mouth was hanging open and his eyes were wide as he stared at the cauldron and the pair of legs clad in cherry red pedal pushers and black stiletto heels rising from it.

Chapter Two

The floor of the front porch was becoming a sea of black and orange as I removed the Halloween decorations. I slipped a black grapevine wreath off its hook and replaced it with an orange and teal pumpkin wreath. I fluffed the Buffalo check bow and stood back to allow Mama to exit.

"What do you think, Mama?"

She set the plastic totes down and walked to the edge of the porch, unwrapping a gold chocolate bar. "Hmmm, I love those colors but what about either side of the door?" She wrinkled her nose. and waved with her candy. "It looks bare now that you've taken the ghosts and signs down."

"Yes ma'am, I was thinking corn stalk bundles with mums in front-" I paused as Mama made a face. "No on the corn stalks?"

Mama nodded. "You do what you think best, Holly Marie, but they make such a mess ..."

Which was code for, don't put those things on my porch. I hid my smirk and gave her my second option. "Yes ma'am, they do. How about I put some at the light post by the drive and maybe the other bundle by the mailbox? The leaf blower can take care of the clean-up."

She clapped her hands and smiled. "A wonderful idea. You're so clever." She sat down and sipped her tea while nibbling on her treat.

I cocked my head to the side and frowned. "Mama, where did you get that?"

"Oh!" She broke off a piece and handed it to me. "Come get some, it's quite good." She looked down at the large piece still in the wrapper. "I didn't hold out much hope, considering ..."

The chocolate melted in my mouth. I swallowed and then asked. "Considering, what? Where'd you get this?"

"That church is selling them door to door, and they stand outside some of the shops."

"Which church is that?" I wiped my fingers on a napkin and then returned to packing the decorations. "I don't think I've seen them ..."

"I can't imagine how you've missed them ... In any event, they just did a write-up in the paper about how the pastor is a reformed delinquent and he's dedicated to keeping kids from following in his footsteps. I forget his name ... Luke? No, Duke, like the mayonnaise. Duke Mobley and I don't know what denomination he could be. Certainly not one of the regular ones." She shook her head and sighed. "Long hair on a preacher, what is this world coming to?"

I hid my grin and refrained from commenting that art throughout the ages had depicted Jesus with long hair. Silence fell and, for a few minutes, I was enjoying the sounds of nature. I jumped as Mama came up behind me.

"What will you place beside the door then?"

My sigh was barely heard, or Mama chose to ignore it. "We have the black signs with Welcome and Gather on them ..." I glanced up to see Mama smile her approval. "And in front of those I'll place the, well Dewey can move them, but I'd like to use the two iron urns that are in the garden."

"That sounds delightful." Mama leaned forward and lowered her voice, "Now tell me what happened last night. Dewey has said very little. I called around but no one knows." Her mouth pursed. "It is vexatious!"

"Hmmm, the nerve of Megan Hearn. Inconsiderate to die on a weekend. Didn't she know the gossip mill is only fully staffed during the week?" I smiled to take the sting out of my words, but Mama still scowled at me.

"Stop it, gossip is a sin." She straightened in her chair. "I am merely concerned with the safety of our community." She arched an eyebrow. "And also, with your reputation. Having someone die in your Halloween display can't be good for business."

I couldn't disagree with that, even though I didn't consider myself in business, per se. "I'm sure Megan didn't die in the cauldron on purpose."

Mama frowned. "Well, what was she doing? I managed to pry enough out of your brother to know that she was found head-first in that witch's cauldron you set up." Her eyes widened. "However, did she manage to fall in and why didn't she get herself out?"

"Um ...," Her questions ran through my mind while I finished hanging a garland of silk maple leaves.

"Well?"

I huffed and joined my mother in the seating area. "I don't really know all of the details, Mama." I poured a glass of tea. "It's possible she fell in and was unable to get out before succumbing to the dry ice ...."

Mama's eyes widened. "Not get out of-why couldn't she-Holly! Please tell me your display wasn't faulty. You could be sued; they could charge you-"

"What? Mama." I grabbed her hand and squeezed gently. "Stop getting upset. I am not responsible for her death."

Her gaze searched my face for a second and then she drew a deep breath and nodded. "Well, thank heavens for that! But how did she fall in?"

"Ehh," My gaze skittered away as I debated my answer.

Mama cleared her throat. "What are you not saying?"

I sighed. "I said it was *possible*, but I don't think she fell into that cauldron."

Her eyes widened and her voice rose. "You think it wasn't an accident?"

"Who had an accident?"

Dewey, with The Colonel at his heels, climbed the steps and set down one of the urns I'd requested. I rose and scooted it into position and then began filling it with potted mums and mini pumpkins. While Mama and Dewey discussed the death of the podcaster.

"Your sister thinks it wasn't an accident."

Without the other urn I was done decorating, so I returned to my seat, resigned to discussing last night's events. Until Mama's curiosity, and now Dewey's was satisfied I'd never get anything done.

"What do you think happened to her, Holly? How else did she get into that pot?"

I frowned. Did it really need saying? If it wasn't an accident … I shook my head and stated the obvious. "Someone put her in there, of course."

Mama gasped and Dewey choked on his drink. I shook my head and helped myself to an apple cider donut, breaking a piece off for The Colonel. They seemed shocked by the idea of murder. That I wasn't might have been a reflection on the cynicism that came with having been a cop.

"I don't understand. How would that have killed her?"

A sarcastic retort was on the tip of my tongue, but I pushed it away and tried to gently explain. "Mama, that cauldron was full of dry ice, if her head was forced down inside it for more than a few minutes she wouldn't have been able to breathe."

"Gracious!" She raised her hand to her chest. "Who would do such a thing? I don't know what this world is coming to, why we aren't safe in our own homes. I was just telling Maybelle we have got to be careful-"

"Mama," I waited until she ran out of breath. "You do need to be careful because crime can happen anywhere but this ..., Mama, this wasn't random."

Dewey huffed. "What, you saying one of those fancy guests did her in?"

"Uh, who else?" I shook my head and rose from my chair. "Can you bring me that other urn? I need to get this done and then we've got to get out to Rosedale and start cleaning up."

He grumbled something I chose not to hear and shuffled off to the side garden leaving me to straighten up and start packing away the Halloween items. I was snapping the tote lid into place when Mama cleared her throat.

"One of the guests." She lowered her voice almost to a whisper. "Who do you think is responsible?"

The whisper drew a smile from me. Our nearest neighbor was several hundred yards away, so who did Mama think was gonna overhear? I pondered the best response.

Any speculation on my part would provide her with weeks of gossip and might also hinder the investigation, not that I had high hopes of that being a success anyway.

Discovering Megan's body had ended the party. No beer launch, no dancing until dawn; just a dozen or so people kept waiting under the tasting pavilion for more hours than I cared to recall.

Craig had jumped in and secured the scene and I'd called 911 and then requested everyone sit down and refrain from discussing the death.

Once the guests were seated, I sent Dewey to get the catering staff along with whatever refreshments they could muster, and then I joined Craig by the stage.

"Not a pleasant way to go."

Megan Hearn was face down in a cauldron of dry ice, unpleasant was an understatement. I snorted. "Uh, no. It wouldn't be my first choice."

My eyes widened as I noticed The Colonel snuffling around the base of the faux fire I'd built under the cauldron. Crud Monkeys, he was supposed to have been with Dewey!

"Hey, boy come here." The Colonel acknowledged my calls with a wag of his nubby tail, but he continued his inspection of the stage, not even bothering to lift his head.

"Holly, get that dog away from the crime scene!"

"I'm trying to-Colonel, come here!" He was the sweetest of animals but within days of sharing a home with him, I'd learned why bulldogs had the reputation for being stubborn. I sighed and stepped onto the stage.

"Dude, you are gonna get me into-hey, what's in your mouth?"

The Colonel wasn't inclined to release his treasure but with some coaxing and scolding, and a handful of dog drool I managed. "Boy, you'll eat anything!" I patted my leg. "Come here and sit down."

"What's he got? That dog better not have -"

"It's nothing, just a piece of plastic or metal." I squinted. Even with the stage lighting on, it was difficult to see clearly. Whatever The Colonel had found was round and slightly metallic.

"Silly dog," I looked down at my unrepentant friend. I started toward the pavilion in search of a trashcan. The Colonel followed along, trying to nudge me into returning his found snack. "No, I know you're hungry, I'll send Dewey to the car for your treat when he gets back-"

"Holly, can you keep watch? I need to hit the head."

I sighed and returned to the stage, shoving the bit of trash into my pocket; my leg was aching too much for more than one trip across the courtyard.

"Sure, no one is gonna mess with anything. I'm gonna sit on the edge of the stage and rest my leg."

Craig nodded and took off for the brewery restrooms. Leaving me to twiddle my thumbs and wait for law enforcement. Dewey arrived along with my friend Marlena and her crew. I sent him and The Colonel to the Scout for the bones I always kept and let the catering staff set up a beverage station under the pavilion.

The offer of snacks halted the grumbling of guests, but I hoped the authorities would shake a leg or Craig and I would be facing a mutiny; the servers were already talking about not being paid to sit around.

Fidgeting under the stares of the guests, I rose and stretched my leg. I steered clear of the witch's circle and cauldron, confining my pacing to a short stretch of path that ran alongside the boathouse, but the stage was in constant sight and the body of Megan Hearn kept drawing my eye.

How had she managed to fall in there? It made no sense. Careful not to trample any potential evidence, I moved closer and peered at the Halloween display.

The cauldron was resting on a cinderblock I'd hidden with birchwood logs. I'd woven strands of orange and yellow lights amid the wood. Inside the cauldron, I'd placed a few strands of green lights and then added four blocks of dry ice. The effect was perfect.

A glowing fog of green rose from the pot. The witches dancing behind it added to the scene and my last-minute addition of the witch's legs made it slightly humorous; well, it had until they'd been replaced with legs still attached to a body!

I backed away, intending to find a place to prop my leg when I noticed the podcaster's hands. A perfect manicure of hot red artificial nails was marred by one finger missing its tip.

Damaging an acrylic nail wasn't difficult especially if doing strenuous work, though what kind of work could she have been doing at a party? I was scanning the path and stage, looking for the missing acrylic tip when a crunch of gravel drew my attention.

I turned to find Glenda and Mark Timmons standing behind me. "Evenin' folks, can I help you?"

Mark scowled. "Yes, when are they going to release us? My wife has a very important video call tomorrow and-"

"Mark, honey it's not Holly's fault." Glenda frowned at her husband and then gave me a rueful smile. "Sorry Holly, we're all on edge."

I smiled. "Understandable. Um ...," I searched for something to break the awkward silence. "So, you have an important meeting?"

Glenda's brown eyes sparkled as she nodded. "Yes, I'm so excited. I'm being interviewed by the search committee for Dean of Saint Anne's. I've made it to the final three!"

My eyes widened; I'd forgotten Glenda was a Doctor of Education. "Congratulations! That's a great school." I suppressed a snort. Prestigious and elite was a more accurate word for the all-girl college located in neighboring Culver County.

"Mmm, I feel like this is what I've been working toward all of my life, it's-"

"Glenda," Mark huffed. "Now isn't the time ..."

Her gaze flitted to the cauldron and then scurried away. "Oh, of course. It's almost sinful to be happy under these circumstances ..." She bit her lip. "This is just tragic. I don't understand how it could have happened." She winced. "I guess I should have inspected it before the guests arrived -"

"Yes, you should have! This party was all your idea ..." He waved his hand toward the stage. "I hope you have liability insurance, Ms. Daye!"

He turned on his heel, scattering gravel as he stomped away. I cocked an eyebrow and met Glenda's gaze. She winced. "Sorry about that, he's upset ..."

Under the circumstances, and more so with the body still in situ, every feeling human on the premises would feel *off*. I'd make an exception for anyone else's behavior, but since meeting Mark a few months ago I'd reached the conclusion he was what Mama labeled high maintenance; I just called him pompous.

Still, apart from having poor taste in men, Glenda was a nice woman, and I didn't hold her husband's actions against her, well, I'd try not to, but that liability comment wasn't going to wash. "This wasn't my fault, Glenda. You know that, right?"

She was quick to nod her head in agreement, but her expression suggested she wasn't confident with her decision.

The last thing I wanted to do was comment on Megan Hearn's death, however, if people were going to start spreading rumors that involved me ... "Glenda, I haven't done more than glance at the crime uh, the scene, but I've seen enough to suspect this wasn't an accident-"

"Attention please," All eyes turned to a sharply dressed man standing in the middle of the courtyard. "My office will be handling this tragic accident and I want you to know that we are cognizant of how valuable your time is." His gaze went to Mayor Tomlin, as a smarmy smile graced his lips. "To that end, we ask that everyone cooperate by giving these officers your name and contact info, and then you'll be free to go."

Glenda joined her husband under the pavilion as a cheer spread through the crowd and the guests started milling around the officers' table.

Joe Brannon. I rolled my eyes and wondered for the umpteenth time how the arrogant fool had made detective, even in a county the size of ours! Detective or no, I was about to step in and point out his first mistake of the night when Craig returned. Since I was resting my leg, and I always avoided talking to Brannon, I briefed Craig on what I'd heard in the shrubs and let him handle it.

The two men had a heated discussion for several minutes, punctuated with scowls from Brannon and head shakes and rolled eyes from Craig. I could only guess as to what they'd talked about, but judging by the way Brannon stalked off to the tasting pavilion and the subsequent groans from the guests I assumed he'd found the first of the flies in his ointment.

Craig shook his head and grinned at me. "What an idiot. Finally convinced him to send forensics over to those hedges." He pointed toward the parking lot. "Coroner will be pullin' up in a minute, gonna get some cars moved so they can back down here. You okay holding down the fort?"

I rubbed at my leg. "Yep, so long as I don't have to do anything, I'm good."

Craig and a few uniformed officers escorted the owners of the cars needing to be moved while the others started taking statements. My only job was to guard the stage, so I sat back down and tried to keep my blood pressure under control as I watched Detective Brannon with the mayor and Councilman Vandershall.

Even in the low light, I could see the obsequious young man was laying it on thick for the pols. Vandershall ate it up, but Lou Lou looked like she'd caught a whiff of manure.

I had seen many colleagues advance through the ranks, most of them deserving it, but Brannon? My lip curled. Barely thirty-five, only three years on beat patrol then straight into a detective. Rumor had it the brass were looking to move him into leadership.

People wondered why their taxes kept going up, but crime never went down. One look at the bloated administration full of incompetent but politically savvy swindlers was all the explanation needed. The stench of corruption in Noble County wasn't strong enough for the average person to demand action, yet; but it was only a matter of time.

The beep of backup alarms signaled the arrival of the coroner. I hopped up and helped guide them through the narrow courtyard and then went to greet Dr. Sawyer.

"Evenin', Tate!" I'd known Tate Sawyer since high school, he'd been a friend of my husband's but, over the years they'd drifted apart. We'd been colleagues and casual acquaintances but, after the shooting and my divorce, he'd become a closer friend.

"More like good morning, Holly." Tate grabbed his bag from the back of the SUV and then his eyes narrowed as he looked at me. "Not takin' it easy, I see." He clucked his tongue and headed toward the stage.

I sighed and hobbled after him. "In my defense, I'd planned to be home soaking in the hot tub by now."

A teasing twinkle appeared in his blue eyes as he wagged his eyebrows. "You ever want company, I'm a phone call away."

Tate's interaction with me had recently changed. Our friendship had grown as he checked on my recovery after the shooting. But lately, he'd been hinting that he wanted to be more.

I'd met him for lunch once and we'd run into each other in town and gone for coffee but, I wasn't sure how I felt about his subtle flirtations. On the one hand, it offered me a confidence boost I sorely needed after having my husband leave me for a girl younger than our son but on the other, I wasn't sure I'd ever be interested in a relationship much less entering one that put a solid friendship at risk.

As usual, I responded to Tate's innuendo with a quick smile and a change of conversation. "Craig and I contained the scene. Not sure when she died but I'd put it between..." I did some mental calculations based on when I recalled seeing Megan last. "Probably a bit after eleven and Dewey-" I smirked at Tate. "Dewey managed to find the body, are you surprised?"

Tate chuckled. "That man has a knack for being in the wrong place ..." he shook his head and rifled through his kit.

"Doesn't he just? Anyway, Dewey called me at twelve twenty-three so, add about ten minutes to that and you have a window-"

"Thanks. We'll see if the liver temp agrees with you." Tate winked at me and mounted the steps, directing his assistants to take photos and then remove the body.

I hung back and watched. The forensics guys were quick. They'd set up lights and a canopy within minutes of their arrival and were now combing the stage and surrounding area for evidence. My gaze drifted back to the pavilion.

Guests were being interviewed and dismissed, while Detective Brannon continued to hobnob with the big wigs. I rolled my eyes and looked for Dewey and The Colonel.

After he'd fed my boy his snacks, they'd taken off for a walk. At the time it had seemed to be a good idea but as usual, Dewey was not where he was supposed to be; uniform would need to account for his whereabouts before we could leave!

My leg had gone from mild protest to dull throb, to shrieking ache. All I wanted to do was go home and go to bed yet the prospect of that happening before dawn kept getting slimmer.

Craig strolled up as they were pulling Megan's body from the cauldron. A sour taste filled my mouth. I gulped and turned my head but not before I caught a glimpse of something shiny in her hand. I was about to point it out when a shout from Tate drew my attention.

"Don't touch that, you fool!"

Joe Brannon's turned a mottled red under his spray tan. He snatched his hand away and rose to his feet, coming to stand toe to toe with the much taller and more physically imposing coroner.

It appeared he'd reached capacity in the sucking up department and had decided to play detective. That he'd neglected to don any kind of protective gear before hovering over the body was typical Joe Brannon behavior; However, challenging the coroner was not.

"I'm in charge here-"

"Until I've released this scene you have as much purpose as tits on a boar hog now get off of the stage!" Tate jabbed his finger in our general direction and then stomped back to the gurney holding the victim.

Tate read the thermometer and glanced at me. "Right again, Daye. Time of death between eleven thirty and twelve forty-five."

Brannon's scowled. "That information is privileged. You are compromising my investigation by giving civilians pertinent information before I've-"

"Pipe down, you twit, Holly is far from a civilian regardless of employment status and Everette is a cop." Tate shook his head and packed up his bag, ignoring the huffs of indignation flowing from the detective.

"Now it's your crime scene." Tate mock bowed. "Cause of death is probably asphyxiation-"

"So we came all the way out here for an accident?" Brannon made a disgusted noise and turned to the forensics team. "You guys can stop now; Doc says it was an accident-"

"I said no such thing," Tate nodded for the hovering techs to continue their work and then scowled at Brannon. "And don't call me Doc."

He pursed his lips and stared at Brannon until the other man squirmed. "It's a questionable death, likely homicide but I won't know for sure until I get her on the table. Postmortem tomorrow ...," Tate paused and stared at the detective for several seconds.

Brannon was leaning forward, his expression intent as he waited for Tate to set the time. I snorted as an unholy grin spread across my friend's face.

"Let's say ten o'clock." Tate's lips twitched. "That'll leave me plenty of time to wet a line."

Time for fishing, but not for golf. It was common knowledge Joe Brannon loved to hit the links with the big wigs every Saturday morning. Brannon's face turned seven shades of scarlet and if looks could kill ..., my friend merely spun on his heel and joined Craig and me by the SUV.

"He's going to blow a gasket and wind up on your slab if you don't stop jerking his chain."

Tate snorted. "Hate to say it, but Noble County would be safer."

Craig smirked. "No argument from me. So, what do you think happened?"

Tate glanced at me. "She suffocated on Holly's dry ice."

I gulped. I'd known it from the moment I saw her legs hanging over the side of my cauldron but hearing it stated as a medical fact didn't make me feel better.

"So, I killed her. Some decorator I turned out to be."

"What?"

"Don't be ridiculous!"

Both men were quick to absolve me. I appreciated it but facts were facts; if not for my party decoration, Megan Hearn wouldn't be in the back of the meat wagon. I said as much and was shot down for my trouble.

"Holly Marie Daye, if that isn't the start of a pity party –"

"Hey, I'm not-"

"Oh, yes you are!" Tate folded his arms across his chest and held my gaze.

I glanced at Craig, but his expression said don't look at me. Men! And supposed friends, to boot.

"You've been moaning about this job for weeks now you're gonna try to take the blame for this just to strengthen your own doubts." Tate cocked an eyebrow. "Tell me I'm wrong."

I opened my mouth then let it snap closed; darn but the truth hurt. I scowled at Tate. "This your idea of tough love?"

He shrugged. "Only kind you seem willing to accept from me ..."

Craig snorted. "Aaand, that's my cue to skedaddle. Think Deputy Dog is gonna release us and Marla is anxious to get home."

He shook hands with Tate and then pulled me in for a hug. We'd never been the touchy-feely kind of friends but, since I'd almost died, Craig had been a bit clingy; to be fair, so had I.

"Daye, behave yourself and call if you need me." He grinned. "Just not too early; spending the night on Osprey Point."

I laughed and shooed him on his way then avoided Tate's pointed stare by watching Brannon stumble his way through the crime scene. Why was he trying to wreck a good friendship? My stomach rolled. I needed the drama and complications like I needed another hole in my leg.

I shook off the uncomfortable thoughts and focused on the investigation. Boy, I'd never worked a homicide, but I'd cordoned off my share of accidents and also watched enough TV to know Brannon was doing some questionable things.

I gasped and instinctively grabbed Tate's arm as Brannon stuck his head down into the cauldron. "Oh my gosh, what is he-"

"Idiot." Tate started to yell at Brannon but one of the forensic team stepped in. Brannon jerked back gasping for breath and gagging.

"Look at him." I nodded towards the stage. "He's spitting into the shrubbery! Does the man know nothing about contamination?"

"No, he's an arrogant young man who should be riding a desk preferably not in an occupation that requires results."

I laughed. Tate was always good for a dose of plain speaking, I just wished none of it involved me. I knew he hadn't left the scene because of me. I also knew that he was gonna try and get me to go out for dinner; he had asked four Sundays in a row. I hated to reject him, so I chose the easy route and changed the subject.

"You really aren't sure about her cause of death?"

For a minute I thought he'd call me on my diversion tactics, but he stared at me for several seconds and then sighed.

"I know the effects of dry ice inhalation are what killed her. What I can't say is how she kept her head in the pot long enough to stop breathing." He shrugged. "I'll know for sure tomorrow. I'm outta here, you coming?"

I nodded. "Just a sec, gotta see about my props." I approached the forensic lead, but Brannon stopped me.

"This area is off limits to civilians."

"I just wanted to know if they are planning to take that cauldron to the lab."

He crossed his arms over his chest. "That is privileged information at this time-"

"Detective, my question is in no way privileged." While I didn't deliberately poke the bear, as Tate did, I was tired and in no mood for Brannon's haughty attitude. "If the team feels it is necessary to do, whatever, that's fine only I need a receipt-"

"For a pot? Don't be ridiculous."

"Joe?" I smiled, though I'd had to force my lips to comply. "That pot was made in the 1830s and is worth almost two grand so yes, I'd like a receipt."

His lips pursed and for a second I thought he'd refuse but, after dealing with Tate's jibes the fight must have gone out of him because he merely nodded and turned back to the crime scene.

Receipt in hand, I told the brewery owners how sorry I was that things had not gone to plan, and then took my leave.

A grunt from Dewey brought my attention back to decorating Mama's porch. I helped him place the other urn and started filling it to match its mate.

"Thanks, Dewey," I added a few pumpkins and stood back to assess the arrangement. "As soon as I finish here I'd like to leave for Rosedale. About ten minutes?"

A heavy sigh was my answer. I turned and met his gaze. "Problem?"

"Uh, yeah. Me and Whopper had plans. Once I get that job, I won't have much free time, so he got tickets to the tractor pull and-"

"Sounds like fun, but I need you to help me take the party stuff down," He was about to argue so I rushed on. "Tell Whopper I'll pay him if he wants to tag along. More help means we'll be done that much faster."

Dewey rolled his eyes but nodded. He pulled out his phone and walked around the side of the house. Mama sidled up and handed me a small green pumpkin and I should have known she wanted something, her helping me decorate was rarer than hen's teeth.

"Well?"

"Well, what?" I frowned and dug in the plastic tote for another string of silk maple leaves.

Mama huffed. "Don't be obtuse. Who do you think killed that woman?"

"I have no idea. Hand me that big white pumpkin, please."

Mama huffed but did as I'd requested before returning to her chair. It wasn't long before she started peppering me with more questions, which I continued to dodge.

"But you must have some idea-"

"Mama," I sighed and straightened, rubbing the small of my back. "It isn't for me to speculate-ah ah," I held up a hand as she started to interrupt. "To even guess the perpetrator, I'd have to know more about Megan Hearn aside from the fact that she put people's backs up."

Mama's eyes widened and she leaned forward in her chair. "What do you mean? Did something happen at the party?"

Dewey snorted as he came up the steps. "What didn't happen?" He joined Mama in the seating area after informing me that Whopper Gilroy would be waiting for us to pick him up and I had to pay him fifty dollars.

Fifty dollars to Whopper for a couple of hours and I had to pick him up? I silently fumed as I continued decorating, though I would have been hard pressed to say if my irritation was due to paying Whopper extortion rates or hearing Dewey feed Mama's need for intel.

"Way I see it; silly woman was asking for it."

"Oh, surely not!"

Shaking my head at her nosy ways, I bent to clean up the decorating supplies. I stacked the totes in the foyer for Dewey to carry up the steps if he could tear himself away from spreading titillating tales.

"So she yells at me, scratches me ..." he pointed to the red marks on his cheek. "And then tries to kick The Colonel and falls on her rear, and blames me- hey, what are they doing here?"

The crunch of gravel announced the arrival of a car. I poked my head out the front door and frowned. Two uniformed officers followed Detective Joe Brannon up the walk.

I stepped onto the porch as they halted at the bottom of the steps. "Can we help you?"

Brannon's eyes narrowed as he climbed the stairs. "Ms. Daye," he glanced at Mama and tipped his head. "Ma'am. Sorry to interrupt your Sunday afternoon."

Mama looked at me. I shrugged. I could think of no reason for Brannon to visit, much less to bring officers.

Brannon crossed the porch and wrapped his hand around Dewey's bicep. "Dewey Charles Barker, we've been looking for you; you're wanted for questioning in the suspicious death of Megan Hearn, you coming voluntarily or-"

"What?" Dewey pulled away. "Why you lookin' for me? I –"

"That's a no then? Boys ...,"

Both officers shuffled their feet and glanced between me and Brannon. One gave me a rueful smile.

I scowled at Brannon. "What is going on here? There's no need for-"

"Daye, are you interfering with an officer of the law?"

"Oh please," I rolled my eyes. "Stop the posturing, there are no cameras here."

The officers snickered and walked away to lean on their patrol car. I crossed my arms over my chest and looked down my nose at the detective. "What did you tell a judge to get a wanted order for Dewey? You must not have looked very hard because he's been here all morning!" I frowned. "For that matter, why would you need to question him? You took his statement last night-"

"And now I have more questions." He motioned for Dewey to head to the car. "This doesn't concern you, Daye. Barker, let's go."

My mouth pursed. As usual, Brannon used vinegar when a bit of honey would have gone a long way to easing the situation. I gave up reasoning with him. "Dewey? You have no obligation to answer his questions. Brannon, he's invoking his right to remain silent and have counsel present-"

"I didn't hear him say that Daye."

He continued to escort Dewey to the patrol car. I gritted my teeth and yelled. "Dewey! Tell him you won't speak without an attorney, and I'll meet you at the station."

Wide-eyed, Dewey followed my instructions to the letter. Brannon scowled and shoved him towards the waiting uniformed officers before turning to meet my gaze.

Mama leaped from her chair and started down the steps. "Where are you taking my boy? How dare you-"

"Mama, leave this to me." I nudged her back up the steps and turned to Brannon. "What's the meaning of this?"

He cocked an eyebrow. "Your brother was seen in a heated argument with the victim. He pushed her to the ground-"

"That's a lie!" Dewey shouted from the car. "I never touched-"

"You people think because your last name is on a road you get special privileges." He motioned for the officers to leave and then looked at me. "Your brother has no job, no visible means of support, and a record-"

"A couple of misdemeanors as a juvenile?"

"I don't have to answer to you and if you continue to impede this investigation I'll run you in as well."

I breathed through my nose and fought for calm. My hand itched to wipe the superior smirk off of his face but that would only leave Mama to bail us both out. A few more deep breaths and I felt semi-capable of being civil enough to keep myself from being incarcerated.

"I'll meet you at the station with our attorney, and if you try to question him? I'll have your badge for breakfast."

Chapter Three

The bell above the door jingled as The Colonel and I stepped through to find Connie Rogers hip-deep in boxes of Christmas decorations. The only craft shop in the county, Glitter and Garland, had done brisk business since it'd opened six months ago.

If my opinion had been sought, I would have advised against renting space in J.T. Minton's Cannery Wharf though. His proposal to turn the old DeMarco Canning Company into luxury condos and retail space had been a hit with the public and many had rushed to invest however, a year and a half later only a handful of shops occupied the ground floor, and the condos were still nowhere in sight.

While still a deputy, I'd answered a disturbance call at the Cannery; Minton and old Mr. Archelaus had been fighting. Neither man would admit to it being anything more than a misunderstanding, but I'd overheard them discussing money and lack of development as I was leaving. My gut said something about the entire project was fishy. Still, none of my money was invested and Connie was only renting space.

As happy as I was to have a supply store just around the corner, I was more excited that my best friend was back in the Lowcountry. We'd been inseparable in high school and had planned to attend art school together but, my pregnancy and then marriage to Brooks had put an end to my dreams.

Not so with Connie. She'd graduated college but instead of returning home, she'd married a man from Ohio. Over the years, we'd talked on the phone, vacationed together once, and done a few girl's trips, but her return to Sanctuary Bay just after I'd been shot was heaven-sent; I wasn't sure I'd have kept my sanity without her presence.

In the few short days since I'd last visited, Glitter and Garland was beginning to look a lot like Christmas. Connie had started assembling artificial trees for the display windows, twinkling lights were draped along shelves, and the whole place smelled faintly of pine due to the presence of several wax burners.

If not for the mess with my brother, walking into the shop would have put a smile on my face and a skip in my step; I loved all holidays, but Christmas was my favorite.

"Hey Holly, come to play in the Christmas goodies?"

"In my present mood, anything I'd create would be more in line with *A Nightmare Before Christmas*." I motioned for The Colonel to sit, and then pushed aside an empty box so I could perch onto the stool she kept behind the service counter. "All this stuff to make wreaths?"

Connie nodded. "Yeah, and centerpieces." She pulled a plastic bag full of artificial evergreens from a box. "Could also do some swags. What do you think?"

"Sure."

Connie wrinkled her nose. "Well don't hold back your enthusiasm on my account."

I laughed. "Sorry. I'm in a foul mood. Here, let me help." I grunted and grimaced but eventually managed to get down on my knees. The Colonel took my lower position as an invitation and within seconds I had a lap full of wiggling chub.

"Oh, you silly boy. Go sit down-no, I do not need a kiss!" I giggled as he ignored my protestations and snuffled my face. "How am I gonna help Connie if you-"

"Here boy, come see Auntie Connie." She patted her leg and walked over to the work counter. The Colonel's ears twitched. A ping of metal and he shot off across the room as Connie pulled a dog bone from a canister.

"Who's a good boy? You are, yes sir." Connie loved on The Colonel and then left him to his treat.

"You spoil him!" I shook my head at her unrepentant grin.

"Oh, look who is talking!"

I laughed. "True, but someone should be the adult and make him behave without bribery."

Connie snorted. "Think of him like a grandchild you get to spoil rotten."

"Uh, that only works if you get to send them home with the parents!"

She smirked and continued counting inventory as I started rummaging through the stock, handing Connie some items, and creating piles for others. I filled her in on the Dewey saga as we worked.

"How did you get everything packed up from the brewery if the police took Dewey?"

I snorted. "Alvin Gilroy. Do you know, I had to pay that rascal a hundred bucks to help me clean up? And he managed to break the frame we made for the pumpkin arch so there goes the idea of repurposing it."

"Whopper. I can only imagine the *help* he provided."

"Oh yes. He also managed to find what I think is part of Edison Marlow's Sherlock Holmes costume while we were removing the witch's circle so now I've got to go by the sheriff's department and turn it into Brannon, and seeing him now will just …," I sighed. "Never a dull moment with Whopper."

Alvin, Whopper, Gilroy was my brother's oldest friend and he'd earned his nickname by the *tall tales* he gleefully told. Mama called the pair high-spirited; I preferred man-child. The two of them were always in trouble or looking for it and neither of them ever kept a job long.

Dewey's employment or lack thereof was at the heart of my current annoyance over the handling of Megan Hearn's murder. Via Craig, favors had been called in to get Dewey an interview with a local company that provided security for various businesses and events in our area.

My brother had scoffed at the idea of being a rent-a-cop, but the job wasn't strenuous, mentally or physically, a boon for Dewey. Add in that the pay was decent, they offered healthcare benefits and a retirement plan, and it was an offer too good to pass up. Only, they wouldn't hire anyone with a criminal record let alone someone charged with murder.

Getting Dewey that job was high on my priority list, and I told Connie as much. "So, I don't know what I'm gonna do if they charge him." I shook my head. "I had such high hopes that my brother would finally enter the land of adulthood and now this. If only I hadn't taken him with me ..."

"Holly, it's not your fault and you needed his help!" She leaned over and wrapped her arm around my shoulder. "I'm so sorry you're going through all of this!" Connie straightened and began to sort the new inventory. "But I've heard great things about your displays!" Her eyebrows rose as she glanced at me. "Several people have called to see about hiring you ..."

"Seriously? One of my designs killed a guest! Who is dumb enough to hire me?"

Connie shook her head. "Stop it. Your decorations were perfectly safe, it isn't your fault someone killed her!" Her brow furrowed. "Speaking of which, who do you think did it?"

My eyes widened. "Oh, not you too!"

"What?"

I huffed. "Mama has been pestering me to find the killer, can you believe that? She is convinced Brannon will railroad Dewey and not bother to find the real killer, and then there's Tate."

"Oooh," Connie's eyes went wide as she leaned toward me. "What about Dr. Tall, Dark, and Handsome?"

I silently cursed myself for bringing Tate into the discussion.

My friend had not failed to notice the doctor's interest in me was more than that of a casual buddy and she never missed an opportunity to nudge me towards accepting a deeper relationship.

Connie tapped her nails on a box. "Ahem, don't hold out, give me all the deets."

"Ugg," I tipped my head back and groaned as Connie laughed. "Give it up." I met her gaze. "We are just friends! It's never gonna happen."

She wrinkled her nose and returned to the inventory. "Never say never. Now spill, what did Tate have to say? Was it about your case?"

I sputtered. "Connie, it isn't my case and yes, Tate called because he'd heard Brannon was trying to charge Dewey."

She had a dreamy look on her face. "Ah, so he was offering you support."

"Eh, not exactly." I fiddled with the flap of a cardboard box and debated how much to tell my friend. "he told me there were bruises on Megan's neck. That confirms she was murdered, and she was clutching a piece of gold chain."

"Oh!" She blinked. "Well, that's sad. I mean, I never believed she accidentally fell into that pot but still, better than knowing we have a murderer in our midst!"

"Yes, but the reality is, one of the guests killed her." I snorted. "And Brannon thinks he's got his man."

She clucked her tongue. "Which is why you gotta find out the truth."

"What? No, why would I-" I stopped as Connie gave me a pointed stare. "What's that look for?"

She cocked her head and shrugged. "Well ...,"

"Well, what?"

Connie snorted. "Holly, you've told me several times you think that detective is *incompetent.* "She shrugged. "Tate must have misgivings about him, why else would he have called to tell you that? And that's probably why your mama is pushing you to look into it, too!"

The words to dismiss her statement were on the tip of my tongue but I bit them back. She was right, my lack of confidence in Brannon's abilities as an officer of the law was no secret. I frowned, thinking of my experience with Dewey at the station.

The patrol car hadn't left the driveway before I was on the phone with Brooks Jr. getting a recommendation for a criminal attorney. Being late on a Sunday, I'd figured Dewey was gonna be sleeping in a cell, but my son had made a call and a smart young man from Beaufort County had shown up at the station in under an hour.

Brannon had taken me at my word and not attempted to question my brother but as soon as Maxwell Bernard arrived the gloves came off, or so I'd been told hours later when Dewey was released.

According to my brother, Max was a legal eagle and he'd put Brannon in his place. Dewey may have been confident the worst was behind him but, after speaking with the young attorney my unease grew.

According to Max, Brannon had let slip that they had evidence linking Dewey to the murder, but when pressed, he'd backed off and said the DA was still considering the charges. Had he been bluffing? Dewey seemed to think so but neither Max nor I were so certain.

"Holly? Do you think they'll charge Dewey?"

I shook off my ruminations and focused on my friend's question. "I'd like to say no, but realistically?" I shrugged. "From what I've seen, Detective Brannon has shown himself to be lazy and more interested in rising in the ranks by sucking up than by good policing."

Connie's eyes widened. "Oh, my goodness. That's not good."

"No, and it's possible Brannon is bluffing about having evidence that Dewey was involved, Max is trying to confirm that through connections in the prosecutor's office, but knowing Dewey ..."

"Holly, you don't think Dewey had anything to do with that woman's death?"

I shook my head. "Of course not, but Dewey ... Connie, all of that man's life he's been in trouble because he was in the wrong place at the wrong time or worse, he was with Whopper Gilroy!"

Connie laughed. "You're not wrong." She picked up a bundle of evergreen boughs and headed towards the work counter. "So, what will you do?"

I grimaced and got to my feet. The Colonel snuffled and joined me by the counter. I patted his head and considered her question. "Guess I'll poke around? I mean, Max is a smart guy. He'll do his best to hold the D.A. off but it'd be better for my brother if another suspect was presented sooner rather than later, especially since he's up for that job."

Connie frowned. "Well if that detective isn't going to look for another culprit, how will someone other than Dewey get charged?"

"And that's the million-dollar question." I sighed "Looks like I'm gonna have to find a murderer."

Chapter Four

I left Glitter and Garland with good intentions but in the end, thinking about who killed Megan Hearn took a backseat to everyday life. After running Mama around hell's half acre, I'd had to buy a snake to unclog the kitchen drain and ended the evening with a stressful phone call from my son. The following morning was little better.

I'd dropped Mama at the Kut and Kurl and then decided to grab breakfast at the Country Kitchen, and I regretted it within seconds of sliding across the plastic seat of a booth.

"Holly! Girl am I glad to see you."

I could have heard a pin drop as the busy diner fell silent. Chairs scraped across the linoleum as people twisted in their seats to direct curious glances before a low hum of chatter filled the diner.

Settling The Colonel on the floor under the table, I cursed the waitress' vociferous greeting and hid my face behind the laminated menu she tossed onto the table before dropping onto the seat across from me. I pretended absorption in food choices as Everleigh Tucker filled my coffee mug and then straightened condiments in a half-hearted manner until her patience ran thin.

"The usual, Holly?" She bent and patted The Colonel on the head. "Hi ya Sweet Boy, I'm gonna bring you a lil snack, yes I am ..."

"That'll be fine." I tossed the menu aside and ignored her intention to fatten up my dog because half of the town seemed to have made that their life's goal.

I could feel Everleigh's gaze on me, so I let mine wander to the left in an attempt to evade her and the prying eyes of the other patrons.

My avoidance technique had the added benefit of soothing my frazzled nerves. The Country Kitchen held prime real estate in Sanctuary Bay. Most of the town faced the Indigo River but alongside that major water route ran Burton Creek, a smaller tributary flanked by acres of marsh. On any given day you could watch dolphins frolic and egrets look for their next meal.

A Blue Heron poked his head out from among the Spartina. I watched as he tentatively waded farther into the creek and began poking his beak into the water. They were such majestic creatures. Stoic, reserved, elusive- Everleigh cleared her throat and I reluctantly met her gaze.

She scrubbed at a nonexistent speck on the table and began pumping me for information. "Everyone's talking about the death of that podcaster!" She glanced at me; perfectly drawn eyebrows arched to her bleached blond hairline. "They're saying Dewey killed her."

Her statements came as no surprise, but I still closed my eyes and prayed for strength. "And what do you say."

"Dewey Barker?" Her mouth twisted as she rolled her eyes. "Girl, please. He wouldn't hurt a fly, mostly cuz that'd be too much like work but still ..."

Leave it to Everleigh to hit the nail on the head. I chuckled. "No truer words." I emptied two plastic containers of cream into my cup and cautiously sipped. Nope, still too hot. I pushed it away. "So, Brannon's stupidity is all over town."

It wasn't a question. In Sanctuary Bay, gossip traveled faster than a minnow evading a dipper net, and ninety percent of the time it was embellished beyond coherence before it went a city block. My family was well known and well-liked, so far as I knew, but that wouldn't stop a sensational story from making the rounds, if anything, it added fuel to the fire.

Being the subject of gossip would mortify my mother; she could dish it out but ... I, on the other hand, could not care less what people might say but preventing wild rumors or even the truth from reaching the ears of Sentinel Security was a top priority.

Everleigh's lips turned down at the corners. "Yeah, Sug. I'm tryin' my best to put 'em straight but you know what folks are like." She tapped the table with her hot pink nails. "Let me put your order in and get the baby boy a snack, then I'll take my break and we can have a chat."

I nodded and settled back to sip my somewhat less scalding coffee and watched the other diners. The novelty of my arrival had worn off and everyone appeared to have returned to minding their own business. I snorted. Or moved on to discussing other poor souls.

The feeling of being watched returned with a vengeance. I let my gaze roam around the room, smiling and nodding at a few acquaintances as I searched for the culprit.

Ah, the back corner farthest from the window. I tipped my head down and pretended to be absorbed in my phone while I watched from beneath my lashes.

A woman, mid-fifties or early sixties, sat with her chin resting in her folded hands. Long, blue-black hair framed a shockingly white face. I was no expert, but my gut said she was wearing a wig. Thick black eyeliner competed for attention with crow's feet and deep grooves bracketed lips painted a red so dark it would pass for black.

All she needed was a long black dress and she'd have the perfect Morticia costume, but Halloween was over so what was with the garish getup? The woman's gaze barely shifted from me as she sipped cola through a straw. Curiosity aroused; I was halfway out of the booth when Everleigh returned with my meal.

I sat back and waited for her to place the multiple plates of the hearty man special in front of me. I gulped and looked at Everleigh. "Grab a plate and help me eat this."

She grinned. "Ah, don't be silly, it's what you usually have. Gonna clock out, be right back."

Two eggs, over medium, three strips of bacon, three links of sausage, cheese grits, and a short stack of pancakes. How had I ever eaten all of that? I stood, motioned for The Colonel to stay, and hobbled my way over to the service area for another plate. I'd meant what I said, no way I could finish that meal.

Everleigh had been right, before the shooting I'd polished off the Hearty Man at least twice a week, but I'd also been slightly overweight and working a full-time job. My days were more sedentary now and, months of recovery had left me twenty pounds lighter, I had no intention of gaining that back. Keeping one egg, two pieces of bacon, and a quarter of the pancake stack, I dug in as my friend returned to the table.

She huffed. "Now I told you-"

"It's going in the trash if you don't eat it."

My blunt response shut the argument down. We ate in silence for several minutes and then Everleigh leaned on her elbow and lowered her voice. "So, who do you think killed that woman?"

I finished my breakfast and sat back with a sigh. "I have no idea." I ignored her sneaking The Colonel a piece of bacon and continued. "Logic says it's one of the brewery guests, but I don't know enough about her or them to guess who might have hated her that much." I cocked an eyebrow. "What have you heard?"

She finished the pancakes and washed them down with a swig of milk before answering. "Well, you know she had that true crime podcast, right?"

I frowned. "I knew Megan had a podcast but not what it was about. True Crime? What's that?"

Everleigh laughed. "Oh, girl you gotta get out more! She talked about cold cases, mostly ones that happened here in the Lowcountry," she cocked her head and her brow furrowed. "Though, I think she did a couple that occurred across the river in Georgia."

"Huh, so was the cold case division cooperating with her? How did she choose cases and if they were unsolved, what did she have to talk about?"

Everleigh started stacking the dirty dishes. "I don't know all of that. I just listened while I cleaned or worked out, ya know?" She rose and grabbed a bus bin to clear the table as she continued. "But it was real interesting. She'd start by telling ya about the crime and how it wasn't solved, and about the poor victim's life and all. After that, the episodes would be about clues or things the police had done at the time, and she'd poke around and visit the places ..., oh! And sometimes she'd have interviews with people that were connected to the old case."

The feeling of being watched returned. A glance around the room and sure enough, the lady in the black wig wasn't even trying to hide her interest. What did she want? I was sure we'd never met- "Everleigh, who is that woman sitting in the corner booth-no! Don't look."

She huffed. "If'n I don't look, how am I ..." She looked down and turned her head slightly to peep in the direction I'd mentioned. "Huh, I don't know who she is, Holly but she was asking about the murder when I served her." Everleigh cocked an eyebrow. "Want me to find out who she is?"

My first instinct was to tell her no, that it was none of my business who the woman was or why she was staring at me but that was before the Halloween Party and my brother being the number one suspect in a murder. I debated another second and then nodded. "See what you can find out, but be casual about it!"

She snorted. "I know!" Everleigh mumbled under her breath. "Not like I'm just gonna march right over and ..."

I tuned her out and replayed what we'd been talking about before the interruption. According to my friend, Megan Hearn's podcasts were based around cold cases. If she was interviewing old witnesses she had to have information or at least access to the police files.

"Hey, Everleigh? How was Megan finding out about these old crimes? And the witnesses. How did she investigate? Was she connected with law enforcement? Did she have a legal background?”

Everleigh snorted. “Heck no, she was a journalism major I think, or maybe it was broadcasting?” She shrugged and rested the bin on her hip. “Not sure, but she weren’t no lawyer.”

I nodded and considered what I’d learned. “Did Megan give her opinion on who might have been responsible for these old crimes?”

She wrinkled her nose. “Weeell, it’s hard to describe. She didn’t come right out and say, this guy is guilty or nothin’ but she’d kind of hint?” She shook her head. “I’m not explainin’ it right; you should listen to the shows. You got a music app? She’s on all of ’em.”

“Uh, yeah, I’ll look them up.” My phone chimed with a notification; Mama was finished at the beauty parlor. I rose, tossed a twenty on the table, and clicked my tongue for The Colonel to wiggle his lazy and overfed tail out from under the table.

“Come on, boy. Thanks, Everleigh, good talkin’ to ya.”

“Holly, hold on!” Everleigh set the bin down and rushed across the room. “Who do you think-”

I waved and strolled out the door, rolling my eyes at her attempts to get fodder for the gossip mill.

A fender bender on Bay Street dragged out my two-block drive to the Kut and Kurl. I used the time to consider Everleigh's information. It sounded as if Megan Hearn had picked the scabs from old wounds and then publicly aired her opinions on the long-dead cases.

Could she have stumbled on a criminal that hadn't been caught? Perhaps the answers to her murder were in one of her podcasts. I shrugged and looked for a place to parallel park. There was a possibility that Megan had kicked a hornet's nest, and since I had nothing else to go on, listening to her podcasts was as good a place to start as any.

I'd always heard that the road to hell was paved with good intentions; in my case, it was the front walk that lead to Mama's porch. My plan had been to sit in the hot tub and listen to Megan Hearn's podcasts, but Mama wanted to stop at the nursery on the way home; Just my luck, It's About Thyme had a two-for-one sale on flats of Fall flowers.

Scout loaded with seventy-two Dianthus and Snapdragons; we arrived home to find Dewey pacing the driveway. Turned out all of my fears were grounded. The supervisor for Sentinel Security had gotten wind of the murder and the fact that Dewey was a suspect. They'd *rescheduled* the interview until the issue was resolved.

Dewey threw up his hands. "Well, that's that. I shoulda known, nothin' good happens to me ..."

Head down, my brother started shuffling back to his apartment over the garage. Mama was fretting and fighting tears and Dewey had lost all hope. "Don't worry, Dewey, It'll all work out."

"How?" He spun around and stalked back to the truck. "How is it all gonna come right, Holly? That dumb detective won't listen and now I gotta pay an attorney and I got no job-"

"Oh Dewey, this is terrible, just terrible." Mama wrung her hands. "When I walked into Kitty's, the other ladies were talking about that woman gettin' herself killed, and then when they saw me-" Her voice broke into a sob. She dabbed at her eyes and sniffed. "The shame! Your poor father must be rolling in his-"

"Mama, that's not helping." I gave her a quick hug and then nudged her towards the porch. "You make yourself comfortable and I'll bring out some tea." I waved for Dewey to help me unload the flowers. "I'm sorry about the job, Dewey but don't let it get you down, I'll get Craig to talk to them-"

"What's he gonna do?" Dewey accepted a flat of Snapdragons and toted them over the porch, setting them on the bottom step.

I followed with my share of the load. "I didn't tell you, but it was Craig that suggested they interview you." I set the flowers down and straightened, rubbing at the ache in my thigh. I'd been sitting too long, and the muscle was starting to stiffen. "The owner is a former cop from Charleston and he and Craig were at the academy together-it doesn't matter, just ..."

"Just what, Holly? They're gonna convict me of murder and all you got is a friend who can help me get a job! They gonna give it to me after twenty to life?"

Another sob from Mama stopped Dewey's rant. I scowled at him and rushed to comfort her. "Mama, you have to stop this, it's gonna be fine. Dewey did nothing wrong and the police will realize that soon but you getting upset is just going to raise your blood pressure and you know what the doctor said ..."

She hiccupped and swallowed several times before managing to speak. "I can't help it, Holly Marie. They're going to lock my baby up and-"

"See? Mama knows! They aren't even looking for the real-"

"For the love of Mike will y'all just stop?" My screech brought all conversation to a halt. I glanced at Mama, she was staring at me with wide eyes, Dewey was standing on the top step with his mouth hanging open.

I pursed my lips. So I might have been a bit harsh, they'd just have to get over themselves because my leg was hurting and now their fussing had given me a headache.

"Y'all just calm down. Mama, stop borrowing trouble, and Dewey? You are not going to prison, at least not over this."

"Holly," Mama whined. "Everyone is saying it's an open and shut-"

"You predict the future now, Holly? Gotta crystal ball?" Dewey interrupted. "Or is this another friend in the right place? You friends with the judge and jury?"

It was all too much, my mind had been running in circles since Brannon had hauled my brother in for questioning- actually, I corrected myself. Things had started going haywire when I saw Megan Hearn's legs sticking out of my antique pot!

I gritted my teeth as Mama started crying and Dewey continued to goad me. My mouth ran before my beleaguered brain could catch up. "Of course not," I sighed. "But I am going to find the real killer of Megan Hearn."

My announcement was like the sun breaking through the clouds during a hurricane. Mama, wreathed in smiles, jumped up and offered to fix a tray of snacks, to keep me fueled for the investigation, and Dewey peppered me with dozens of questions.

In the end, I only found a moment of peace by convincing Mama that she'd be of more help if she were well rested and treating Dewey to a round at the bar by tacking an extra twenty onto what I owed him for helping me at the brewery.

Once I'd sent my family on their way, I found myself at loose ends. With the sun hanging low in the sky it made little sense to start planting Mama's flowers, besides my leg was too achy to get down on the ground. I debated calling Connie, thought of Tate, and quickly vetoed that idea for fear of giving him hopes in the wrong direction, and ended up opting for a soak in the hot tub.

My divorce had been traumatic, but the shock and pain were lessened by the big fat check Brooks had to write each and every month. I'd used some of my settlement to build a deck in the garden and install a spa; my injured leg had rejoiced in my decision.

Sinking into the warm, bubbling water chased away my aches, though not my stress. I tipped my head back and cursed my stupidity in committing to find the killer of Megan Hearn.

What had I been thinking? I didn't have the first idea where to begin, anyone could have murdered the woman, and judging by the little I saw of her that night, she'd made tons of enemies-huh, that was probably a good place to start.

In the handful of hours between my completing the decorations and the party ending with Dewey finding her body, I'd seen her in some kind of unpleasantness with no less than three people and I suspected she was the cause of the argument between Rae Ella and Griff Reid. A woman that created that much animosity ...

She'd started the evening by fighting with Dewey- well that was the first I was aware of, and from there I'd witnessed her be catty and provoking to Glenda Timmons though I wasn't sure what she'd been taunting her about, Megan had been toying with her earring and it had looked like Glenda was staring at them when she'd gotten upset.

I wondered if the earrings had been a gift from an admirer. Why else would she wear them to that party? They were too fancy for it and were not remotely appropriate 1950s attire. Could they have been from Mark? Someone else that Glenda was or had been involved with?

I sighed. So many questions and I had no real idea how to get them answered. After dinner, Megan said something to Griff Reid that made him look sick and his wife cry. To round out the evening, Megan had a heated discussion with Edison Marlow.

Were those people my suspects? It didn't seem possible that any of them would have been angry enough to hold a woman's head in a cauldron of dry ice until she suffocated; none of the altercations I'd witnessed were that inflammatory.

Still, Whopper had found Edison Marlow's pipe near the crime scene, and he'd had words with the victim ... I pulled myself from the tub and dried off. Time for bed and, for lack of any better place to start, I'd track down the author tomorrow and, as much as it pained me, I'd turn the pipe into Brannon.

Chapter Five

Waking to a text message reminding me that I had my first appointment with a personal trainer was not a great way to start my day but, my doctor refused to refill my pain meds unless I tried physical therapy.

My aversion to working out notwithstanding, I could admit that I was tired of being limited by my weak leg, tired of the stares when I used my cane, and worried I could get hooked on the muscle relaxers and nerve blockers; I just wished the workouts didn't have to be in a public place.

The gym appointment wasn't until two which left plenty of time to stop by the Sheriff's Department and then to visit the set of the television series being filmed downtown and talk to Edison. After seeing to The Colonel's morning ablutions, we set out to complete my errands.

The village of Sanctuary Bay was only a few blocks from the house and before the shooting I'd have happily walked. I could still make the trek but now it took twice as long and today I didn't have the luxury of time. I loaded The Colonel into the Scout and, after fighting traffic snarls, pulled into the Sheriff's Department lot.

It felt odd to be coming back to the place I'd worked for over twenty years and not be in uniform. Greeted with smiles and hugs from former colleagues put me in a benevolent mood that was quickly soured two minutes after Brannon walked into the room.

I'd requested an audience with the legend in his own mind, telling the desk sergeant that I had evidence pertinent to the case. Brannon walked in with a scowl on his face and my hackles raised.

"What's this about, Daye? I'm a busy man."

The implication that my time was not valuable set my teeth on edge, but I forced a smile and explained what Whopper had found. I also told him about Edison's costume and the argument I'd overheard with the victim.

"Let me get this straight." He crossed his arms over his chest and looked down his nose. "Your brother is accused of murder, and you just happen to find evidence that points to another suspect." He pointed to the door. "Get out of here, Daye, and leave the real police work in more capable hands." He snorted and rolled his eyes. "When you carried a badge, you were little more than a glorified paper pusher."

Several pithy replies crossed my mind and a few almost escaped my lips but, in the end I knew anything I did to further antagonize Brannon would only hurt Dewey. I got an evidence receipt from the desk sergeant and stalked out of the building. I chuckled and got back into the truck. Brannon was good for something after all, his arrogance had lit a fire in me, and I was now more determined to find the real killer.

Minutes later, we arrived downtown to find the business district slammed with people and not a parking place in sight, handicap or otherwise.

Taking a chance, I looked for parking at the marina and was rewarded. I frowned and wondered at the number of out-of-state license plates I'd seen while hunting for parking.

Our islands were year-round vacation destinations but from Fall through Spring the area was usually quiet, and locals outnumbered tourists. The last event to draw a crowd beyond locals had been September's Piratefest. If the pattern held, the next celebration guaranteed to draw thousands wouldn't be until March's Azalea Festival.

Sanctuary Bay was a true harbor town. Founded in 1714 as a haven for the pirates that roamed the Atlantic, most of Bay Street's businesses stood opposite the Indigo River, with nothing blocking the view except a tree-lined green space that had been turned into Goodwin Park.

I let The Colonel sniff and explore the shrubbery as we made our way to the street. Filming equipment and trailers were scattered around the area, and at the other end of the park, I could see barriers had been placed to keep intruders from wandering onto the set. Ah, now the out of towners made sense!

The production company and what they were filming had fueled conversation for weeks, but I'd paid little attention. After chatting with Edison during the party I knew that he'd moved away from Sanctuary Bay, written a book that I hadn't read, and now he'd moved back and his book was being turned into a movie, or was it a television series?

Regardless, since Whopper had found what I believed was a piece of the pipe Edison had carried as part of his Sherlock costume, I had questions. The only trouble was I didn't know if Marlow was on set and, if he was, how was I going to get passed the guards?

The sweet smell of freshly baked pastries drifted in the breeze, making my stomach grumble and giving me an idea. Perhaps I could butter up a crew member and gain access to Marlow.

Convincing The Colonel that he wanted a treat got him moving and in minutes we were entering The Split Bean coffeeshop. The shops that lined Bay Street dated from the 1800s and had maintained their ornate facades. The Split Bean was a corner shop with banks of windows overlooking the river and fluted molding painted an eye-catching powder blue. White, wrought iron bistro sets sat under a blue and white awning, and potted palms and seasonal flowers softened the concrete and brick sidewalk.

As much as the curb appeal enchanted me, the interior was like a soft sweater on a blustery day. Ten-foot ceilings covered in white shiplap met white brick walls trimmed with decorative molding painted a soft grey.

The original floors of heart pine added warmth, while the coffee station, dark blue wainscoting with a counter of pristine white marble, anchored the space. After my divorce, I'd needed a haven when living with my mother and brother became too much; Glitter and Garland and The Split Bean had fit the bill.

The Colonel trotted inside like he owned the place, and judging by the greetings and offers of treats, he did. Once the girls at the counter had finished spoiling my dog I got to place my order.

" Mornin' Holly, haven't seen you in a while."

I smiled at Maisie, a twenty-something working her way through drama school, and ordered coffee with cream. "Aaand, are those chocolate croissants?"

"Yep, Bill made them this morning."

"Oh my, throw one of those on a plate, please."

"Sure thing, have a seat and I'll bring it over."

Grateful for their low-key offer of assistance, The Colonel and I took the coveted window seat. I was watching the film crew set up for another shoot across the street when a warmed pastry and a cup of coffee slid across the table and owner Wanda Graves took the seat opposite me.

"Good morning Holly, what brings you into town today?"

About ten years older than me, Wanda and Bill Graves were New Jersey transplants. Retiring from corporate life, they'd chosen Sanctuary Bay and we were all the better for it, though the collective waistlines of Noble County were probably increasing due to Bill's artistry in the kitchen.

"Hey Wanda, got a few appointments this afternoon, thought I'd come in early and see what everyone is fussing about." I tipped my head toward the window, indicating the commotion across the road.

She snorted. "That crew has been at it since dawn. Thought the filming would increase sales but they have that catering truck ..." She shrugged. "They asked to shoot an interview in here though. We'll be known as the birthplace of the novel that started it all. That should bring in the customers, dontcha think?"

I nodded though hearing the crew had an onsite caterer scuttled my bribery plans. "Sure sounds like good publicity. So, it's Edison Marlow they're going to interview? I didn't know he was a regular here."

Wanda's springy gray curls bounced as she laughed. "You kidding? Marlow haunted this place; Him and his friend, Amber Price, such a sweet girl." She pointed at a bistro set to the left of the window. "That was their spot when the weather was nice. Once it got too hot, they'd sit over in that corner. Ate breakfast and lunch here for over a year. Sipping tea and pounding on their laptops," She frowned. "Don't know how you coulda missed them."

I reminded her that I hadn't frequented The Split Bean until after the shooting.

Her brows rose above her wire-rimmed glasses. "Oh yeah, I forgot. Well, I never did know what she was working on, but Edison wrote Bernie Deveraux and the Honey-Baked Curse, and the rest is history. That was about seven years ago?" She nodded. "Yep, I remember because he signed with a publisher the same week my daughter got married- did I tell you we're expecting the first grandchild in the spring?"

I managed to get in congratulations as Wanda continued talking about Edison Marlow. "Such a nice man, very funny and do anything for you. Now that he's moved back he comes in every morning like clockwork, though it seems strange to see him working alone." She tsked. "Such a shame about Amber!"

My brow furrowed. "Did something happen to her?"

Wanda's eyes widened. "You don't know?" She continued as I shook my head. "Well, it was not long after his series took off, this was a few years before it got picked up for the television show, they were living out west somewhere, not L.A. but near there I think." She waved her hand. "Anyway, by then they'd married and one day Edison came home to find Amber had fallen to her death. They ruled it an accident, something about the bolts on the balcony rail and sea air corrosion?"

"Oh my gosh, that's horrible! That poor man."

Wanda nodded. "Yes, but as if that wasn't enough ..." She looked around and then leaned in and lowered her voice.

"Right after it was announced they were gonna make a television show based on his books ugly rumors started circulating."

I frowned. "What about?"

Wanda's mouth pursed. "It's lies, total nonsense but they are saying Edison wasn't the author of the Bernie Deveraux books."

"People think he plagiarized the work? Is someone suing him over it?"

She shook her head. "No, because she's dead." Her eyes narrowed. "The rumor is he stole the books from Amber and now there is speculation that he killed her to keep it quiet."

"That's a horrible thing to accuse someone of, is there proof? I mean, you can't just go around saying things like that, you'll get sued for slander."

She scowled. "You can if you're Megan Hearn."

My eyes widened. I had not been expecting that. "The podcaster who was murdered?"

"Yes, and by the way, I don't believe for a minute your brother had anything to do with it, our sheriff's department is run by fools." She rolled her eyes. "I know one shouldn't speak ill of the dead but that woman ... do you know she had the nerve to come in here and upset Edison with her lies? Bill threw her out."

"Really? What did she do?"

"Well, I don't know what was said but Edison told me afterward that Megan has been pestering him for weeks about a podcast. She wanted a statement or an interview? I don't recall, but she's just a witch. I'm sure it was her that started those rumors! Hmmph, calls herself a journalist. Maybe so, but no decent paper would have her. She's worse than the grocery store tabloids. It's no wonder someone killed her."

I nodded. "I haven't listened to a show, but watching her at the party I thought she enjoyed stirring up trouble." I refrained from adding that Wanda had just pushed Edison Marlow to the top of my suspect list.

After nudging The Colonel from his barista-induced sugar coma, we walked across the street and joined the crowd of on-lookers behind the film set barricade. I watched them block the scene for a few seconds as I thought about what Wanda had told me.

Edison Marlow was an author with a series being turned into a television show but, what if the books hadn't been his? Was bestseller and tv show success really worth killing your wife over?

Wanda's guess that Megan Hearn was behind the rumors of plagiarism and murder was spot on, I would bet good money. But did she have proof? Unpleasant personality notwithstanding, would Megan have risked a defamation suit? My gut said no, but then, why start the rumors? If she'd repeated them in a podcast ...

Whatever her reasons, I had no doubt that Megan had argued with Edison on the night of the party. What it'd been about was another riddle to ponder. I leaned against the metal fence blocking my way and tried to remember what I'd overheard.

Whomever she'd been arguing with, and I was assuming it to be Edison Marlow because he had exited the garden shortly after Megan stormed out, had said *I don't have,* and Megan interrupted with *find it,* but what had they been referring to? What did she want that the writer claimed not to have?

Talking to Edison might have gotten me closer to an answer but, after walking around the perimeter of the set and not catching sight of him, followed by a fruitless attempt at coaxing a guard to let me in, and finally stopping a crew member to ask if Edison was on the set I gave up.

Wanda had mentioned he still frequented The Split Bean, and it was no hardship for me to drop in for one of Bill's delicacies. I'd talk to the writer later; it was time to hit the gym.

The drive across town was brief and all too soon I was shifting my weight from one leg to another and tugging on my workout shorts as my trainer, Lance, demonstrated how to use the leg press. I watched him push the plate out with his legs, hold it, and then control its return to the starting position but a glance at myself in the mirror to my left distracted me.

God, I could scare children! I'd never been overly fussed about my appearance but retiring and being critically injured had increased my slacking in that department. I shoved a stray lock of hair behind my ear and wondered when I'd gone so gray.

Probably when you stopped routinely coloring it said the snarky voice in my head. I wrinkled my nose and admitted Mama had been right to suggest I join her at Kitty's Kut and Kurl; I'd make an appointment for later in the week.

Unfortunately, my battered leg couldn't be repaired with a bottle of hair dye. The bullet had entered my leg halfway between my hip and knee, leaving a dimple and puckered skin to clash with my cellulite.

The whole area was a dull reddish purple and looked horrible enough to draw the eyes of the fit young women by the free weights. I cursed and tugged at the biker shorts and promised myself I'd buy some of the yoga pants they were wearing. I jumped as Lance patted the vinyl seat on the machine.

"Okay, Holly? Do three sets of ten and I'll be back to check on you."

My turn? Crud, I really didn't want ... Lance's smile was bright and expectant. I succumbed to the peer pressure and assumed the position, earning me a *you got this* before he sauntered off.

He was chatting with the woman manning the check-in desk and I realized I was on my own. The Colonel rose from his makeshift bed and snuffled at my hands. I patted his head, told him to go lay down, and myself to quit stalling. I placed my feet against the metal plate. Lance had left the added weight off but just moving the machine was enough to tax my strength.

I gritted my teeth and focused on using my leg muscles to move the square my feet were resting on. My thighs trembled, I tightened my stomach muscles and grunted; the plate made it to the end of the track, and I was triumphant.

Then I remembered I had to control the rate of return. I blew out a breath and bent my knees, letting the plate come toward me slowly as Lance had instructed. My muscles burned, I was gonna feel it for days, but I had to admit I was proud of myself.

Sheer determination saw me through one set of ten, but it left me shaky and sweating like a pig. I was starting the second set when giggles and laughter rang out. The plate slammed back to its resting position when I saw it was coming from the girls I'd seen earlier.

My face grew hot. I really didn't want to continue, at least not in public. I shouldn't care what anyone thought-oh, but they weren't laughing at me! I squinted and realized the laughter I'd heard was directed at a muscle-bound man partially hidden by the weight rack.

I was about to return to my exercise routine when the man turned, and I saw his face. Dale Scruggs, wasn't that convenient? I grinned. He was in his element, doing curls and goading the girls into feeling his biceps. It looked as if he'd never outgrown the high school jock persona.

Speaking of his glory days ... Wanda had told me Megan Hearn was harassing Edison Marlow over his past and I'd seen her talking to Dale during the party; his expression had suggested he wasn't happy.

I wondered if she'd done the same to Dale. He'd lived a checkered life for one so young and something told me Megan's interest in cold cases might have put Dale on her radar.

Either way, he'd been a guest at the party, and I'd take the opportunity to talk with him. I did another set, putting less effort in as my focus was on Dale Scruggs. The girls left and he settled into his workout. Lance came back as I finished up my last rep.

"Great job, Holly!" He glanced at his watch. "That's enough for today, you remember the stretches I showed you?"

I nodded and he sent me on my way. I coaxed The Colonel into following me and went to grab a floor mat, an elastic band, and a five-pound weight. I settled my dog near the weight stand and then set my things down.

Taking hold of the elastic band, I slipped one end under my foot, and lifted my leg, using the bar mounted in front of the mirrored wall for balance. My gaze met Dale's and he blinked.

"Oh, hey Holly, I didn't know you came to this gym."

I smiled. "First day. I have to do PT with a trainer." I nodded in the direction of my damaged leg. "Got to get this leg back in working order."

His eyes widened. "That where you got shot?"

My face flushed but I tamped down on my embarrassment and nodded.

Dale shook his head and returned to his arm curls. "Ouch!" He glanced at me. "They ever figure out what happened?"

My eyes narrowed. Why would he ask that? It was common knowledge. I'd gone to serve Shawn Dupree. He'd shot me, and I shot him. He died, I barely survived; what else was there to know?

I said as much to Dale, and he shrugged. "Yeah, I read that, but it never made sense to me."

I stiffened. "Why is that?"

"Well, cuz I knew Shawn, went to school together, played on the same team ... he was an entitled jerk but shooting someone? Especially a cop? Not something I'd have thought he'd ever do but ..." He shrugged again and concentrated on his weights.

Dale's nonchalant statement set my thoughts on a track I studiously tried to avoid. The elastic band slipped through my moist hands as my breaths became shallow and rapid. Before I could stop it, I was reliving the night my whole world tipped on its axis.

"Brooks, I'm gonna be late. I've got to deliver a notice to appear-" I bit my lip as he cursed and grumbled something about my lack of organization.

"It fell between the seats, Brooks!" I swallowed and forced my voice into a friendlier tone. We were supposed to be meeting for dinner to celebrate our thirtieth wedding anniversary, fighting over the phone would just make an awkward meal that much worse.

I waited for a break in the griping. "Anything or *anyone* else and I'd leave it until tomorrow but it's the Dupree kid-yes,

Roland's son, he'll use the lack of proper notice to get the kid off on a technicality and he deserves to pay after what he did."

My husband was a corporate attorney, but he knew what personal injury lawyers were like, especially Roland Dupree. The man's face was on billboards all over the Lowcountry, he was the best of the bunch in that field, or at least he made the most noise.

His son had taken the family boat out while intoxicated and caused the death of a young woman. Daddy's influence had gotten him off of the criminal charges, but there was less burden of proof in a civil damage case. With any luck, the Duprees would be several million lighter in the wallet, but it wouldn't happen if I didn't get the notice served.

"Look Brooks, just go on to the restaurant and I'll meet you there." I gritted my teeth as he launched into how my plan would leave me dining in my uniform. In Brooks' mind, my being a deputy had never been good enough for the senior partner of a law firm, much less one that now had a founding member running for congress.

"That'll be fine. I'll change when I get there." I shuddered to think what he'd bring for me to wear and ended the call, setting off for the northern tip of the county.

The clang of weights jolted me. I gulped and examined my reflection in the mirror. Blue eyes, large in a pale face, a sheen of sweat on my upper lip, my frizzy brown and gray hair falling from the elastic band I'd secured it with.

I forced air into my lungs, holding each breath for a count of three before releasing it just as the shrink had taught me. A whimper drew my gaze. Big brown eyes stared at me as The Colonel nuzzled my hand. I stroked his head, concentrating on the feel of my nails combing backward through his short hair but the usual comforts didn't work. I couldn't shake off the memories.

A vision of the dirt road winding through a thick forest crept before my eyes and before I knew it, I was back in the squad car, unaware of the horrific future just ahead.

Dusk had turned everything hazy; the dense canopy of trees didn't help. I bit my lip and thought about turning around; there was no telling if Shawn Dupree was even on the premises.

But the gate to the hunting camp had been open, my sources said Shawn and his father were spending the weekend at their hunting camp, and I was already on site. Might as well check it out.

The weather was mild for January. I loved driving with the windows down. The smell of pine drifted on the breeze and flashes of white suggested the camellias would soon be in bloom

The main road ended at a fork. I'd never been to the Dupree hunting camp, and they hadn't bothered to mark the roads ... I drummed my fingers on the steering wheel and tried to decide which way would take me to- a single gunshot, followed by three more in quick succession made my eyes widen.

It was a camp meant for hunting, logic said to follow the sound. I took a left and kept my eyes peeled for running deer. The forest was denser, ambient light almost nonexistent. Something moved up ahead.

I slowed the car and leaned forward, squinting as I looked through the windshield. Something was on the ground. A deer? Two people, a pickup truck- was that Shawn and Roland Dupree? My stomach tightened. Something wasn't right, though I couldn't define my unease. I unclasped my gun from the holster.

Closer now, the people are gone, run away into the forest or hiding in the shadows? What is that on the ground?

The headlights of the pickup are blinding. I step from the car, my gun is drawn, the other hand shields my eyes. I leave the door open, keeping my body behind it as I try and assess the situation.

I announce my presence, a snap of branches, I turn my head. My eyes widen, a flash, searing pain ... I fall, my skull cracks against the door jam, darkness pulls me under.

"Holly!" My body is shaken so hard my teeth rattle. "Hey, snap out of it!"

I gasped and coughed. Through a veil of tears, I meet Dale Scruggs' green eyes, they are wide with terror. "What," I cleared my throat. "What's going on, what happened-"

"You lost your shi-er, you freaked out." Dale's hands fell from my upper arms. He took a step back and ran his hands through his hair. "You better now? Was it your leg? Do you need a doctor?"

My mouth was dry, and my tongue felt thick and fuzzy. I bent and retrieved my water bottle, guzzling the contents in one go. I shook my head and stepped back as The Colonel wedged his chubby self between us and proceeded to lick any part of me he could reach.

I bent and rested my head on his warm back. "I'm fine, thanks, just ..." I drew a few more breaths and let the last one out slowly. I stood up. "Sorry about that, I-I don't like talking about the uh ..."

Dale gulped. "I'm sorry, I shouldn't have-"

"No, it's, you couldn't have known." I forced a smile, beyond embarrassed about my mini panic attack. I rubbed my dog's velvety ears and willed my pulse to return to normal.

Thank God The Colonel had been with me ... something about the wiggly little potato grounded me, especially when my mind went to dark places. A group of teens walked in, and I realized how much time must have passed for them to be out of school.

I was wasting time and my anxiety was distracting me from the matter at hand. I was searching for a way to turn the conversation to the murdered podcaster when Dale inadvertently gave me my opening.

"I, uh, could show you some coping techniques for that," He shrugged and looked down at the floor. "If you want."

I frowned, not following. "Coping?"

He met my gaze. "Yeah, you know, for the anxiety. After I lost my scholarships I kinda went off the deep end and ..., well, I learned how to rein myself in."

I bit my lip. "Uh, thanks, maybe not today." A nervous chuckle escaped me. "Still feelin' a bit, shaken."

"Oh sure, I understand, any time, just ask."

"Thanks, I will." I lowered myself to the mat and lay flat, intending to continue with the stretches. My focus was now firmly on getting answers about Megan Hearn, but I managed to go through the motions.

We exercised in silence for several minutes until I completed a set and cleared my throat. "So you went through therapy?"

Dale grunted through a lift and then nodded as he reached for a towel. "Yep, best thing I ever did." His gave met mine before darting away. "After that whole thing with Coach Carlson I drifted for a few years, drugs hooked me pretty bad."

He shrugged and loaded weights onto a bar. "But rehab and therapy taught me a better way. I don't really look back but if you want those relaxation techniques ..."

I nodded and before I could consider them, my thoughts tumbled out. "Did Megan Hearn plan to do a podcast about you?"

"What?" I winced as a ten-pound weight bounced on the floor. Dale's mouth was hanging open but anger, not shock was rising in his eyes. His jaw was tight, and a nerve ticked in his cheek.

"Her podcast, you mentioned Coach Carlson and that's an unsolved murder ..." I shrugged. "You and Megan were talking at the party, and it looked like something she said upset you so, I was just putting two and two together?"

My eyes widened as Dale's hand clenched into a fist. Before I could blink he'd punched the wall beside the mirror. "That bit- she promised ..."

He was flexing his fingers and mumbling under his breath. I took a step closer and tentatively touched his red and bleeding hand. "You should put some ice on that."

He nodded and pulled away, grabbing his water bottle before sinking onto the weight bench. Hands dangling between his spread knees, Dale stared at the floor for a long minute before meeting my eyes. "She was going to go ahead with the podcast?"

I gulped. The way he phrased his question let me know my hunch had been right. I held up my hands in a stop motion. "I could be wrong, only I know she was dredging up some questionable things about someone else and threatening to put them in her show ..., I was just guessing."

A look of pain crossed his face, and I regretted bringing the subject up. The anger was gone, replaced with heartbreaking sadness. "It never ... the past drags me back no matter how far I climb."

My hand twitched to offer him comfort but I fought my instincts and continued to probe. "So that's what she said to you the other night?"

He ducked his head, and his voice was barely above of a whisper. "Yes, she came in here a week ago and introduced herself, started asking questions I refused to answer." He snorted. "I kept my cool until she started to threaten me. Said she knew all about my drug problems and how I'd lost my gyms." His eyes were blazing with anger as he met my gaze. "She said if I didn't help her she'd suggest I was the murderer ... she was-"

"Not a nice person."

His eyes widened. "Yeah, good way of putting it."

"What did she want from you?"

He sighed and looked away. "She wanted to know about Mark."

I frowned. That had come out of left field. "Mark. Mark Timmons?"

He nodded. "Yeah, about some business he's invested in. Said if I got her a copy of his computer files she'd leave me out of her podcast on the coach's murder."

His expression was haunted as he met my gaze. "I ... I refused at first but when she threatened me I ..." he shrugged.

"Did you give her what she wanted?"

"Yes!" He jumped up and started to pace. His uninjured hand clenched and unclenched in a rhythmic cycle and I wondered if the wall would gain another hole. "But she was lying. She was pushing me for more information or she'd ... you know." He sniffed and let his head fall back so that he was staring at the ceiling. I had to strain to hear as he continued. "I betrayed my partner for nothing!"

I jumped as he spun around and met my gaze.

"I'm glad she's dead!"

My eyebrows shot up. There had been clear menace in his voice. I'd pushed him to tell me about Megan, so it seemed anticlimactic to shove him over the cliff. "Dale, did you kill Megan Hearn?"

I'd expected shock maybe anger but not the weary sadness he projected as his shoulders slumped and he stumbled back onto the weight bench.

"No," He dragged a hand through his close-cropped brown hair. "But I wish I had."

Chapter Six

I'd left the gym feeling like I'd kicked a puppy. After his admission I'd questioned him a bit longer, mainly verifying his whereabouts during the estimated time of Megan's death. He'd claimed to be with the others walking from the tent to the brewery. As that was easily checked by asking Craig or Jessica if they'd noticed him I let it go and we talked a bit longer about his years in therapy and how he was in a better place now.

Just before I said goodbye, Dale had asked me if Megan had recorded the podcast concerning the murder of Coach Carlson and if it'd air even though she was dead. It was a good question and one I should have thought of.

I mulled it over until after dinner and then decided to listen to one of her podcasts. Within minutes I realized what Wanda Graves had been talking about. Megan had sensationalized the cold cases and if the Friendly Fire episode was indicative of her style, she liked to speculate and allude to the perpetrator.

After talking with Edison Marlow and Dale Scruggs my gut said Megan Hearn was blackmailing people. So far, I knew she'd pressured people to give her information in exchange for not publicly accusing them of murder but there was nothing to say she hadn't also done so for money. Her investigations dredged up dirty laundry, people would pay to keep it from being aired.

I'd slept on my jumbled thoughts and had a eureka moment while walking The Colonel. After each episode, Megan thanked her sponsors and listed those who'd helped in the making of the show. She'd mentioned the local radio station and a sound engineer. With no other leads, I figured it was time to answer mine and Dale's question; what happened to her recordings now that she was dead?

After an internet search for an address and a drive across the county, I walked into the radio station only to have the receptionist inform me that the engineer I needed to speak to was doing a live broadcast and I'd have to wait.

I'd only flipped through a month-old magazine for a few minutes when the magic of English bulldogs stopped the office manager as she passed by the lobby.

"Oh my goodness, he is precious!" A rotund lady with short flaming red hair bent at the waist and clasped her hands between her knees. "Can I pet him?"

My permission was not needed. The Colonel snuffled and snorted his way to her and was soon basking in the attention like he was starving. I rolled my eyes and told him he was a drama king.

The office manager met my gaze and laughed. "That face!" She cupped his chubby jowls between her hands and grinned. "How on earth do you keep from spoiling him rotten?"

"Uh, isn't it obvious that I don't?"

She laughed and sank onto the seat beside me. "What a love." Keeping one hand on the rotten one's back, she offered me the other. "I'm Lis Overby."

"Hi, um, Marie Sinclair." My middle and mother's maiden name popped out before I'd thought about it.

"Are you waiting for someone, or can I help?"

I considered the pros and cons of telling her my business and figured it couldn't hurt. "I'm not sure. I wanted to talk to someone about the Lowcountry Crimes podcasts."

Her expression morphed to sadness. "Oh, haven't you heard? The woman that did those shows has died." She shook her head. "Shame. She could be difficult, but no one deserved to die like that. Did you know Megan?"

Decisions, decisions. I wasn't sure how to proceed. Did I tell her what I really wanted and my opinion of the dead woman or play dumb? Mama's admonition that I would catch more flies with honey ran through my head, fueling my decision.

"Uh, I didn't know her well, no. I did listen to some of her shows, however, and I had hoped to talk to her about a cold case I think she was looking into."

Her eyes widened. "Oh! Are you a police officer?" Again, I debated how to answer. "I, uh, used to be and I'd heard Ms. Hearn was asking about a case I'd been involved with ..." I shrugged. "I thought she might have uncovered something that could shed more light on what happened." I ducked my head and pretended to be upset. "Some things you never get over, ya know?"

I'd played my cards right because she patted my arm and rose. "Oh, you poor thing! Was she doing a show about a case that haunts you?"

I bit my lip and nodded. "I think so. I had thought to compare notes with her but if she's passed on ..." I sighed. "I guess some things aren't meant to be resolved ..."

"Nonsense! Come with me."

We entered the office area and Lis led me down a narrow hallway. After passing several glass-walled rooms where people were broadcasting, we turned down a short corridor and she opened a door to a small office.

"This is a spare office Megan rented from us. I don't see why it'd hurt if you looked over her notes ..."

She might not have seen the harm, but I could guarantee Detective Joe Brannon would. I refrained from telling her that, however. "Oh, thank you. That's her computer and file cabinet? I wouldn't want to intrude on anyone's-"

"It's fine, honey. We haven't been told what to do with her things yet, so I just locked the door, but you go ahead and see if there's anything about your case. Maybe you'll finally catch a killer!" Hand on the doorknob, she was about to leave when she turned. "What's the case you're interested in?"

Oooh, for a split second my mind was blank. "Uh, the uh, Coach Carlson murder?"

Her eyes widened. "Well, you're in luck then! Megan and I talked a bit, and she was indeed looking into that poor man's murder." She graced me with an approving smile. "You sit on down there and look through her notes, I know Megan would want you to! If you need anything my extension is 5875."

I nodded. "Thank you, I will … " I turned the computer on and watched as a password prompt appeared. Crud! I glanced at Lis. "Well, there went that idea … she used a password."

Lis laughed. "Oh, that's alright honey, it's P E R P, get it?" She laughed again and left the room, closing the door behind her.

Unbelievable luck and a bit of dissembling had gotten me access to more than I could have dreamed but I wasn't going to take it for granted; the sooner I was gone, the better.

Once the desktop was loaded I clicked on her file explorer and scrolled through the listings. If the file names were any indication, Megan Hearn had kept meticulous and copious notes. A file named Production Schedule caught my eye.

I opened the schedule and stifled a curse. Megan had merely listed her show topics for the next six months. I read the list and tried to decipher what the intended content might have been.

From what I'd been told, Megan's podcasts had been sensational, bordering on tabloid fodder, and that theme was represented in her proposed show titles.

October   6 episodes   <u>Fatal Fire</u>

Fire takes the lives of all but one family member on All Hallow's Eve.

Was a son's dabbling in the occult to blame?

The October topic referred to a suspected arson that occurred just over the state line in Georgia. I'd listened to part of an episode, and nothing jumped out as being linked to any of the brewery guests. I scrolled on to November.

November 4 episodes   <u>What Ever Happened to Baby Jane?</u>

An aspiring actress disappears while working as an au pair on Rose Island.

Try as I might, I couldn't recall any cold cases that matched those descriptions and that meant I had no way of knowing if they were related to anyone in attendance at the party.

I moved on to December.

December 5 episodes   <u>Deck the Halls</u>

Hanging Christmas lights takes deadly
turn for a prominent Charleston
family's housekeeper.

There was no need to wonder what she was referring to with that description. Everyone in three counties knew the story of the Anderson family and the housekeeper that fell down the stairs while decorating for the holidays. It'd been ruled an accident but rumors that the youngest son had pushed her off of the ladder still circulated.

January's topic made my eyes widen. Pay dirt.

January   <u>The Breakfast Club</u>
A jock with a bright future falls in with
the wrong crowd and a beloved coach
pays the price.

The Breakfast Club. A nod to the 80s movie about a disparate group of teens spending their Saturday in detention and one of the teens had been a jock. Having spoken with Dale Scruggs, I had no doubt, that Megan was alluding to the unsolved murder of Coach Drew Carlson.

Coach Carlson had been shot at a public boat ramp one Sunday morning over a decade ago but every year a fundraiser was held for the scholarship created in his name and periodically, his family offered rewards for information leading to an arrest.

Dale Scruggs had been a star running back and local golden boy during Coach Carlson's tenure but, after a drug bust, he'd been suspended and removed from the team. That had ended Dale's potential college and pro career.

I wasn't sure how that could tie into the murder of the coach, but Dale had said Megan was blackmailing him over his. Seeing her files, I was now positive that was Hearn's modus operandi for creating her podcasts.

I scrolled down to see who else might be a victim.

February   8 episodes   <u>A Novel Murder?</u>

An author perishes in a freak accident but what happened to her unfinished novel?

Edison Marlow. Here was proof she'd been planning a show based upon the rumors she had likely started. I hadn't felt like Marlow had a murder in him, but when pushed anyone could snap. I put the author at the top of my suspect list, not that I'd made one yet.

Below the monthly schedule, Megan had added what I assumed were titles for future podcasts.

<u>The Vanishing Senior from Noble County High</u>
Three friends go out for a graduation celebration, and only two come home.

Hmmm, I was unfamiliar with any case-I jumped as a door closed and voices grew louder. Someone was coming. I closed out the index and frantically thought of a way to copy the files. Could I email them to myself? I started to open her email account when my gaze fell on a thumb drive hanging off of her pencil holder. Bingo!

A few clicks and the files were transferring. I pulled the drive, shut down the computer, and dragged The Colonel from the room. We'd just turned the corner when a familiar voice reached my ears. I blew out a breath and sent a silent thanks skyward. I'd made it out just in time; Detective Brannon and a uniformed officer were being escorted down the hall.

I left the radio station with more questions than answers but one thing I felt certain of; Edison Marlow was a strong suspect. He'd argued with the victim, part of his costume was found near the scene, and there was a strong possibility Megan was blackmailing him. If I had a list, he'd be at the top.

Thinking about lists sent me to Glitter and Garland, checking in with Connie had been on my daily to-do. The bell sounded as The Colonel and I walked through the door. Connie was with a customer, so I guided the boy around to her office and propped my leg. I was fiddling with a stapler when my friend entered carrying a tray with tea and the canister of dog biscuits.

"Oh my gosh, that dog will need a motorized scooter if y'all don't stop feeding him!"

Connie laughed and slipped him a biscuit. "He's so cute though, look at those sad eyes ..." She grinned at me. "We couldn't have a snack and leave him out!"

I shook my head and accepted the mug of tea. "How's business today?"

"Pretty good for a weekday! I have three orders for custom wreaths, I want your opinion on some floral picks so don't let me forget, I sold a couple of Thanksgiving centerpieces, and ..." She glanced away and made herself busy fixing her tea.

She was too quiet. My radar went up. "And? Might as well spill it."

She chuckled and rolled her eyes. "Okay, but just hear me out before you say no."

My mouth opened to say that if she put it that way it was a definite no, but Connie rushed on before I could get the words out.

"I had a call from Edna Simms, the Grande Dame of Oyster Point?" I nodded and she continued. "Well, they were unable to attend the brewery party but her friend and steering committee member for the Plantation Club was there and she's been bragging on the decorations ..."

My stomach rolled. I had a feeling I knew where this conversation was going. "Connie ..."

"Come on Holly, this is a great opportunity for you! A new career path! Start an event decorating business! You can call it, Coast*yle* Events!" She set her tea aside and leaned across the desk, her face alight with excitement. "Ms. Lou Lou stopped by to say that the council has approved her Christmas Village in Goodwin Park idea and she wants you to submit a bid, combine that with the Plantation Club's Silent Auction and you'll have two jobs lined up, oh and she mentioned a new friend ...," she bit her lip and avoided my gaze.

My mouth went dry at the mention of the mayor. I already knew why she'd come to Connie but ... "You might as well spit it out."

My friend's gaze flew to mine. She licked her lips. "Okay, uh, don't eat me but, Ms. Lou Lou told me about her friend wanting you to call her and she was pretty sure you wouldn't, so I did it for you and you have an appointment this evening at six."

The words were jumbled together as Connie rushed to get them out, but I had no trouble understanding. "You didn't."

Connie winced. "Come on, Holly! You weren't gonna call and Ms. Lou Lou said-"

"You're right, I wouldn't have because my last job KILLED SOMEONE!"

My friend rolled her eyes. "Oh stop! You did no such thing. Just go meet with Heather, she sounds sweet and it's another job! They're pouring in! It's a sign." She reached across the desk and squeezed my hand. "Each job you do will probably get you more. Please don't turn your back on such great opportunities Holly ..."

Her blue eyes pleaded with me, but I shook my head. "This is your field, you can expand and- what, why are you shaking your head?"

"Because I just opened the store. It would be a bad financial decision to expand at this time."

I scoffed. "But you want me to take a risk!"

"Yes, because there won't be any investment aside from materials for each job and I can extend you credit if you need it but if you bid the job like you did the brewery, though you should charge more, I told you that was too low-"

"Too low!" I snorted. "A woman died in my Halloween display, Connie!"

Her nose wrinkled. "What's that got to do with anything? It wasn't your fault."

I sighed and rolled my eyes. My friend was being deliberately obtuse. I changed the subject. "I'm too busy to think about taking on a new business-"

"Too busy doing what?"

"Trying to find a killer and keep my brother out of prison."

"Oh, right." Connie bit her lip and glanced away. She was quiet for a couple of seconds, and I thought that was the end of the 'why don't you start a business conversation' but she looked up and grinned. "If I help you solve the murder will you at least meet with Heather and put in a bid for the Christmas Village job?"

My mouth hung open and my brow furrowed as I stared at my friend. "What does one have to do with the other, and how can you help me solve a murder when you weren't at the party?"

She shrugged. "You said you were too busy solving a murder so, I'll help you and then you won't be too busy!" She rooted around in a desk drawer and tossed an ink pen and legal pad at me. "Here, let's start."

My confusion must have shown on my face because Connie huffed and snatched the pad back. "Okay, let's start with a list of suspects ..." She glanced at me. "Who had a motive or hated the woman?"

"Oh let's not-"

"Come on, toss out some names!"

Her gaze never wavered, and I knew she wasn't going to let up. I sighed. "Okay, Edison Marlow ..." I told her what Wanda Graves had said about Megan and the plagiarism, the pipe Whopper had found, and finally, what I'd learned at the radio station.

Connie's eyes widened. "Gosh, that would make a good book!"

I laughed. "Hadn't thought about it, but you're right." I shrugged. "I plan to stop in at the Bean tomorrow morning and chat with Marlow, Wanda says he's a regular. Other than that I don't know who might have wanted her dead."

Connie frowned. "One suspect? That's it?"

"Eh, I copied a couple of files to a thumb drive, but I haven't had time to really look at everything and now that you've made me an appointment ..."

Connie tapped her pen against her lip. "Leave it with me, I'll look through it tonight."

I dug in my bag and handed the drive to her. The clock above her desk caught my eye. "You made an appointment for six?"

Preoccupied with making a copy of the drive, Connie nodded. "Yes, and don't even think of backing out, come on ok, it's running ... drive E, copy all ..." her brow furrowed as she murmured, "Lot of megabytes for only two files."

I waved a hand. "No idea, my knowledge of computers extends to turning the thing on and point and click."

Connie laughed and handed me the bag. "Don't worry about it, I'll look over the whole drive tonight and let you know if I find anything." She rested her forearms on the desk and leaned forward. "You've got forty-five minutes or so before you need to meet Heather Rudd, back to suspects."

The twinkle in her eyes made me laugh. "You're awfully chipper about discussing murder."

She shrugged. "If you think about it as a game …"

"Fair point." Though it wasn't a game. A real woman had been murdered and the method was up close and personal; someone had truly hated Megan Hearn. However, my friend was right. If I was going to keep Dewey out of prison I needed to buckle down; talking it over might help.

I glanced at the legal pad Connie had pushed to the middle of the desk. She'd made a T chart with Suspect on the left and Motive on the right. Edison Marlow was the only name listed. I considered what I'd learned today along with what I'd talked about with Dale Scruggs.

"Connie, put Dale Scruggs under Edison Marlow."

Her eyes widened. "Ooh, the brewery owner? Why would he kill her?"

I hit the highlights of my conversation with Dale. "I walked away believing he was innocent, and I still lean that way, but he did have a motive, she was blackmailing him just like Marlow."

Connie scribbled the name down and then looked at me. "That's starting to look like a pattern. I wonder if she used those tactics with everyone featured in her podcasts?"

"I'm beginning to think she did." I thought back to the night of the party. "She liked to pick fights, too. I remember thinking she could start an argument in an empty house because I heard her in the garden ...”

Connie whistled as I finished telling her about what I'd observed at the brewery event. “You think it was Edison that said I don't have it?”

I nodded. “Yes, no proof, but he came out of the gate just after Megan. Wouldn't stand up in court.”

“No, but it builds a case. It sounds like she was asking him for something and based on what we know from you talking to Dale Scruggs ... what do blackmailers ask for?”

“Money of course, information, influence?”

Connie frowned. “Not following.”

“I'm just thinking out loud but, Griff Reid was there that night and I remember passing him and Rae Ella as The Colonel and I were leaving the tent.” My brow furrowed as I cast my mind back. “I was worried they'd want to stop and chat but when I looked at them Griff looked ill and Rae Ella had been crying, I'd swear to that.”

“Oh wow, poor thing, but where does Megan come in?”

“Not sure that she does, only I saw her talking with Griff during the happy hour. I didn't think much of it, they didn't argue or anything, though I remember thinking he'd had a shock. He was trying to hide it, but his hand shook when he tossed back his drink, and he was definitely pale.” I shrugged.

"Couple that with Rae Ella looking like she'd been crying and I'm suspicious and Griff is favored to win the congressional seat. Maybe Megan wanted him to do something for her once he was in office?"

Connie cocked an eyebrow. "Oooh, that's a possibility!" She frowned. "But how are you going to find out what was bothering them?"

"Probably talk to Rae Ella. We always got along. I'll have to figure out a reason to drop in on her though ..."

"Okay, so Edison Marlow, Dale Scruggs, Rae Ella and Griff Reid." She looked up from her tablet. "Anyone else act oddly that night?"

"No-Yes!"

"Connie laughed. "Which is it?"

"A bit of both. Mark was a jerk after we found Megan's body, but that isn't why he should be on the list." I motioned for her to write his name. "Dale said it was something on Mark's computer that Megan wanted. Stands to reason he's doing something sketchy if she was on to it."

"Didn't you say he insinuated Megan's death was due to your decorations?"

I nodded. "Uh-huh, but I set him straight on that right off. He was posturing and talking about liability insurance."

Connie scribbled again and then turned the page toward me. "Okay, did I miss anything?"

"Might as well add Glenda Timmons." Connie gave me a puzzled look. "I don't think she'd have it in her, seemed nice enough, fretting over the guests, making sure everything was perfect, but if her husband was threatened?" I shrugged. "We have Rae Ella down for the same reason so ..."

"I see your point." She pulled the table back, made a few notes, and returned it to me. "Alrighty then, looks good to me. What do you think?"

I read over her chart.

Suspect/Motive

"That's a good start- add a question mark at the bottom of that list though."

"Why is that?"

I stood and rustled The Colonel from his snooze under Connie's desk. "Because someone was in the camelia hedge just before the body was discovered. At the time I dismissed it as someone using the shrubs for a bathroom but now ... I called out to them, and they ran off. Not sure it means anything, but it could have been any one of the suspects listed or someone else altogether."

"Come on, boy-no, don't look at me. It was your Aunt Connie that made the appointment so up you get."

Connie giggled and rattled the biscuit canister. "Here precious, come get a little snack for the road."

The Colonel jumped up and gobbled the biscuit then looked at me for more. "Oh no, I'm trying to keep you from getting any fatter."

"He's just big-boned!" She smooshed The Colonel's face between her palms and kissed his head. "Don't you listen to her, she's a grouch."

I snorted and snapped on his leash. "Come on before you're so spoiled rotten I gotta throw you away."

Connie laughed and followed us to the door. "You meet with Heather Rudd, and I'll look over that thumb drive. Want to meet for coffee tomorrow?"

"Um, I was gonna stop by the Bean and see what I can pry from Marlow-wanna tag along?"

"Sure! Should we write our choice of the killer on cards and seal them in an envelope? Miss Scarlett in the library with a candlestick?"

I snorted and headed to the truck. All jokes aside, the murder of Megan Hearn had been brutal, she'd have kicked and struggled for several minutes before succumbing to the dry ice fumes. What type of person could watch their victim suffer like that? I shivered as a gust of cool air ruffled my hair. Civility was a mask that someone used to hide a cold heart.

Chapter Seven

The house was dark when I arrived home from my meeting with Heather Rudd. I thought that would provide undisturbed time to uncover more secrets from the thumb drive, but I'd barely set foot in the back door before Mama pounced.

She was making cocoa and wanted to update me on what everyone in town was saying about the murder. An excuse was on the tip of my tongue but when she mentioned the rumor that Megan had been asking questions about the Cannery Wharf development I settled The Colonel in his bed and then pulled up a chair and accepted a mug.

"Mmm, you make the best cocoa, Mama." I took another sip. "Now then, what did your spy network have to say?"

Mama gave me *the look*. "Don't be offensive, Holly Marie." She sniffed and picked at her bathrobe. "If one of my friends observes something that might be of benefit to keeping my precious child out of prison-"

"Yes Mama, I'm sorry. Tell me what your friend saw."

Her eyes widened and she leaned toward me. "*Well,* Bernice and Pug Ziggler were down at the old courthouse getting a permit, you know he's promised Bernice a Florida room for the past twenty years!" She pursed her lips. "That man, always claiming he's so poor he can't jump over a nickel to save a dime when you only have to look at those stores he owns to see-"

"Yes ma'am, so Ms. Bernice is gettin' a sunroom, what does this have to do with Megan Hearn-"

"I'm getting to that!" She huffed. "As I was saying, Bernice and Tug were in the Planning Department getting their forms or whatever you need to build-Holly, do you think we'll need a permit to expand the potting shed -"

"Mama!"

She sat back and looked at me as if I'd grown two heads. "Whatever is the matter with you?"

So many replies to her question sprang to my lips but having been raised to respect my elders I bit them all back. "It's getting late, and my leg is aching, could you just tell me what the Zigglers saw?"

Her chin hiked up a notch, but she nodded. "Of course, as I was trying to say when you interrupted, that podcaster woman was in an office-Bernice didn't know whose it was but it's just to the right of the counter if you should-"

"Yes ma'am, I'll find it, now what did Ms. Bernice see?"

"Well, it was what she heard really. It seems the young woman was pitching a fit and their voices got loud, which is why Bernice noticed it because you know she isn't one to gossip-"

"Yes ma'am, because gossip is a sin." I managed to hide my smirk behind the mug of cocoa, but Mama's eyes still narrowed. She watched me for several seconds and then continued.

"Hmmm, yes it is. But that is neither here nor there as Bernice doesn't *do* it, however, she couldn't help but notice that the Hearn woman was angry and laying into the person in the office, so she commented on the behavior and the clerk said that they were used to it." Mama's eyebrows rose. "It seems, that woman was asking for records and inspections several times a week for the past month and *all* of it was on the Cannery Wharf project, now what do you make of that?"

I replayed the conversation with Mama, discarding the Ziggler's sunroom and financial status to be left with the fact that Megan Hearn had been seeking information on J.T. Minton's pet project. Was that a reason to kill her?

There was no denying I'd been suspicious of that project, and J.T. Minton in general. Because of that, I wasn't inclined to run with it as a line of investigation. Mama didn't see it that way.

"But Holly, it makes perfect sense! Many of us- er, I mean the investors have been questioning where the money has gone."

Many of us ... , was Mama invested in Minton's project? My brain immediately rebelled and said don't be ridiculous, my mother had no head for figures or money for that matter. Over the past year, I'd had to step in several times when she overdrew her bank account ... my brow furrowed as something about her finances nagged at me-

"I believe there is something unsavory about that wharf project."

Mama's comment set my thoughts back on track, though I made a mental note to think about it again later. "I'm not disagreeing with you, Mama, but what specifically has he done?"

She took our empty mugs to the sink and began to wash them. "It's not one particular thing ..." she shut the water off

and returned to the table. " I suppose it's the lack of progress and then, when you ask questions it's always something about holdups in the permit department or supply line issues." She scoffed. "Then he comes around with his hand out because of cost overruns or some such nonsense."

That sounded very specific to me and, once again I was questioning my mother's involvement in the Cannery Wharf project. I opened my mouth to ask her a point-blank question when Dewey burst through the back door.

"She thinks my tractor's sex-hey, Holly, just the person I wanted to see ... ah!"

Dewey stumbled across the threshold and face-planted on the kitchen floor. Mama rushed to his side, clucking like a hen, but I followed more slowly. Regardless of how hard the stone tiles, he was feelin' no pain.

Mama helped him to a sitting position and then gasped. "Dewey Barker, are you *inebriated?*"

I snorted to stop my outright laughter. My mother's naivety, in particular when it came to my brother, never ceased to amuse me, well, when it wasn't getting on my last nerve.

"Me? 'Course not ...," Dewey grabbed onto the counter and hoisted himself to his feet. "Well, not over much anyway. Nah, now don't fuss Mama, it's just a little beer ..."

Dewey waved away our mother's concerns and stumbled his way over to the table. Dropping into the chair beside me, he leaned on one elbow and gave me a Walleyed stare.

"Guess who killed Megan Hearn."

Half of what Dewey said came out as one long, slurred word. I hesitated to engage with him, but he sat up straight and repeated it.

"Go on, ask me who killed that woman." He scowled and waved his hand before I could reply. "Never mind, I'll tell you who did it! Cricket Morrison."

He sat back, arms crossed over his chest and a triumphant look on his face.

"Cricket Morrison?" I rolled my eyes. "Dewey, go to bed, you're drunk."

"No I ain't, well maybe just a little, but that don't mean I ain't right, tell her Mama."

Mama fretted over the coffee pot. "Well now, I can't say as I know her all that well but if you think so son ..." She looked over her shoulder and directed a pointed stare at me. "You should look into it, Holly Marie."

She would say that. I could count on one hand how many times our mother did *not* take up for Dewey. I drew a deep breath and then took another to insure I replied with a civil tone. "Mama, I am looking into the murder, but I hardly see how Cricket Morrison could be responsible." I scowled at my drunken brother. "She wasn't a guest, Dewey!"

His expression turned mulish. "Well I know that, but she coulda done it just the same." He tapped the table for emphasis. "She had motive!"

Motive. Cricket Morrison was a thrice divorced forty-something-year-old barfly that I strongly suspected had been the anonymous poster of a personal ad looking for her lost panties a few months back. Much head scratching and cogitation yielded no clear reason for her to have killed Megan Hearn. I hesitated to even go down the road but ...

"Dewey, she has no clear connection to-"

"Ha, see now that's where yer wrong!" His smile was smug. "Cricket works for Peachy Clean, don't she? She does them big fancy houses out on Osprey point and," he frowned at me when I started to interrupt. "*And* she also cleans offices, like fer Coastal Construction and Minton Equipment." He sat back with a nod. "See? Motive. She did it."

"Oh Dewey, that's genius, isn't that clever of your brother, Holly?"

I closed my eyes, so I didn't have to see the beatific smile my mother was gracing Dewey with. In her eyes, all he needed was a halo. But either I was lacking all good sense, or they were because I still didn't see a connection between Megan Hearn and Cricket Morrison.

Dewey huffed. "How can you not see what's right in front of yer face?" He rolled his eyes. "Didn't I tell ya Cricket cleans fer J.T. Minton's companies? Huh? And didn't I also tell ya she was there the day that podcaster walked in and tried to get an interview with Minton only he refused because, according to Cricket, Minton told Hearn she made mountains out of molehills for ratings, so Minton had her thrown out." He sat back. "There, clear as day now, ain't it?"

Clear as mud, more like. "hey, first, you left out the part where Minton threw her out but even so, how is that relevant? He wasn't at the party!"

"Nah, but Dale Scruggs was. I'm goin' to bed. " Dewey struggled to his feet and wobbled his way to the door.

"Hold on, " I shook my head. "What on earth does Dale Scruggs being at his own party have to do with J.T. Minton and Cricket Morrison?"

My brother turned and gave me an incredulous look. "Jeez Holly, like with J.T. Minton, Megan was poking around asking about those gyms Dale lost and ..." he shrugged and waltzed out the door. "Dale was Cricket's second ex-husband." The screen door slammed as he headed off to his apartment over the garage.

My jaw dropped. Of all the convoluted ... I turned and met Mama's gaze.

She quirked an eyebrow. "Close your mouth, Holly, you'll draw flies."

A quick dog walk to the park and back, followed by a shower should have relaxed me enough to sleep like a baby but my brain was determined to run in circles. Every time I shut my eyes I heard Dewey's rambling theories about Cricket Morrison and her second ex-husband, Dale Scruggs.

If I managed to shut down that train of thought, I'd end up ruminating on what Mama had learned concerning Megan Hearn and J.T. Minton; that track was stronger due to Dewey's inadvertent addition that the podcaster had been thrown out of Minton's office.

Could J.T. have been responsible? Logic said no, he hadn't attended the party and if I was sure of one thing, it was that the murderer had been a guest.

There was a tiny possibility someone had arrived by boat and killed her but that was too fantastical to give much credence to; anyone arriving by car would have been seen by the valets, we'd verified that when they'd made statements that no one had arrived after the party started except for Dewey.

No matter what Mama and Dewey thought, I still felt that the answers to Megan Hearn's murder lay in her relationships with the party guests. I considered the suspect list Connie and I had created.

Marlow was still at the top, but much as I hated to admit it, Dewey had a point; Dale could have killed the podcaster to keep her from dredging up his past. My gut still said he hadn't, but I'd need to check his alibi before I crossed him off.

Speaking of alibis, seeing the statements each guest made that night would be a tremendous help. I bit my lip and considered my options for getting the information. I could ask Craig to access the files but doing so would put him in an awkward position should Brannon find out. Which meant, I'd have to conduct my own interviews and I wasn't entirely comfortable with the idea.

Prying into people's personal lives was not something I made a habit of doing; that was more my mother and her friends' idea of a good time. But Dewey was headed to trial if I didn't put aside my reservations. Maxwell Bernard had called to say the evidence the prosecution was using to proceed was DNA under her fingernails and no amount of being told she'd done that with witnesses around was swaying them.

I sighed and turned off the bedside lamp. Tomorrow's chat with Edison Marlow would be the first test to see if I'd inherited any of my mother's busybody genes.

Chapter Eight

The Colonel and I strolled into The Split Bean minutes after they opened. Bill came out of the kitchen long enough to offer me a hot from the oven piece of quiche and then I was left to sip my tea in solitude. Connie and I had agreed to meet at eight but late last night I'd realized I had no idea what time Marlow frequented the cafe, thus my awakening at the butt crack of dawn.

Morning commuters started to filter in around six-thirty. The coffee shop had a lounge area, so I took my book to a cushy armchair and settled The Colonel at my feet. I was six chapters into a thriller when a barista welcoming Edison Marlow drew my attention.

Edison Marlow was not my idea of a writer. His wire-rimmed glasses and blazers with patches on the elbows gave him the air of a professor but his bubbly personality seemed at odds with the stereotype of a solitary soul pouring his heart onto a page.

Over the top of my paperback, I watched as he casually flirted with the girls behind the counter. If I had to choose one word to sum him up, it would have been smooth. His even white teeth, ready smile, and quick wit were a hit with the coffee shop employees and patrons alike.

His voice echoed off of the high ceilings as he regaled a small crowd with a story about the filming occurring across the street. He chatted for a good twenty minutes before excusing himself to work. I watched as he took his coffee to the booth Wanda had pointed out yesterday. He'd settled in and opened his laptop when his phone rang.

The expression on his face went from cheerful and open to closed and sullen within five minutes of saying hello and I wondered who he was speaking with. He'd lowered his voice, but I managed to hear him furiously whisper something about *damn store* before he snapped the computer closed and stalked outside to pace, and if his animated gestures were any indication, rant at his caller.

Being more than a little curious, I roused The Colonel and headed outside for a potty break. As I'd figured, Marlow paid me no mind as my dog sniffed and shuffled his way along the sidewalk looking for good places to lift his leg. The writer continued his conversation, and I eavesdropped under the cover of pet care.

"Look, she's dead and that's the end of it-no, I won't be-" Edison sighed and dragged a hand through his shaggy brown hair.

He held the phone away from his ear as someone on the other end spoke. They were yelling or he had his volume up because I could hear the tone but not the words.

A few minutes and Edison returned the phone to his ear and spoke through gritted teeth. "I'm- what?"

I glanced at him from the corner of my eye as The Colonel tugged me closer to a nearby Crape Myrtle. Edison got quiet, listening intently to whatever the person on the other end of the phone line was saying. His complexion had gone a funny shade of yellowy-green. For a minute I thought he might toss up his breakfast. He gulped and looked up, meeting my gaze.

I nodded and then turned, pretending interest in a poster hanging on the café window as I watched him through the reflection in the glass. He started walking back and forth, keeping pace with the words streaming from his mouth.

"I had nothing to do with it!" His hand waved like a symphony conductor as his volume increased. "This is on you- is that a threat?" The last words came out in a strained whisper. He walked farther away and, with his back to me, I could only catch broken phrases. " ... deserve to know ... sorry."

Edison walked toward me, and I hurriedly turned my back but not before I saw the scowl on his face. He pulled open the coffee shop door as he finished his call. "Don't ever call me again!"

I gave The Colonel a few more minutes and then followed the author into the Bean, choosing a table by the window since it was almost time for Connie to arrive. My seat gave me a clear view of Edison's corner booth. I opened my book and watched as he tried to work on his computer but every few minutes he'd stop and stare into space. Writer's block or was he still upset by the call he'd just finished? I was considering what I'd overheard when Connie startled me by sliding into the seat opposite mine.

"Good morning!" She bent and hugged The Colonel. "Hello, my little potato, are you being a good boy? Auntie will give you a bite of her cake, yes she will-"

"Connie, that dog is going to need a motorized scooter if y'all don't stop feeding him!"

My friend pouted. "But look at that face, how can you say no to those sad eyes?"

I rolled mine. "Because I have to pay the vet bills!"

She scoffed and sat back as the server set a piece of cinnamon streusel coffee cake and a cappuccino in front of her. "Spoiled sport." The Colonel grunted and started to beg. "Sorry buddy, your mom says no."

She held out for all of two seconds before breaking off a tiny piece of cake and slipping it under the table. I pretended not to notice and launched into what I'd just heard from Edison Marlow's one-sided conversation.

Connie's eyes widened as I finished. "He said, *she's dead*. You think he was talking about Megan Hearn?"

I shrugged. "I don't know, could be but his late wife also fits that bill and I know Hearn was dredging up Marlow's past ..."

"Yeah ..." She sipped her coffee. "Hey, didn't you say he was also talking about a store?"

"Uh-huh, but I don't know if that is what he said, it was hard to hear, it could have been something else that sounded like that?" I shook my head. "All I heard for sure was the curse word and then the *sto* sound."

Connie's mouth twisted and her brow furrowed. "Hmm, stow? Stoic?"

I shook my head. "Nah, that wasn't it ..."

"Stone? Storm-"

"That's it! I think he said damn storm and it makes sense because a few seconds later he said something about cleaning."

Connie's eyes widened and her gaze went to the corner where the author was staring at his computer. "But what was it about? Why curse the storm?"

"No idea. Maybe the person on the phone needs stuff done in their yard or house? Damage from the hurricane?"

Connie shrugged. "That's probably it." She leaned across the table and lowered her voice. "So when are we gonna interrogate him?"

I bit back a laugh. "I don't know, but should I bring a rubber hose and bright light?"

"Oh very funny." She stuck her tongue out at me and leaned back in her seat. "Okay then, smarty. How do you want to handle it?"

Well, she had me there, I couldn't think of a legitimate reason to strike up a conversation with the man. He'd waved at me when he arrived and then made it clear he was working by setting his table up like a mini office. Other than just marching over and telling him I wanted to talk I was at a loss.

"For Heaven's sake, Holly, we can't do that!"

"Duh, I just said that, but I don't know-"

"Leave it to me." She rummaged in her tote bag and pulled out a paperback copy of Bernie Deveraux and the Honey Baked Curse."

"No thanks, I prefer thrillers." I snorted and finished my tea. "Murders in small towns full of nosy people is completely unrealistic."

Connie cocked her head to the side and pursed her lips. "What?"

A roll of her eyes followed by a snort was her reply. She rose from her chair and motioned for me to follow. "Come on, let's play fangirls."

The Colonel and I trotted behind my friend, he no doubt happily anticipating more treats and me, baffled but willing to go along for the ride. As we approached the table, I heard Connie gushing with enthusiasm and the fangirl comment slid into place.

"I don't want to interrupt your work, but my friend Holly mentioned that you're the author of my favorite book and I just had to say hi and," her expression turned sheepish. "I have a copy of Bernie Deveraux and the Honey Baked Curse." She bit her lip. "Would you mind signing it?"

The author turned on the charm I'd witnessed at the party. One on one, he was low-key but with a rapt audience he sparkled; it was clear he loved the attention his writing garnered.

"Goodness, it's no imposition!" He gestured for us to take the seat opposite his, he smiled and nodded at me before turning his attention to Connie's paperback. "Hey Holly, and you too, Sad Sack."

The Colonel wiggled over for the obligatory head pat as I slid onto the seat beside Connie. Edison gave my bulldog his attention before retrieving an ink pen from his messenger bag. "Ok, to C O N N I E?" My friend nodded. "To Connie, enjoyed our conversation at The Split Bean, Regards, Edison Marlow." He grinned and slid the closed book across the table. "That do?"

Connie smiled. "Oh yes, thank you again."

Edison smiled. "My pleasure." He glanced at me. "I wanted to tell you how lovely everything was at the party; people are talking about the decorations as much as the murder!"

That wasn't a good thing, in my opinion, but I kept it to myself and forced a smile. He'd given me the perfect opening to bring up the pipe Whopper had found. "Thanks! Though I think everyone missed the full impact of what I think was the best part."

His brow furrowed as he cocked his head to the side. "What would that be, then?"

"The tasting pavilion decorations of course! The launch presentation was to showcase Witch's Brew which is why I set the stage as I did, but it barely got noticed with all of the commotion ..."

His eyes widened. "Oh, that sounds cute! I glanced over that way but seeing her legs sticking out ..." he grimaced. "After that, I did my best to avoid looking in that direction, ghastly."

"Understandable but you're sure you didn't go over by the stage that night?"

He swallowed convulsively and looked away. "Of course I'm sure!"

"Hmm, odd." I narrowed my focus as I delivered my punch. "Are you missing any pieces of your costume?"

Wide-eyed and a little bit pale, Edison met my gaze briefly before staring at his laptop. "My costume ..., no. Look, it was lovely meeting you Connie, but I really need to get back-"

"Are you working on Bernie's next adventure?" Connie busted into the conversation, keeping her fan persona going as she shot warning looks at me. "Does she end up with the Sheriff?"

A cloud seemed to dim the light in Edison's eyes then he blinked, and the familiar twinkle was back, brighter than before. He continued to chat with Connie about a fictional world I knew nothing about, and I used the time to observe him.

He'd been bright and bubbly until I started talking about where Megan Hearn's body was found and when I'd hinted about a missing piece of his costume his body language gave him away, even if I hadn't known the pipe was found near the witch's circle.

He'd glommed onto the change in conversation, but when Connie mentioned the next book in his series he once again looked uncomfortable. I couldn't help but wonder if his change in mood had anything to do with the allegations Megan Hearn had made. Was his conscience pricked or was I just looking for clues where none existed?

I tuned back into their conversation in time to hear Connie gently probing the author. God bless my friend; I'd let my mind wander from the point of the whole meeting.

"So, you were at the brewery party." She rested her arms on the table and leaned forward. "Can you believe someone murdering that woman?"

I braced for Marlow to rebuff my friend but after a second's hesitation, mirrored her posture and replied. "No, such a brutal way to go." He gave a mock shudder. "One would have to be very angry to kill someone that way but, if you knew Ms. Hearn at all, you'd see that she often put people's backs up."

"Then you think she was asking for it?" Connie and Edison gasped at my question, with my friend also shooting me daggers. I just shrugged. Yes, I could have been more tactful, but I'd been up early and wasted hours sitting in the Bean. I was tired, the dog was restless, and my patience was hanging by a thread.

Marlow frowned and sat up straight. "Well now, I don't know if I'd go so far as-"

"But you do think her actions might have gotten her killed."

He stared at me for a few seconds, his face morphing into a more guarded expression. I was just about to back off of my question when he sighed.

"Yes, I'm sorry to say it, but she was not a nice person." Edison glanced at Connie as if in need of support. Encouragement? Either way, my friend smiled and nodded her head and he continued. "I think she enjoyed provoking people."

My brow furrowed. "In what way?"

Edison shrugged. "She just ... would do or say anything for a story."

I nodded and was about to pepper him with another question, but Connie nudged me with her foot and presented the author with a sympathetic smile and a pat on his arm. "Mmm,

I'd heard that too. In fact, someone mentioned she'd been spreading tales about you."

Marlow jumped as if she'd shocked him with a cattle prod. "Wha-how, who said that?"

Connie cast a panicked look my way. I interpreted it to mean she was floundering and jumped in. "Wanda said Megan had been in recently and Bill tossed her out for harassing you. She seemed to think Hearn was questioning your claims of writing those books ..."

His eyes widened. "Wanda said that?" He shook his head and flashed a rueful smile. "What utter nonsense! I wasn't friends with Ms. Hearn but she never-"

"Edison, the conversation was overheard. According to Wanda, Megan Hearn was threatening to do a series of podcasts on you plagiarizing your late wife's books and even hinting that you killed her. Are you trying to tell me Wanda is lying?"

The author's cheeks flushed scarlet, and his Adam's apple bobbed as he gulped several times. A glance at the table showed his fingers curling into fists and his posture was rigid. I braced for him to explode with rage but, without warning his expression crumbled and tears filled his eyes.

I glanced at Connie. She shrugged and both of us turned our focus back to Marlow as he groaned, head in hand he muttered. "I just want this to end!"

Connie made a sympathetic noise and patted his arm. "What to end, Edison?"

He lifted his head. Red-rimmed and tear-filled eyes met Connie's. "The guilt!"

The Colonel sniffed the air and then tugged on the leash until I allowed him to move closer to one of the swings that lined the boardwalk overlooking the Indigo River. After ensuring there was nothing he could ingest, I left him to explore the shrubbery and let my mind wander back to the conversation Connie and I had engaged Edison Marlow in.

He'd been genuinely distressed when pushed to admit Megan Hearn had intended to pursue the topic of him plagiarizing. Connie had been sniffing and wiping her own eyes as the author had begged for absolution. Turned out, he had stolen his late wife's work but only the first novel.

According to Marlow, she'd written Bernie Deveraux and the Honey Baked Curse, and it'd been shopped around to publishers with no success. Just as she was about to try again, she'd fallen to her death, and he claimed the submission was done to honor her and things had been misconstrued, and by the time he'd noticed the error …

Edison had sworn on all that was holy he hadn't killed his wife and that all the subsequent books were written by him. I wasn't a fan of the books, so it was of no concern to me one way or the other, but Connie and I agreed he'd been telling the truth; he was only guilty of plagiarism.

How far would he go to keep his secret was a matter of contention, however. Connie insisted Edison wouldn't have killed to keep Megan from doing the podcast. Her reasoning was the fact that he was guilt-ridden over stealing his late wife's work and subconsciously welcomed the truth coming out.

She had a point, but I hadn't been content with striking him off of the suspect list based on intuition. He'd lied about missing the pipe from the Sherlock costume and lied about being near the stage. Then, before we'd left him to blubber in solitude, I'd asked him who he'd been arguing with on the phone. He hadn't been expecting the question. Surprise showed in his eyes, and he hesitated before claiming it was his agent.

His body language said he was lying again but I let it go and asked where he'd been when Hearn was likely being murdered. My question caught him off guard. He'd looked everywhere but at me, wiped his wet cheeks, and blew his nose before stammering a reply that he'd been with Rae Ella Reid.

The answer surprised me. I hadn't realized they were friends, but when I commented, Marlow casually replied that they'd been at school together, but Rae Ella had been more Amber's friend than his. With no reason not to believe him, Connie and I had left.

She returned to Glitter and Garland, and I'd had every intention of speaking with Rae Ella anyway but a trip out to Rose Island required my boat, decent weather, and an early start. Not a problem but before Edison claimed her as an alibi, I'd had no reason for showing up unannounced and I'd pushed the task aside; now, checking Marlow's alibi gave me the perfect excuse. After I'd carried out a boatload of errands for Mama, it was too late to head for the island.

Pushing the task of visiting Rae Ella to tomorrow's list, I dropped onto the swing and contemplated my other source of anxiety. Connie's interference had netted me another decorating job. Heather Rudd's home was a turn-of-the-century mansion built for Josiah Adams. The two-and-a-half story clapboard home was designed in the Queen Anne gothic style.

Sky blue with loads of bright white gingerbread trim, complete with a turret, the home was a well-known landmark in the Bayview neighborhood and word would get around that I'd decorated it for the holidays; I had to be on my game.

The trouble was, I had no idea where to start. Aside from wanting a coastal Southern theme, Heather had left the details up to me. I hadn't had the heart to tell her Southerners decorated for Christmas the same way everyone else did so now I was left to interpret what coastal and Southern meant to a recently transplanted Yankee.

When decorating Mama's porch, I tried to respect the historic nature of the home: no blow-up characters on the lawn or anything else pop culture. A tug on the leash drew me from the swing. The Colonel perused the oyster shells serving as mulch underneath a cluster of palms and inspiration struck.

I'd never used native greenery before, but if Heather wanted coastal I couldn't think of a better representation than palms. I could order some from It's About Thyme nursery. Along with being coastal, they were perfect for a late Victorian-style home because potted palms had been all the rage!

The Colonel and I took our time walking home. The weather was pleasantly cool, and the setting sun painted everything in shades of pink, purple, and gold. I passed the Adams house. The Rudds were on the porch. I waved and then crossed the road to avoid being hit up to buy candy from what I assumed were the congregation from Mama's long-haired preacher church, and then let my imagination run with more ideas for decorating the Rudd's house.

Once home, I'd eaten a quick meal with Mama and left her to watch her shows. I settled The Colonel on his bed and spent the rest of the evening making rough sketches before turning in. As I drifted off to sleep I realized I was excited to embark on another decorating job. Perhaps Connie's idea of a business had merit if I could avoid another body in my display.

Chapter Nine

The housekeeper ushered me and The Colonel onto the terrace, murmured something about refreshments, and left us to wait for Rae Ella to complete her laps. The former beauty queen crossed and recrossed the infinity pool with a butterfly stroke so aggressive it appeared she was trying to pummel the water into submission.

Dedication to burning calories or was rage her fuel? I hadn't missed the raised voices as I approached the front door, nor Griff's thunderous expression as he stalked past me without so much as a by your leave.

The poor housekeeper had stammered and stuttered her way through a semblance of an apology before giving me a rueful smile and escorting me to her employer. Dropping in on people unannounced was not something I routinely did, but calling ahead would have demanded an explanation for visiting, and putting Rae Ella on the defensive was not on my agenda.

A pitcher of cucumber and melon-infused water along with a plate of fruit kabobs were set on the table without a word, leaving me to assume it was a standard post-workout routine. The tray held two glasses and I had no idea when Rae Ella would finish, so I helped myself to some water and settled back to enjoy the amazing view afforded by the Reid's backyard.

The home was at the end of Rose Island and looked out at the Intercoastal Waterway. A few boats came in and out of view and then I was left to peruse miles of unspoiled coastline on the opposite shore. I yawned. No matter how early I went to bed, I never seemed to feel rested.

The sun glinting off of the rippling water was mesmerizing and, coupled with the gentle breeze ruffling my hair and setting the palm fronds creaking my eyelids began to droop.

"Holly?"

The Colonel grunted and got to his feet as I jolted from my stupor and swung my gaze to the end of the pool. Rae Ella waved and then pulled herself from the water.

I sat up straighter and sipped my water. "Hey, Rae Ella! Sorry to barge in on you but the housekeeper ..."

She waved away my apology and reached for a towel. "Don't be silly, it's great to see you, and you too little pork chop!" She patted The Colonel's head and then leaned over to fashion the towel into a turban before donning her coverup and taking the seat across from me. "Haven't seen you in forever-well, that brewery party doesn't count since we didn't get to talk." Her smile waned. "I'm sorry about your brother."

I looked out at the river and bit my lip as I debated the best way to broach the subject uppermost in my mind. My upbringing said I should ease into it with small talk but, she'd brought it up ... "Thanks, that's actually why I came by."

Rae Ella's perfectly arched brows rose. "Oh? I don't see how-"

"I was wondering if you can recall anything happening that night that might lead to who killed Megan Hearn ..." I shrugged and tried to decide if I should tell her I was looking for the murderer.

Rae Ella's gray eyes widened. "Gosh Holly, I don't think-" she frowned. "Why are you interested?" She gestured toward the platter of fruit, "Help yourself."

I smiled. "No, thank you. Um, I was wondering because, well ..." I drew a breath and sighed. We'd never been close friends but neither had we been enemies. There was no reason to beat around the bush with her unless she'd killed the podcaster, and I still thought that was a stretch. I laid my cards on the table.

"I'll be honest, Rae Ella. The detective on this case isn't even looking for another culprit and Dewey did *not* kill her ..."

The sparkle in her eyes dimmed and she squeezed my hand. "I understand." She snorted. "Griff was just saying the competence in the department is questionable, especially since Sheriff Goodwin retired- oh!" She bit her lip. "I shouldn't have said that! Please don't repeat it, Griff will be so mad. I'm so stupid, his rivals would use that-"

"Hey, hey it's okay!" I touched her arm. She was shaking and fear was evident in her expression and quivering voice. My brow furrowed. I'd dealt with my share of domestic violence issues while carrying a badge, my radar was clanging.

"Rae Ella, has Griff hurt you?"

Her eyes about jumped from their sockets. "No! No, of course not! Why would you-"

"Because you seem scared of Griff. I heard y'all arguing as I arrived. If he's harming you we can get you help, you don't have to-"

"No, no Holly it's nothing like that." Her lips turned up in a parody of a smile. "He's just got a lot on his mind right now and the least thing will set him off ..." She shrugged. "Griff would never hurt me, but he does fly into rages more often lately ..."

My mouth pursed. I wanted to shake her for defending him but there was nothing I could do; Rae Ella would have to stand up for herself. She'd mentioned him being under stress though, and I could prod her for more information on that.

I cleared my throat. "Rae Ella? You said Griff has a hair-trigger temper? I've never known that about him, is it the election? Is the stress too much ..."

"No." Her gaze dropped to the glass tabletop. She fidgeted with a skewer as she replied in a voice barely above a whisper. "It's ..."

"It's what, Rae Ella?"

She met my gaze for a split second and then looked out toward the river. "Nothing, it's just the election ..."

I didn't buy her answer. Griff Reid was predicted to win by a margin of thirty percent. If he was stressed over the election it was because he feared an October Surprise and Megan Hearn was just the woman to deliver one.

"Rae Ella? Was Megan Hearn blackmailing Griff?"

Her gaze swung back to mine as she sucked in a breath. "Wha-why would you ask such a thing?"

I cocked my head to the side and studied her before answering. Shoulders hunched, spine stiff, hands clasped ... her body language reminded me of a turtle trying to get back into its shell and instinct said she was going to clam up, regardless of what I said.

I decided to go for broke. "The other night, at the party, I saw Griff talking with Megan Hearn and whatever was said didn't make him happy. I would call his expression shell-shocked."

I'd been watching Rae Ella as I spoke. She'd moved so that her arms were crossed like she was hugging herself and she'd lowered her chin closer to her chest. "Not long after that, I passed you and Griff at the entrance to the tent. Rae Ella, you looked like you'd been crying, and Griff was very angry. Care to tell me what that was all about?"

Rae Ella's head sprang up and her angry gaze met mine. "How dare you? Why can't you people leave us alone?"

"You people? Who is bothering you, Rae Ella?"

"Just leave us alone! You think Griff killed that horrible woman? Huh? Or did I do it?" She jumped up, sending her metal chair crashing to the concrete. "I thought you were a friend but you're just like all the rest."

My mouth fell open as the turtle came out of its shell, snapping for all she was worth. I started to speak but Rae Ella cut me off.

"Poking your nose where it doesn't belong!" She snorted. "You're just trying to pin the murder on someone other than that lazy brother of yours! Well, how about the others? Tons of people hated that woman!"

Rae Ella paced across the pool deck, waving her arms as she settled into an epic rant. "What about Mark Timmons? Did you bother to pry into *his* life?" She glanced at me but didn't give me a chance to get a word in edgewise. "The brewery is in trouble; did you know that? Mark's been all over the county begging for investment capital! We dined at Indigo the other night and he was with J.T. Minton." She rolled her eyes. "Griff said Mark's trolling for big fish. But where did the money go? He was bragging about how successful the brewery was just last year so what changed? I saw him and Hearn going at it in the garden just before we all went to the tasting pavilion, why isn't he a suspect? Huh?"

"When will it end?" As quickly as she'd flown into a rage, Rae Ella deflated, sinking onto a lounge chair with a sob.

I rose and tentatively touched her shoulder only to have her flinch and mumble. "Leave me alone, Holly. I thought you were my friend but you're just looking for dirt like everyone else ..."

"Rae Ella ..." This wasn't what I'd planned, and I felt about two inches tall. "I am your friend, and I'm sorry I upset you." I crouched down to meet her gaze. "I'm not looking for dirt to use on Griff, I actually think he'll be a good representative for us! But I do need to find out who killed Hearn. I came by to see you but also to check Edison Marlow's alibi."

That brought her head up. Rae Ella frowned. "Edison? I don't understand ..."

"He claims to have been talking to you during the time police estimate Hearn was killed ..."

Her eyes narrowed. "What time was that?"

"Between 11:15 and 11:45? Give or take a few minutes ..."

Rae Ella worried at her bottom lip as she considered my question. "I did talk with Edison but ... I don't think-no, I know it was earlier than eleven."

Her expression showed no doubt. "How can you be so sure?"

"Well, I wanted to go home, especially after that whole thing with Hearn- I mean, I was tired and I asked several times if Griff was ready to go. He kept saying it was too early, it'd look bad ... " she rolled her eyes. "The last time I asked to leave I checked my phone first so I could use the time against his argument. It was a few minutes before eleven. I rounded up and told him it was eleven and the boat ride home is always longer in the dark which meant we wouldn't get home until one in the morning ..." She snorted. "We argued for nothing because by the time the police let us go ... we ended up staying at Griff's apartment in Sanctuary Bay."

That had been a very specific ramble and Rae Ella's description of prodding Griff into leaving was a familiar routine. I'd seen it countless times when Brooks and I had been out with the couple. Which meant that Edison was mistaken about the time of his chat with Rae Ella, or he was lying.

I smiled and patted her knee before I rose. "Thank you, and thanks for telling me about Mark. I've heard a few things that had me wondering but added to what you've said he is definitely a suspect." My eyebrows rose as things from her earlier tirade clicked in.

"Rae Ella?" She glared at me, but I ignored it. "What were you saying about Mark Timmons and Megan Hearn in the garden? That's the first I've heard about it ..."

Rae Ella sniffed and swiped at her eyes. The mulish expression on her face made me think she wasn't going to answer but she drew a deep breath and cleared her throat. "If I tell you will you leave us alone?"

I wanted to know what she'd observed between Mark and Megan, but I didn't want to lie to Rae Ella, regardless of what she thought, I'd always liked her. "If I can, Rae Ella ..." Her expression turned stormy, so I hurried on. "I'm not out to get Griff or keep him from being elected; this isn't political! I am trying to keep my brother out of prison and I'm just following where the clues lead me, so I promise not to bother Griff unless I have to, okay?"

Her lips pursed and I braced myself to be thrown out on my ear, but Rae Ella surprised me. She wasn't cordial and I resigned myself to having ruined a casual friendship, but she sighed and accepted my caveat. "I'm not sure what time it was ..." she paused. Her eyes looked slightly unfocused and then she nodded. "Okay, I'm pretty sure it was just before I told Griff it was time to go which means it was before eleven. Let me think ..." Once again she looked off into the distance for several minutes. "I'd been to the restroom." She glanced at me. "Were you also annoyed that the closest facility was in the brewery? I swear, whoever thought that was a good set up for a party with the tent all the way across the-" Her expression turned apologetic. "Oops, sorry, was that part of your job?"

I grinned and hoped her lighter tone meant I was forgiven for prying into her personal life. "No, and for the record, both myself and the caterer pointed out the bad location, but Mark insisted. He said Glenda wanted to show off the renovations to the house. Pretty sure she was giving tours earlier that night."

Rae Ella nodded. "I must have missed it. Either way, it was a pain to have to walk through that garden, which was pretty dark, even with your luminaries. But that's why I remember ..." She shrugged and picked at the fruit still on the tray. "I was complaining to myself as I came back from the bathroom and wasn't paying much attention and came up on Mark and Megan Hearn."

I frowned. "Were they arguing?"

She shook her head. "No, that's what was odd. They were standing pretty close and when I came around the corner they jumped apart and they looked guilty. To be honest I figured they were having an affair and what happened a few minutes later confirmed it."

The idea that Megan, a woman barely thirty years old, was romantically involved with a man close to sixty didn't sit right with me. It happened of course, but Mark wasn't one of the stereotypical wealthy older men that attracted young women. He wasn't a big name in business or society circles, he wasn't flashy with cash, cars, boats ..."What happened after you surprised them?"

"Well, I'd excused myself for intruding, you know how you do when these things happen, and Mark said something about hoping I was enjoying myself ... just small talk. I walked on, but as I was nearing the fountain their voices got louder and something in his tone made me turn around." She chewed on her lower lip and frowned. "I can't define why I came back, it was just a feeling but, anyway, I did and arrived in time to hear Megan call him a nasty name and then she raised her hand, like this ...," Rae Ella bent her arm and raised it near her ear. "I thought she was going to hit him but instead she extended her arm straight out in front of her and something she was holding sailed off into the garden." She snorted. "Girl had a good arm on her. Whatever she threw arced in the air and landed a good ways away."

"Wait, she threw something? What was it? Where did it land?"

Rae Ella chuckled. "No idea what she threw, it was too dark to see, but it was small, like a rock maybe? Must have been important though because Mark called *her* a nasty name and then rushed to look for it and Megan stalked past him toward the brewery."

Mark had been in the shrubbery looking for something. I'd heard someone just before finding Megan's body. The Colonel had even tried to chase them-but no, what Rae Ella was describing happened earlier so it couldn't be the same thing.

"Thanks, Rae Ella. I'm not sure if it helps but every little bit, right?"

She shrugged and turned her back on me.

I bit my lip. "Rae Ella, I appreciate your help and ..., I meant what I said. I'm your friend and if you need to talk ..."

She looked over her shoulder. The eyes that met my gaze were like shards of flint and I knew I'd over-stayed my welcome. I sighed, mumbled another apology, and showed myself to the door.

I let the little I'd learned from Rae Ella simmer as I prepared for the return trip home. Traveling by boat with The Colonel took a bit more effort than in the Scout. Ten minutes of wrestling his pudgy butt into a life jacket and I was finally ready to cast off.

Once out of the No Wake Zone, I opened up the motor. Hardly anyone was on the river, so I hit the throttle another notch. The skiff's bow rose and The Colonel, who always sat on the seat directly in front of the wheel, braced his fat butt against the windscreen and tossed his head into the wind. Jowls flapping, cinched into a bright blue with dancing sea life safety jacket, he was a comical site.

We were enjoying our ride and had just passed the tip of Elloree Island when a large wake caused me to slow. A flotilla of boats, a cruiser, and several smaller boats, along with a barge were heading out toward the Atlantic. Puzzled, I grabbed my binoculars. State police logo on two boats, another from DNR, along with the barge and their course ... best guess was more clean-up and evidence gathering out on Shell Point.

Once the way was clear and the river again calm, I hit the throttle and in short order, we were docking back at the Marina. Matt, the dock hand tied me off and soon enough The Colonel was leading me to the Scout.

Aside from making an enemy of Rae Ella Reid, my morning had been productive. It'd been a glorious day to be on the water and I'd have liked nothing better than to anchor near the marsh and cast a line, but I had an appointment with the shrink at three. It'd taken an hour to get back to the marina, leaving me just enough time to grab a bite at the Country Kitchen. A full belly with a side of gossip was just what the doctor ordered.

Chapter Ten

A quick bite at the Country Kitchen filled my stomach as well as my ear; Everleigh had taken to her task with gusto. According to my friend, Megan Hearn had been asking about the Cannery Wharf project. That wasn't news to me, but it did place another virtual star next to the J.T. Minton involved in her death theory.

While she'd found more ties for the Minton theory, Everleigh hadn't been able to turn up much on the Morticia Adams wannabe that had been staring at me the other morning. All anyone seemed to know was that she was staying in a vacation rental near the interstate, she'd been seen eating lunch with that *long-haired preacher,* and some said her name was Jan or maybe it was Jen Smith.

Since the mystery woman hadn't been seen in several days I dismissed her and focused on J.T. The evidence for his motive was stacking up but nothing by way of means had presented itself, though one old man had suggested a killer for hire scenario, bless his heart.

The Colonel finished his after-lunch bathroom break and trotted beside me as I entered the therapist's office. Talking with Dr. Miriam Styles was a condition of my settlement. If my financial security wasn't dependent upon it, I'd have quit the appointments after the first month.

With The Colonel stopping to smell every tree, bush, and fire hydrant, we'd made it to her office in the nick of time. The receptionist ushered us into Styles' office and closed the door.

"Holly, so nice to see you!" Dr. Styles rose and gestured for me to take a seat on the leather couch across from her desk. After I made myself comfortable, she took the seat opposite and patted The Colonel on the head. "And hello to you, too! Have you been doing your job?"

She looked at me for a reply. "Oh, uh, he's a great comfort?" I winced as she cocked an eyebrow. Probably shouldn't have ended that more adamantly.

Dr. Styles sighed. "Holly ..., have you had any panic attacks since our last session?"

I considered lying but she always seemed to know. "Yes, but The Colonel helped me take control. I think I'm making real progress." I forced a smile. "You were right to suggest he act as a support animal."

Her answering smile told me she wasn't buying my act. "Good, I'm glad he's helped you." She sat back in her chair and met my gaze.

"Other than that incident, how have you been? You started physical therapy, has that helped with your sleeping issues? Still having nightmares?"

My answers were non-committal, earning another sigh. I knew I was being stubborn, but I resented being forced to attend the sessions. I just wanted to be left alone. All of the sharing of feelings and being asked to analyze every thought or emotion was stressing me out.

Styles started to speak, and I just knew it was gonna be more mumbo jumbo. Without much thought, I announced my new decorating client and Connie's suggestion that I start a business.

Dr. Styles' eyes widened. "But that's wonderful! How do you feel about this?"

Oh, here we go with the feelings! I managed to refrain from rolling my eyes and forced my tone to acceptable levels for common civility. "It's fine." I shrugged. "Wasn't looking for a new career though, and frankly I'm surprised anyone would want to hire me after what happened at the brewery."

She nodded. "Now that you've brought it up ..., I understand you were present when the body of the podcaster was found?

What was her point? I frowned and gave a quick nod. I didn't have to wait long for an answer.

Her expression was solemn as she leaned forward. "How did that make you feel?"

Again with the feelings? I smirked. "Um, okay? How should I have felt? It was sad, I don't like to see anyone die."

She murmured a soft hmmm and sat back in her chair. Her gaze held mine until I looked away. God, I hated shrinks!

A few seconds of silence and then the doctor cleared her throat. "Circling back to the day you had an attack. Were you able to define what triggered the anxiety? If so, what actions can you take to avoid those triggers?"

I looked over at her and then turned my head to look out the window, though her only view was of the upper floors of Prince Street businesses. I could feel her staring at me, expecting me to answer, and my temper flared. Why couldn't she leave well enough alone? The dog helped me calm down, the panic attacks were less frequent, all was right with the world; the end, time to go.

"Holly, where were you when you had an attack? What were you doing?"

I glanced back at her and wondered if her expression was taught in college. Framed by salt and pepper hair pulled into a loose bun at the nape of her neck, Dr. Styles' lightly lined face was arranged into a bland mask, revealing no emotion. I was sure she meant to appear nonjudgmental but all it did was give me the creeps; it was like talking to a robot.

Knowing she wasn't going to end the appointment unless I cooperated, I thought back to the last attack. My mouth went dry. I hated talking about it, hated that it had happened ..., "Someone asked about the shooting, and images of that day flashed in front of my eyes, and I started to panic." I blurted out the facts in a single breath. My hands curled into fists and a nerve ticked in my cheek.

Dr. Styles nodded. "I see, and how did that make you feel?"

My reply came through clenched teeth. "Angry, weak ..., I don't know, frustrated!"

"Let's start with anger." She smiled. "What made you angry? That the person asked about the shooting or your body's response to the question?"

Her emotionless smile got on my already strained nerves. I jerked my head to the right and went back to staring out the window as I tried to rein in my emotions. Her question lingered, though, and my brain kept replaying it over and over until I got tired and addressed it. I sighed and met her unwavering gaze. "I was angry at myself. I shouldn't be this weak."

Her eyebrows rose. "So you think you shouldn't have these panic attacks."

I nodded. "Of course, it's been ten months. Time to get over it."

"But your mind isn't agreeing?"

My glare was met with an unblinking stare. I rolled my eyes. "No, it isn't, and I come here week after week and get no results so perhaps we should call it a day." I'd stood up and gathered The Colonel's leash when Dr. Styles' hand came to rest on my arm.

The gentle restraint didn't sway me, but the smile that reached her eyes did. I cocked my head to the side as I tried to decide what I'd said that warranted the first semblance of human emotions. It wasn't long before Dr. Styles enlightened me.

"Now that you've admitted you need help ..."

The smile remained bright as her words and their implication filled the silence. My brows rose. "You have a treatment, other than yakking for an hour once a week?"

Dr. Styles laughed out loud. "Treatment? I'd call it more of a method of coping ... if you'd like to take a seat?"

I plopped back down onto the couch with a sigh. "This gonna hurt?"

"Not that I'm aware. Just relax." She rose and removed a candle and a lighter from a cabinet beside her desk. She lit the three wicks of the large white candle and set it on the coffee table. "I'd like to introduce you to DBT which stands for Dialectical Behavior Therapy."

"What's with the candle? Twisted aversion therapy? Gonna burn my hand as you make me recall the shooting?"

She tsked and shook her head. "Don't be silly. I've chosen a candle, but you can use any object that is handy so long as it doesn't have any strong emotions attached to it. A book, the television remote, a coaster, something neutral, okay?"

Her gaze met mine and I nodded, though I had no idea what she was talking about.

"DBT is a method of coping that teaches your brain to focus and to redirect your attention when something triggers you. Do you remember the breathing exercises I taught you?"

"Yes, I actually used them along with petting The Colonel, to break the anxiety attack."

"Excellent! Then you know concentrating on your breathing is helpful. Now we'll add a focus object." She pushed the candle closer to me. "Let's start by observing the object. Take about five minutes and really look at it."

She smiled and nodded encouragement, so I leaned forward and stared at the candle.

"Great, breath in and out concentrating on how it feels to fill your lungs ... perfect. Now, how does the candle look? Is it smooth, does it have edges? Is it round? How about size, is it very small or medium-sized?"

The candle was just a candle, of course, it was round and smooth, and this one was also very large. Dr. Styles chuckled at my observations.

"Indeed, you're right. What color is it? Is it shiny or dull? Does it have an odor? How about weight; heavy or light?"

"It's white and dull?" I sighed. "What does this have to do with-"

"Just consider the questions, Holly. It's normal for your mind to wander. You might feel bored. That's okay. Accept the thought and push it aside. Maybe you'll think of something that happened earlier today or a conversation that made you angry ... again, just acknowledge the thought and push it aside, don't analyze it, just park it in the back of your mind and return to the properties of the object."

Doctor Styles moved to her desk and opened a drawer. I watched from the corner of my eye as she removed a blue journal and brought it back to the seating area. She motioned for me to take it.

"This focusing exercise should be done every day for about five minutes; think you can commit to that?"

I huffed. "Yeah, but how is this going to-"

"Ask yourself the questions I just ran through. Study the object you've chosen and identify its properties, then when the time is up, I want you to make a dated journal entry." She opened the notebook and pointed at the first page. She'd drawn a grid and labeled the columns date, object, qualities of the object, and feelings or thoughts. "Just fill out the information for each column header."

"Okay, but how does this help me combat anxiety?"

"Well, our minds often hop from one thing to the next in a flurry of disorganization. Being more focused is a skill that requires practice and training. If you do this every day and note your thoughts or emotions but gently turn your attention back to studying the object, your brain will slowly start to do this with other things throughout the day. Make sense?"

"Kind of." All I'd felt was frustrated and bored but if it got me out of her office I'd commit to trying just about anything. "Five minutes a day, right?"

"Yes, and write down your observations so we have a record of your progress. Bring the notebook with you and I'll see you next week."

I took my journal, set the appointment for the following week, and then set off for home. I thought the focus exercise was a bit silly, but if doing it would appease the woman into releasing me from further appointments I was all in.

The Scout was acting up again. I made a mental note to get it into the shop and then forced it into gear. My conversation with the doctor continued to irk me. I was fine, she'd made a big deal about nothing. Everyone had nightmares occasionally.

I wrinkled my nose as my know-it-all inner voice piped up to argue. *You haven't had a decent night's sleep since the shooting and that's why you almost fell asleep at Rae Ella's.*

I scowled and down-shifted to make the turn into my driveway as I muttered. "Oh, shut up. Nobody likes a smart Alec."

Chapter Eleven

Everything is hazy in the waning light and because my eyes are only half open. The ground is damp, a rock or something is poking in my lower back but below that, I can't feel anything. I clench my stomach muscles and try to sit up but pain in my head makes me cry out and lay still.

The crunch of gravel makes me turn my head, despite the sharp pain. Someone is coming, voices getting louder. I moan as something connects with my side. Was that a foot? They kicked me? My brow wrinkles. What are they saying?

"... alive

" ... not long ..."

Alive? Yes, I'm alive! I manage to crack one eye open. Light so bright, dancing around, blinding me. The outlines of people, one? Two? I can't tell but I need them.

I lick my lips and try to request help but my mind rebels and screams danger. It urges me to run, to hide, but the darkness is closing in and the shadows their bodies cast are fading as I fall, down, down, into the darkness-

I gasped and jerked upright, shoving the wet covers away as I tried to calm my racing heart. The gap in the curtains showed the night sky was fading but dawn was still hours away and a glance at my alarm clock confirmed I was awake far too early for my comfort.

My hair was plastered to my neck, sweat made my t-shirt cling to my back and a cold, clammy feeling covered every inch of my skin. I shuddered and stumbled into the bathroom. A quick shower eliminated the effects of my nightmare but also brought me fully awake.

Going back to sleep was out of the question. I stripped the bed and crept into the hall for a new set of sheets but even with fresh covers I couldn't make myself attempt sleep; the jumbled remains of the nightmare were running through my mind on a loop.

A grunt from The Colonel drew my gaze. His one raised eyelid spoke volumes about me being up so early, as did his heavy sigh. I chuckled and was heading back to bed when my gaze fell on Dr. Styles' journal. I almost ignored it, but since my lazy bulldog was still snoring and I had no desire to risk another nightmare, I couldn't find a good enough excuse. I grabbed the nearest thing to hand and settled back on the bed.

Staring at my hair brush. I was literally staring at my hairbrush. Worse, I was cataloging its color, length, weight ... my first thought was how stupid and time-wasting the exercise was. The fact that I got to document how stupid and wasteful it was cheered me immensely and spurred me to continue but all too soon the visions of the shooting popped back into my head.

Cold, I am so cold and tired, I can't keep my eyes open. My head is throbbing and I'm panting through the pain. An engine rolls over ... the squeak of brakes, the transmission engages. Help! I try to scream but a croak is all- The brush is black, several gray strands are wrapped around the bristles, I still need to make a hair appointment ... *shake it off, Holly, focus!* About five inches long and three inches wide ...

My heart was racing and the hand holding the pen shook like a leaf. I let it fall from my hand and sank onto the pillows, concentrating on the breathing exercises meant to calm me. So much for the doctor's focus therapy; focused myself right back into terror!

Several more deep, measured breaths had my pulse back to normal. I managed to write a few observations in the focus notebook before my eyelids started to droop. Praying the flashbacks would stay away, I tossed the journal onto the nightstand, clicked off the light, and let sleep claim me.

The blaring alarm roused me a second time. Sunlight streamed through the crack in the blinds, so I dragged myself from bed, took care of my most pressing needs, and then saw to The Colonels.

He made quick work of his bowl of kibble while I scarfed down a container of yogurt. I chucked the container into the trash and then snapped the leash onto his collar. "Come on, buddy. Walkies."

November in the Lowcountry was glorious, my favorite time of the year. We'd slept later than usual, and the sun was high overhead, though dark clouds dimmed its warmth. A brisk breeze blew in from the river, adding a chill to the leaden sky. The marsh grasses had started changing colors, framing the blue waters of the river in shades of harvest gold. Shorebirds waded on spindly legs, looking for periwinkles and frogs while a trawler chugged its way out to sea.

We strolled along the waterfront, The Colonel doing his business while I did my best not to think of anything deeper than what I should have for lunch- ooh, I'd made plans to visit Connie and I was late. I hopped up and used the promise of a treat to bribe The Colonel into trotting back home.

Mama was talking on the phone, enabling me to grab my bag and truck keys without getting the third degree. I boosted the chubby boy onto the passenger seat and cranked the truck. A few choice curse words and a hard shove on the gear shift and we were soon on our way. Since I was nearly three hours late for my meeting at Glitter and Garland, I decided lunch should be on me.

A sign for BBQ set my mouth watering so I steered the Scout toward Cypress Island and tried to keep my mind from wandering any further than what I'd ordered. My intentions lasted through two stop lights and then I was back to worrying about Dewey's situation and how I was going to find a killer.

It'd been nearly a week since the party at the brewery resulted in the death of Megan Hearn and, while I had managed to compile a list of probable suspects, I was no closer to solving the murder. An image of the list Connie had helped me with formed in my mind. Edison Marlow occupied the top of the suspect list. After talking with Wanda Graves I'd learned he was being blackmailed. He'd argued with the victim the night of the party and, when pressed, he hadn't denied Megan's threats of exposure for plagiarizing his late wife's work.

On the basis of what I'd learned, he was still a great suspect. Motive and means he had aplenty, but opportunity was the sticking point. Rae Ella had said they were talking but it was earlier than Marlow claimed. Had he been deliberately lying or just misjudged the time?

I mentally kept him at the top of my list and turned to the next name as I parked beside the cedar plank-sided shack that doubled as the best BBQ joint in three counties, maybe four.

I lifted The Colonel out of the truck and clicked my tongue for him to follow me up the steps to Tyson's. This close to lunch, the line was almost out the door, giving me plenty of time to continue pondering suspects.

Dale Scruggs had just as much motive as Edison Marlow and for the exact same reason. As much as my gut said Dale was innocent, I had neglected to ask his whereabouts during the estimated time of Megan's murder. He'd told me Megan wanted information on his partner and since our chat at the gym, I'd learned a bit more about Mark Timmons and shady business dealings ... It wouldn't hurt to drive out to Rosedale Plantation to chat with Mark. If Glenda was around I'd ask about her alibi, too.

My other suspects were a bit trickier. Rae Ella and Griff Reid. Rae Ella was afraid of Griff, and he was angry. Several times in as many days I'd witnessed or overheard him arguing or looking like he could cheerfully strangle someone. I'd bet good money Megan Hearn had been up to the same extortion tricks with him, but Rae Ella had remained closed-mouthed and all I'd learned was that Edison had a semi-alibi and, by extension so did she.

That left Griff and I resigned myself to dropping by the law office and probably encountering my ex-husband in the process. The things I did for my family. I made a face and stepped up to the counter to place my order.

A short drive back to Sanctuary Bay and then I was coaxing a grumpy bulldog to walk into the craft store. Christmas carols and the scent of Bay Berry candles spread holiday cheer along with several artificial trees Connie had assembled. In the few days since my last visit, she'd made a lot of progress. Evergreen and Magnolia leaf swags bedecked with beads, bows, and ornaments hung alongside several wreaths and her workbench showed she was about finished with holiday centerpieces.

"Hey, I was beginning to think you weren't coming, we did say ten, right?"

I nodded. "Yeah, but I had a nightmare then fell back to sleep ..." I raised my hand and dangled a white paper bag. "But I come bearing gifts."

Connie's grin went from ear to ear. "Ooh, you're forgiven, what'd you bring?" She flipped the out-to-lunch sign around and we took our Tyson's BBQ to the backroom. Connie divvied up the sandwiches and coleslaw and then dove in. "That man can cook a pig!"

"Mmm, so darn good," I mumbled around a mouthful of food. We ate in silence, allowing my mind to continue worrying over my search for a killer. I polished off my sandwich and then asked. "Connie, have you looked at that thumb drive?"

Her eyes widened. She swallowed a bite of coleslaw and shook her head. "Haven't had time, but I'll do it tonight, I promise!"

Once we'd finished, Connie took the trash out and then stuck her head around the door and motioned for me to follow her.

"What?" She shook her head and walked out of sight, leaving me to follow after I'd prodded The Colonel awake.

We stepped out the back door in time to see her entering the store next door. The brisk and chilly wind hastened our stroll and in seconds The Colonel and I were stepping into a semi-furnished retail space to find Connie grinning like the Cheshire Cat.

A cozy seating arrangement of a loveseat and two club chairs were centered near the large display window, providing a beautiful view of the wharf. Across from the grouping was an L-shaped desk configuration complete with rose gold accessories and a fluffy dog bed beside the desk.

To the left of the office area was an archway, with a sign above it. *CoastStyle.* That had been the name Connie suggested when she was bugging me to start a decorating business. My eyes narrowed. "What have you done?"

She shrugged. "You were never going to act so ..."

"Act?" I spun around in a slow circle, taking in the soft blue walls and heart pine floors. "Tell me you didn't do what I think you did. I'm not ready-I can't afford-I am not in business!"

She rolled her eyes. "Semantics, you got another job, didn't you?"

I didn't want to admit it but ..., I sighed. "Yes, Heather Rudd wants me to decorate for Thanksgiving and then for Christmas, but I don't need-"

"Yes, you do!" She walked over to the desk. "The forms for setting up a bank account and stuff are on the blotter and you have to keep records: here is your file cabinet, I even set up the files. Keep all of your receipts, gas, food, any decorating supplies you buy, oh, and write on the receipt what job it was for! Let's see, you can bring your laptop, and use your cell phone ..."

"Connie ..."

She pursed her lips. "Oh, just come and see." She walked through the archway. "This is the storeroom."

My stomach flipped but I didn't have the heart to burst her bubble, so The Colonel and I trooped through the archway. The rear of the space had been set up with metal shelving along two walls, a workbench and storage cupboards occupied the back wall, and the last side was an empty space I assumed was for large items since Connie had already stored the broken pumpkin arch frame there.

Several shelves held unopened boxes with brand labels I knew were items carried by Glitter and Garland. I frowned and met Connie's gaze. "What is all of this for?"

She smirked. "Hear me out. I knew you were never going to set up a business-" she waved a hand at me as I started to speak. "Okay, not going to start a business while there was momentum! Anyway, the suite I'm in is too small, I didn't anticipate the amount of inventory I'd need to keep on hand." She walked over to the shelves. "I've been investigating moving to a larger store, but people know my location and it's the only available one with the two display windows facing the street ...just figured it'd be a bad idea to up and move."

I nodded. "Makes sense, but it doesn't explain this space and the Coast*style* sign ..."

She wrinkled her nose. "I'm getting to that! We can both use this space-"

"Connie, it's too much!"

"Oh, don't be silly." She walked back into the office area and dropped onto the white slip-covered sofa. "As I was saying, we'll both use this space. It's storage for both of us, plus the workshop, and you can meet clients here ... it's perfect!"

The Colonel snorted and sniffed his way around the room and then settled into his new bed. That dog ... Connie had bought him a thick round bed complete with an orthopedic cushion and a monogram. I cocked an eyebrow. "Really? He's spoiled enough ..." I sighed and dragged a hand through my hair. "This is fantastic and amazing ... and you are a great friend but, Connie I can't afford this! I barely made two hundred dollars off of the brewery job and probably won't make more than that from Heather Rudd-"

"Not a problem. When you start making money you can pitch in on the rent, but don't worry about it for now, Mr. Minton gave me a great deal since I already have the shop. Oh, speaking of – good afternoon, Mr. Minton!"

I forced my lips into a smile as J.T. Minton waltzed through the door. Whenever I saw him my lip wanted to curl; there was just something about him. Maybe it was the thick, white hair perfectly coiffed and framing a gently lined and tanned face. Or, it was the starched shirts, tailor-made with a discreet monogram on the cuff, that stood out like a sore thumb in a town where even its wealthiest citizens were most frequently seen in golfing attire or fresh from the boat hair.

Connie gushed and simpered, as far too many people did around Minton, but I merely nodded and then sat in the chair behind the desk. She showed the man around and then they returned to the lobby, seating themselves in the reception area.

"Again, we can't thank you enough, Mr. Minton. This will help mine and Holly's businesses grow and –"

"Think nothin' of it, Sugah, I'm happy to help." He glanced at me. "After all that Deputy Daye has suffered in service to our fair town? It was the least I could do."

Manners and the pointed look Connie was throwing at me, dictated I respond. "That's very kind, Mr. Minton but please have your office send the rental agreement as soon as possible. Connie and I wouldn't dream of taking advantage –"

"Advantage? Nonsense, darlin' you're doing me a favor!" He gestured toward the window. "Why, you've surely noticed that Cannery Wharf isn't yet at capacity. Having a law enforcement presence, even retired, will put other tenants and the investors at ease."

Connie beamed but my smile was still forced. He was just too smooth. "Nevertheless, we want to be treated like any other tenant."

J.T.'s smile slipped for a second and then he was oozing his normal mega-amount of charm, mainly directed at Connie, however.

I ignored their conversation and explored the contents of the desk and file cabinet until they started discussing a recent spurt of crime in the Crystal Cove neighborhood.

"Honestly, I don't know what the world is coming to!" Connie huffed. "The paper said it was a domestic incident but still, a stand-off with guns, in Noble County!"

"I agree dear lady and have been speaking with Sheriff Felton and Councilman Vandershall about that very thing. We must be proactive and keep the crime out of Sanctuary Bay and of course, the Sea Islands too, imagine a murder on Saint Mariana Island ..." His mouth pursed. "Nasty business, though it was surely an anomaly."

"Mmm, yes it is." I hadn't planned to talk to Minton about renting a storefront much less the murder of Megan Hearn, but the Lord moved in mysterious ways and the opportunity was staring me in the face besides, Mama would skin me alive if she found out I hadn't taken her *intel* seriously. "But from what I've discovered, she brought it upon herself."

Connie gasped and looked daggers at me, but Minton merely cocked an eyebrow. "Indeed? I take it the rumors are true then. You are investigating that woman's death."

"Seeing that an incompetent detective is trying to railroad my brother I didn't have much choice."

J.T. chuckled. "You have a point. I don't have much confidence in Brannon, either but, why do you think Ms. Hearn instigated her murder?"

His expression was indecipherable. A hint of amusement in the slight upward curve of his mouth and a relaxed posture yet Minton's green eyes were hard, bright, and watchful, like a fox. Several responses came to mind but, in the end, I decided to go with the direct approach. "Several sources have revealed Megan Hearn wasn't above a bit of blackmail in pursuit of stories for her podcast."

Minton's lower lip thrust out as he cocked his head to the side. "You don't say ..." He sniffed. "Not surprising."

A smirk twisted my lips before I could stop it. "Mmm. Rumor has it she was looking into your businesses, too."

He cocked an eyebrow. A lazy smile graced his face, but his eyes were devoid of warmth. "You know how this town is, people love to make something from nothing. Ms. Hearn was pestering me for an interview, which I politely declined."

"An interview? About what?"

He shrugged. "I really couldn't say. She was a troublesome woman that liked to make up stories which is why I didn't give her the time of day. However, I have nothing to hide in any of my business dealings."

I nodded. "Yes, I'd heard she liked to stretch the truth. Like Mark Timmons and Dale Scruggs."

Minton's eyes widened a fraction. "Oh yes? What was she fabricating about them?"

I shrugged and acted unconcerned. "I don't know if it's true or not, but she seemed to believe Mark was in financial trouble and looking for a way out." I watched Minton like a hawk. "Someone suggested that way out might have been through you ..."

J.T. laughed. "Oh, that's no secret, Sugar. Half of the town saw us at dinner the other night and he was certainly begging for my investment, but I have no interest in a brewery." He flicked an imaginary speck from his trouser leg. "As to why Timmons has money problems. I'm afraid I couldn't say, though it might have to do with his frequent excursions into international waters ..." He looked at his watch. "Y'all ladies must excuse me." He tipped his head toward me but gave Connie a warm smile. "Now, don't you hesitate to call on me should the need arise."

Connie gushed and simpered a reply as Minton left and then turned to me with a frown. "Really? Did you have to be so, so ..." she waved a hand at me and scowled.

My nose scrunched as I frowned. "So, myself?"

She laughed and rolled her eyes. "Yes! Try a little sweetener with your words, Holly, at least for that man, he's helping us!"

"Eh, that may be true, but he still sets off my internal BS alarm." I watched J.T. through the window. He was standing on the dock, waving a hand and pacing as he talked on his phone. He'd never been a true suspect in my book but everything in me screamed he was guilty. The only question remained; guilty of what?

Chapter Twelve

After Minton left, I hung out in my new office for a while, brainstorming a few more decorating ideas for the Rudds with Connie, and then, when she returned to her shop I compiled a list of supplies. I ordered the palms from It's About Thyme and had started making notes on what I could do for the Mayor's Christmas Village when The Colonel let me know it was time for supper.

"Hey lil' buddy, you hungry?" He wiggled and hit my leg with his fat paw, a sure sign I'd neglected him. "Silly boy, hold still while I put your leash on!"

A short struggle later, The Colonel and I were on our way to the Scout when I remembered we'd run out of dog food. I changed direction and two blocks later we arrived at Meows and Growls pet store.

The owner was about to close but took pity on me, or maybe The Colonel's sad expression saved the day. Either way, we made our purchases, which included another set of food and water bowls for the office. I decided to feed my boy and then stop at the Country Kitchen for my dinner so we headed back to Cannery Wharf.

The sun was low in the sky, shadows were covering the sidewalk, and most of Bay Street was closing up shop. Sanctuary Bay was a small town, we had our share of crime, but I'd never felt unsafe walking anywhere, yet several times the hair on the back of my neck rose as The Colonel and I traveled the increasingly deserted street.

The light changed, trapping us on the corner of Chandler and Bay Street. Apart from a couple window shopping along the block ahead of me and a mother and her children entering the ice cream parlor, we were alone. I hunched my shoulders and stuffed my hands into my pockets as a gust of wind came in off of the river. I shivered, though whether from the cold or the feeling I was being watched I couldn't say.

The light changed and The Colonel bounded across. Under the pretext of looking both ways, I searched the area for the source of my unease but saw nothing or no one out of the ordinary.

It made no sense. I gave one last look around and then hobbled after the hungry bulldog as fast as a bum leg and a cane would allow. We arrived back at the Wharf without incident. Connie had already left for the night, so I returned to the CoastalStyle office and fed The Colonel.

The boy made quick work of his supper which left a short walk while he did his business and then we drove to the Country Kitchen. My shopping expedition followed by tending to my pet had pushed me long past the regular dining hour so getting a seat was painless. I'd just placed my order when my name rang out.

"Holly! Mind if I join you?"

Jessica was standing at the hostess station. I waved her over. "Working late?"

She shrugged out of her coat and then slid into the booth. "Yep, just got back from Columbia."

"Oh, something exciting happening?"

"Kinda?" She gave the server her order. "The forensics lab held a press conference, though they had precious little to say."

I frowned. "What was the conference about?"

"You kidding?" She laughed as I gave her a clueless look. "How are you not chomping at the bit and frothing at the mouth like most of the county?"

"Frothing at the-" I snorted. " The only thing I know that's newsworthy right now is the murder of Megan Hearn and I know everyone is gossiping about it but frothing at the mouth?"

Jessica grinned. "That's not the only thing making the rounds." Her eyes narrowed as she cocked her head. "You really don't ... the remains they found during the hurricane clean-up."

My eyes widened. "Oh wow, I forgot all about that!" Our food arrived. I used the time to think about the other big story in Sanctuary Bay. Silly of me to have forgotten about it, especially since I'd noticed officials heading out toward Shell Point when I was coming back from Rae Ella's and Mama had fussed about nothing new being in the paper yesterday morning. I told Jessica as much.

"That's because there have been no updates from law en-forcement!" She took a few bites of her She Crab soup before continuing. "The remains were sent to the state crime lab and nothing more has been said until the conference today."

"Well, that's SOP, regardless of how much the busybodies clamor for details."

"Yep but try telling that to this town. The calls and emails I've gotten ..." She rolled her eyes. "My mailbox is full and I'm still not going to give them much."

"What did you learn today?"

"Precious little. Just that the remains are female, between ages of eighteen and twenty-five, and she's been buried out there for a little over a decade."

"But did they identify her?"

"Yeah, but they won't release the name, pending notification of family-and get this. They can't locate her next of kin so who knows how long ..."

"The old ladies are gonna be upset, brace yourself for more calls!"

"Oh, don't remind me!"

Her frustrated expression made me chuckle, but my mind wasn't on a death from years ago, I had a more recent murder to solve.

Jessica nodded in commiseration. "Yeah, sorry about Dewey. What is Brannon thinking?"

I snorted and took another bite of mashed potatoes. "That's just it, he isn't! I'm trying to find the killer but I'm losing hope of being in time." I looked up and met my friend's gaze. "She had skin under her nails and despite the attorney admitting it's probably Dewey's because she scratched him when he tried to help her when she tripped in the garden they aren't listening. The DA wants another notch in her belt before elections next week and Brannon just takes the easy way ..."

"I'm sorry, Holly." Jessica frowned. "I've been so busy with election coverage and the remains cases-but run through what you've found, maybe I can help."

I briefed her on what little I'd found and added my thoughts and analysis of my findings. We ate in silence as my friend considered the information.

A few minutes later, she tapped her fingernail on the Formica topped table. "You said Hearn was blackmailing people?"

"Looks that way. Marlow was, and Dale Scruggs, too. Something is going on with Rae Ella and Griff Reid, though I have no idea what it's about, and J.T. Minton said she tried to pull her crap on him ... oh, speaking of Minton. He suggested Mark Timmons' money troubles are due to gambling. Know anything about that?"

Her eyes lit up. "Funny you should mention that because I'm digging into who owns those gambling cruise ships that leave out of Minor's Creek just below Charleston ...company called Tropica."

I frowned. "Why are you investigating them?"

"Eh, reports of big losses, accusations of cheating." She shrugged. "The usual. Mobbed up, rigged games, allowing play on credit then muscle when people don't settle their debt."

"Geez, that's a big deal!"

"Maybe? So far I haven't found anything illegal. I'm thinking it's just talk from sore losers. But I can look into whether Timmons has been seen there if you want."

"Yes, please! I'm going to pay him a visit, but he'll probably lie. It'd be great if you gave me proof ..."

"No problem." She finished off her meal and pushed the plate to the end of the table. "So who else is on your list?"

My smile faded. "No one-well, Glenda Timmons but she's only on there because Connie I figured she might do something if her husband was threatened. You know, same reason I put Rae Ella Reid down. Doubt there's anything to it."

"Yeah, you're probably right, but not because she's such a devoted wife."

I frowned. "What do you mean? Is she having an affair or something?"

Jessica shook her head. "Not that I know of, but she is up for the dean of Saint Anne's."

"Oh, she mentioned that! But what's it got to do with her being a suspect?"

"Nothing? Just that school has a morals clause as a condition of employment. Glenda's worked hard for that position; I'd say she'd do anything to keep any and all scandal far from her or by extension her husband."

"Huh. You might have something there ... nah, I still don't think Glenda did it." The creepy feeling of someone staring at me returned. I looked over my shoulder and then around the dining room but found nothing unusual.

"Who's top of your list then?"

I wrinkled my nose. "No one? Everyone?"

Jessica laughed. "You'll never solve it that way!"

"True. Number one suspect I guess would still be Edison Marlow so far, all of the evidence points to him, but I don't think it'd be enough to get Brannon and the DA to leave Dewey alone ..." I blew out a breath and considered my list. "Oh, and Dale Scruggs. All I really have on him is motive and I saw him speaking with Hearn that night in an unfriendly way but heck, that's everyone the woman met! By the way, when I asked Dale where he was around the time Hearn was killed he claims to have been walking down to the brewery with everyone else. Any chance you can confirm that?"

Her brow furrowed as she considered my question and a minute later she laughed. "As a matter of fact, I can vouch for Dale." She laughed again and shook her head. "One of the soaker hoses in the garden was shooting water straight up and Councilman Vandershall got a face full. Dale was all apologies ... you know what Vandershall is like. Craig and I got a kick out of the whole thing."

I snorted. "The drama king made a scene?" Jessica nodded. "I can only imagine. Welp, that moves Dale farther down on my list. Thanks, I think."

She pushed her empty plate to the end of the table and then leaned on her elbows. "Sorry. Now, what's this about the Reids?"

I sighed. "Probably nothing. I only put them on the list because they both looked unhappy at the party. Did you happen to notice anything between them and Hearn?"

Jessica snorted. "Uh, yeah. Where were you?" She waved a hand as I started to speak. "Never mind, you were probably out walking The Colonel, but you missed Griff and Hearn throwing verbal darts."

My brow furrowed as I replayed the night of the party. I couldn't recall ... oh, there'd been the laughter at the bar. I mentioned it to Jessica.

"That'd be it, but not long after that things turned a bit ugly. I'm not sure what started the conversation, but Hearn said something to Griff, and he snapped back with a witty retort that made us all chuckle. Most people were milling about so only a few of us heard what happened next." She laughed. "From zero to sixty in seconds! Megan leaned in and said something to Griff, and he got very still, and all of the color drained from his face; I remember thinking he looked like he was going to throw up. Rae Ella gasped, and her eyes were wide and kinda glassy like she was in shock."

"Wow, what the heck did Hearn say to cause that kind of reaction?"

She shrugged. "Wish I knew. All I heard was Griff's reply and not all of that, unfortunately. Something about Florida I heard that much … oh!" Her eyes widened. "He said people change. Think he meant himself and Hearn was trying to blackmail him about something in his past?"

"Could be? He's a trust fund kid, dad died when he was around ten? I know he was kinda wild in his teens."

Jessica cocked her head. "Wild. In what way?"

"Sorry, I don't know anything except Brooks was friends with him and then Griff started going off of the rails and they stopped hanging out-you know how Brooks is or was-"

I snorted. "Always uptight. I'm thinking this craziness now is a delayed mid-life crisis."

She laughed. "Probably right." Jessica bit her lip. "You know there's a rumor the girl is pregnant."

"I heard that, too." I shook my head. "Unreal if it's true. She's a year younger than Brooks Jr. for heaven's sake!"

"Mmm, I'm sorry, shouldn't have brought it up."

I waved a hand in dismissal. "It's fine. We weren't … it wasn't a shock to find out he'd been cheating and his leaving was only bad because of the timing. I mean, I was just out of the hospital, couldn't walk much … but I will give him one thing; he paid for excellent care and has been generous in the settlement."

"Well, that's good to hear. I can't say I ever liked Brooks much, like you said he's so uptight, but he seemed responsible."

I nodded. "Accurate analysis. That's why I can't help but think he will snap out of this and then regret … poor girl. Junior blames me."

Jessica's mouth dropped open. "What? How is any of that your fault?"

My mouth twisted. "Beats me. He helped me get a lawyer for Dewey and that's the first time I've spoken to him in about six months."

"Oh Holly, that's awful, I'm so sorry. Maybe he just needs time to adjust?"

I stared out at the darkened parking lot, not really seeing it but wanting to avoid the pity in my friend's eyes. "Possibly, I admit I had choice words for his father at first. Like I said, the timing was awful, and it was stress I didn't need but, I shouldn't have told Junior some home truths about Brooks. That boy has had his dad on a pedestal-Jessica did you see that?"

My friend frowned and shook her head. "No, what? I wasn't looking ... something out there?"

Between the quarter moon and a broken lamp, the lot was shrouded in shadows. I'd been staring out at nothing, my gaze resting on my daddy's old International Scout as I'd admitted to being a bad mom when I could have sworn- "The passenger door of my truck just opened." I fumbled for my cane and slid out of the booth.

"What?" Jessica got up and beat me to the door. "Did you see who it was?"

The Colonel wasn't easy to rouse but a few minutes later and we were all cautiously walking toward my vehicle. "I only got a vague impression of someone beside the truck, it's dark on that side ... whoever it was had long hair."

"A woman then."

I put an arm out to stop her from proceeding. "This day and age? Not necessarily." I focused on the lot. My gaze scanned the perimeter and then worked back toward the interior, and my truck. No signs of humans or animals, the wind was barely blowing now, and even if it was, there was no vegetation near my parking place; what I'd seen was no shadow. I was convinced someone had been in my truck.

My hand went to my hip but came up empty. Jessica saw my movement and gave me a rueful smile and murmured. "Old habits."

I nodded. Walking into an unknown situation unarmed was foreign to me. Still, I had good instincts and law enforcement training; that never went away. I shortened The Colonel's leash so he was heeled at my side and then bent so that I could see under all of the surrounding cars. Not so much as a stick under any of them.

"Come on, it's clear."

We crossed the short distance, and I used the flashlight on my phone to peek in the windows. No one inside, nothing out of the ordinary-"What's that?"

I opened the passenger side door and frowned. "I didn't put this here."

Jessica peered over my shoulder. "It's a flyer for that pirate tour."

"Uh huh, but the image of the buried treasure is circled, and something is scrawled above it ..." I picked the glossy paper up and examined both sides but other than the circle drawn in red marker and the words I couldn't read without my reading glasses, nothing stood out. I handed it to Jessica. "Can you make out what's written there?"

She took the flyer and, with the help of my phone's light, deciphered the chicken scratch. "Well, it looks like an F here, that might be a d ... oh, find. Next word is ...," she laughed. "Illegible, sorry. So, *find* and then no idea, think that is a letter u? And the last word is *see* ...not sure what this letter is." She returned the glossy pamphlet, pointing to the letter she couldn't read.

I squinted, cursed the need for glasses, and gave up. It'd have to wait until I got home. I shrugged and tossed it on the console. "Thanks. I'll look at it when I get home." I frowned and looked around the front seat. "No idea why someone would slip that into my truck but either someone is trying to tell me something or, maybe they're putting them out all over?"

Jessica nodded. "Could be. I'd look in mine, but I'm parked over on the street, I'll let you know if I find anything." She gestured toward the diner with her head. "Got to get back in there before the server calls the cops, we left without paying."

I laughed. "Probably having kittens!" I reached into my pocket and pulled out a twenty. "My leg is aching; do you mind going back in and paying for mine?"

She smiled and took the cash. "Sure thing. You headed home?" At my nod, she gave a wave and started back to the restaurant. "Well, keep me informed about your investigation, and let me know if you need anything."

"Thanks, I will." Not that I thought she could help. The way things were going, Dewey would be headed for trial. I snorted. Should be looking for employment, better use of my time; attorney fees were going to eat us alive.

I loaded The Colonel and went around to the driver's side. As I buckled up my hand moved the flyer I'd found. I shoved it into my bag and then began the increasingly frequent fight with my transmission. I rolled my eyes as it finally slipped into gear. One more pressing thing to add to my never-ending list of problems.

Chapter Thirteen

Cold sweats and a racing heart jolted me awake in the wee hours, causing me to sleep in, which stood all of my plans on end. Being up earlier had provided one bonus: I'd done my focus therapy. But after, I'd given in and let the sandman catch me. Now, there was no way I could sneak out before Mama woke up and found a million things for me to help her do.

It was past nine, my mother should have been rocking on the front porch and chatting with all that passed by so why was I hearing her in the kitchen? I paused halfway down the back stairs and frowned. She was on the phone and, was she crying? I trotted down the last few steps as quickly as I could, The Colonel racing ahead. We both arrived to find my mother sobbing at the kitchen table.

"Mama? What on earth is the matter?" Heart in my throat, I looked around for the cause of her distress. "Where's Dewey? Is everyone all right? Who was that on the phone?"

My questions were rapid-fire, and she couldn't have gotten an answer edgewise, not that it mattered. Mama was too distraught to pay me any attention, that was until I mentioned Dewey. His name just made her sob harder.

I knelt beside her chair to the best of my ability and gave her a one-armed hug. "Mama, stop crying and tell me what's happened. I can't fix anything until you-"

"Oh Holly Marie, there's nothing to fix! It's all over, everything is in ruins." Her shoulders shook as another round of tears began. In between sobs she stuttered out the problem. "I ...I don, don't know wh-what your father would say! Oh, the sh, sh shame ..."

Okay, not much of her disjointed sentences made sense but, I'd seen fifty-one years with Mama and had learned to speak a bit of her language. She'd been on the phone, started crying as she hung up, got more upset when Dewey's name was mentioned, and my poor, dead father's feelings were being considered. All of which meant something had happened with Dewey and it had the potential to shame the family name. Basically same as any other given day that ended in Y.

I shrugged and got to my feet. "Mama, what's Dewey done now?"

Like magic, the tears stopped flowing. Mama turned and gifted me with a ferocious scowl. "Your brother has done nothing, and, thanks to you, he's being charged with murder, and Thanksgiving is ruined!"

Hats off to my mother, she'd managed to be succinct in her condemnation. I turned on the coffee pot and fed The Colonel while it brewed. Mama continued to sniff and direct baleful glares at me, but I ignored her until the dog was out in the garden and a steaming cup of coffee was in front of me.

"I take it the D.A. is presenting the case to the grand jury." I stirred cream into my cup as Mama proceeded to tell me about the phone call from Max Bernard.

Her ability for pithy replies must have expired because ten minutes later I knew no more than when she'd started. I poured another cup of coffee; it was going to be a long morning.

Fortified with caffeine, I pondered the rambling dissertation in silence until Mama cleared her throat.

"Well? What are we going to do?" Her last word ended with a sob.

Anxious to avoid another round of weeping, I jumped in without thought. "Basically, there is nothing much we can do-"

"Oooh, my baby is going to be locked away for –"

"Mama ...," I squeezed her hand as she continued to work herself back into hysterics. "Getting upset isn't going to help anything. Please, try and get ahold of yourself."

For expediency's sake, I hid my alarm behind a calm exterior, but Mama had slouched back in her chair and her hair was sticking out at odd angles from running her hands through it. Mascara streaks marred her cheeks, and she'd slopped coffee on her shirt.

Two of us losing our cool wasn't going to help anything but I was secretly worried; never in my life, even when Daddy had been rushed to the hospital for what turned out to be a fatal heart attack, had I seen my mother in such a state. She sniffed and rose, wetting a paper towel to wipe at her cheeks as she returned to the table.

"Now then, let's look at this calmly, shall we? Dewey's attorney is working on the legal end but there isn't much he can do at this point-ah, just listen please ..." She swallowed hard and nodded so I hurried on. "If it goes to the grand jury they'll decide if there's enough evidence to proceed or not. I don't think there is but, either way, the defense can't do much until that is over so don't borrow trouble!"

Her lower lip trembled but she managed to speak calmly. "But Holly, what will we do? We can't just sit around-"

"Sit around? Mama, I've been working on this every day and I'm not quitting. As for you, keep your eyes and ears open for any word on the street but also, plan Thanksgiving as usual."

"Oh, but ..., do you think we should?" She wrung her hands and looked everywhere but at me. "What with this unpleasantness ... everyone will be talking ..."

Ah, so that was her issue. Embarrassment. Every year for as long as I could remember, Thanksgiving was held at Myrtlewood, the river plantation that had been in Mama's family for over two hundred years.

This year I'd invite Connie and Craig and Ms. Maybelle joined us every year. Jessica dined with her family but always stopped by for dessert, and then there were several of Mama's cousins and their ever-increasing clans.

Daddy's side of the family tree was smaller, but my cousin Tommy Barker and his family of four would attend, his sister and her brood, and one of the Barkers would pick up Uncle

Howard from the retirement home ... all in all, we'd sit down to dinner with a little over forty family and friends.

"Mama, no one will be unkind, these are our dearest friends and family!" I had to bite my tongue and tell a little white lie because the wife of one of my cousins would delight in carrying tales but on the whole, everyone would follow Mama's lead and I told her as much.

"Yeees, I suppose you're right and that Deanna creature. Well, no one likes her anyway."

Since Mama was still raw over the issue, I grinned but refrained from laughing. Though she was right. My cousin Warren's wife was not well received at the best of times. "You see? There is no reason not to continue as we always have. But you've left things a bit late so how about spending the day organizing the meal and we'll talk about the plans when I get home."

Mama nodded but stopped me before I could reach the back door. "What will you be doing then?"

Ignoring the tone in her voice that implied whatever I had planned wouldn't be enough, and fastened The Colonel's leash as I replied. "I'm checking on a few leads in the murder case and then I need to stop by the off- er, Connie's shop. I'll bring supper home if you call the order into the Country Kitchen."

I caught myself in the nick of time. I hadn't yet told Mama about my new business venture and if it slipped out now I'd never get to leave. I needn't have worried though. She was more concerned with Dewey.

"Leads? What leads?" She half rose from her chair, but I waved her back. "Please tell me you know who did this awful thing they are trying to pin on my baby!"

"Mama, it's ... I'm still looking into things. It could be one of several people-I have to go, just stop worrying and plan the holiday. Love you, bye!"

I rushed out the door before she could start in again. Too much pressure and I'd crack and reveal that I had several suspects, very few clues, and not much hope. I wondered how many days in purgatory one got for lying to one's mother.

Traffic was light and the drive to Saint Mariana Island was peaceful; something I needed after Mama's mini meltdown. After hurrying out the door I'd been waylaid by my brother and had spent another half hour soothing as well as berating him for going on another bender at Cluck's bar.

The smell of beer seemed to ooze from his pores, and I was more concerned than I let on, hiding it behind a lecture to grow up and act like he had some sense. Truth was, Dewey was scared.

He'd been in trouble many times but all of it simple drunk tank stuff; the reality that he was facing a felony charge was sinking in and he needed a distraction so, I set him the task of cleaning up Myrtlewood.

The home had been closed for months, the last time we'd gathered there being Easter. The plantation was a concern that I'd pushed to the back of my mind since the shooting but at some point in the near future I was going to have to talk with Mama and Dewey about it; it seemed like property taxes rose every year and keeping a hundred acres and a large home on the river seemed like a luxury, especially when no one lived there.

That conversation could wait. My main priority was saving Dewey's hide. I'd succeeded in calming my family, but the result was an increase in my stress levels. Not only did I have to find a killer, decorate Heather Rudd's home, and put together a bid for the Sanctuary Bay Christmas Village but now I also had to get Myrtlewood spit-shined and polished for a huge family Thanksgiving.

Delegating the cleaning to Dewey soothed me somewhat but the decorating all fell on me. The miles rolled by as I considered my options. To save time, I could design a centerpiece for the Rudds and make extra for our family gathering.

Aside from the table, I needed to create a welcoming entry for both homes, and do something for the guest powder room. Heather had also requested something special in her two guest rooms.

I tried to do some mental math for the number of items I'd need but I was too distracted. After my visit to Rosedale, I'd go to my new office and do some calculations and place some orders. For now, the business needs had to take a backseat while I focused on Dewey and the killer of Megan Hearn.

The wrought iron gates that marked the entrance to Rosedale came into view. I downshifted, wincing at the corresponding protest in the transmission, and turned off of the main road.

Rosedale Plantation started life as a sea island cotton farm in the late 1700s. Owner Edward Fuller prospered and in time commissioned the building of the manor house. Constructed of brick to withstand storms, Rosedale survived for over a hundred years, until a fire gutted it in 1929.

Unable to afford repairs, the great home sat empty until 1955, when a Northern industrialist purchased the property and began restorations. The property had changed hands a few times since the Fifties, falling into disrepair by the time it had ended up in the Timmons family, about twenty years ago.

When Mark had inherited Rosedale, people had predicted he'd sell to the developers always clamoring for large chunks of riverfront property but, to everyone's surprise, Mark had started repairs on the manor house, and created River Rat Brewery in the boat house.

The revival of Rosedale wasn't nearly complete. While consulting on the launch party, I'd asked to see the improvements. The upper floors were not habitable, and the main level was a mess of crumbling plaster, exposed wiring, and builders' scaffolding.

Mark hadn't seemed more than politely interested in the project and when I'd commented, he'd admitted making Rosedale a livable home was Glenda's dream, not his. Regardless, the expense would be astronomical, and I had to wonder if gambling wasn't a misguided way to raise more funds for the project.

The drive, sand with a strip of grass running down the middle, wound through land allowed to remain natural, with a small, landscaped area of grass and shrubs to line the route. Just before reaching the house, the drive split. I took the right fork and was rewarded with glorious views of the river and marsh as the boathouse came into view.

"Only three cars were parked in the lot. I was pretty sure one of them belonged to Mark Timmons, but it occurred to me that I should have called before coming out. I'd been to the brewery several times in the weeks leading up to the party, and I'd had to search for a parking space each time. I hoped their lack of business wasn't a result of the murder.

I parked as close to the path as I could, not for the first time I wished the brewery had a few handicap parking places closer to the building and got The Colonel down. A slight chill in the breeze coming off of the river was negated by the warmth of the sun and for the remaining hours of daylight, it was going to be a glorious day to explore the grounds of Rosedale.

I took my time, letting The Colonel investigate every tree, shrub, and structure he fancied. My speed wasn't due solely to indulging the dog. I kept my eyes on the concrete path, watching for loose soil since I'd nearly fallen the night of the party. The last thing I needed was a broken leg or even a twisted ankle.

We arrived at the boathouse without encountering anyone and found the gift shop similarly devoid of life. The sizable room held a bar on one wall but, instead of a traditional setup with numerous liquors and glassware, the area held huge copper vats filled with the brewery's latest offerings.

To the left of the bar were doors leading to restrooms and a hall that gave access to the offices and the main brewing floor. Scattered around the rest of the space were wooden barrels serving as display tables, holding River Rat Brewery logo items.

Thinking of a Christmas gift for Dewey I picked up a bottle opener and then quickly set it back down; for thirty dollars it should be made of gold! There were other barrels holding more souvenir-type items, along with high-end barware. Along the back wall, a shelf held books by local authors or ones on our local life and lore. Edison Marlow's series was front and center, reminding me that by rights that first one should have had his wife's name on the cover.

An old-time soft drink cooler stood next to the hallway. A bottle of water sounded good. I walked over and grabbed one from the case. Five dollars was highway robbery, but I opened it anyway.

"I said I was good for it! I just need time-" I paused with the bottle halfway to my mouth. Angry with a slight edge of desperation, the loud voice sounded like Mark Timmons.

When nothing else was said, I relaxed and took a swig of water. I'd no sooner screwed the cap back on than a shout rang out followed by the sound of breaking glass. I rushed down the hall and stopped at an open door when I heard Dale Scruggs.

"Find it! Three days or I talk..."

I flattened against the door as Dale stalked by me. His expression was like a thundercloud. He never acknowledged me or Mark, who'd followed behind his partner.

"You do and you'll – oh, what are you doing here?"

Hello to you, too Mark! I pushed away my snarky inner self and pinned a smile to my face; I'd catch more flies with honey and the fly I intended to catch was a sizable check for services rendered. "Hey Mark, is this a bad time?"

He looked at the now empty hallway and then huffed and motioned for me to join him in his office. "So, what brings you all the way out here?"

I made The Colonel stay out in the hall and stepped over the broken glass. "Was out this way and realized I hadn't picked up the check."

His brows met in the middle as he frowned. "What check? I don't –"

"The payment for decorating. You paid half up front, and the rest was due after the party." My cheeks were getting sore, but I kept the smile in place. Mark fidgeted with an ink pen and then pretended to look for his checkbook. The jerk was going to make up an excuse to not pay me, I just knew it.

"Uh, sorry Holly …" he flashed a contrite smile. "Our book-keeper handles all billing and payments and she's out until next week. I'd gladly write a check if I figure out where she keeps the book …"

My smile dimmed. He was full of it, but did I call him on it? Maybe subtle was the best option. "Oh, that's fine, Mark. I'm sure she'll cut the check as soon as she gets back. It's for fifteen hundred, remember?"

He looked a bit sick when I rattled off the amount owned which told me the rumors of his money problems were true. Not good for my bank account but perhaps good for finding a killer.

"I noticed the police tape is gone. Have you been able to reopen?"

Mark nodded. "Yes, we opened Tuesday and business has been brisk. Who would have thought? I figured the murder would be a death knell for us."

Just the opposite, people were ghouls. I kept my opinion to myself and merely smiled. "That's wonderful, Mark. Glad this nastiness isn't hurting the brewery. I was kinda shocked to find the parking lot empty…"

He smiled, though it didn't reach his eyes. "It's Sunday."

My mouth dropped open. "Oh my word, I completely forgot what day it is!"

Mark didn't comment on my forgetfulness. His tone was flat as he repeated his instructions "Come by next Wednesday, Gail should be settled in by then."

I rose from my chair. "Fine, I'll do that." I snapped my fingers for The Colonel to follow and headed for the exit. "Oh, almost forgot." I stuck my head around the door and watched Mark closely. "Where were you during the time they think Megan was murdered?"

A nerve in his cheek ticked and if he ground his teeth any harder he would never need to visit another dentist. His gaze held mine for a few seconds and then it slithered away to rest on the floor. "I really don't see ... I mean, I told the police-"

"Uh-huh, we all did, but I'm looking into things and thought it'd be easier to ask while I'm here rather than get the information from the police ..."

He didn't bother to hide his irritation but neither did he call my bluff. "Not that it's any of your business, but I believe I was speaking with um, Griff Reid; it was just before we asked the crowd to make their way down to the pavilion." He drummed his fingers on the desk for a few seconds before continuing. "I assume you're asking because of your brother."

I nodded. "Yes."

Mark sniffed. "Can't say I blame you, now if that's all?"

"Not quite." I bit back a laugh as he pursed his lips and looked daggers at me.

"I was talking with Rae Ella Reid the other day." He stiffened and I knew I was on the right track. "She told me about seeing you and Megan Hearn in the garden the night of the party."

Mark frowned. "And? It isn't a crime."

"No, it's not but I wonder what the police would make of the fact that you and the victim were in a heated discussion that ended in her throwing something at you. What was it, by the way?"

His face turned an ugly shade of red and then purple. His throat convulsed and I thought I might need to call an ambulance. He drew several deep breaths and then, through clenched teeth he replied.

"That is an ugly insinuation, we're done here. Collect your check on Wednesday."

My lips twitched and I had to fight not to smile. His reaction spoke volumes, though about what I wasn't sure. I decided to have one more poke at the bear.

"Hey, Mark?"

He glared at me. "What now?"

"How do you like the Tropica gambling cruise? Is the boat well equipped for the ocean? Thinking about indulging in some gambling fun but I don't want to get seasick ..."

His eyes narrowed. "I've no idea as I've never been. Now, it's best if you were on your way."

"Sure. Have a nice day."

The Colonel and I made our way through the gift shop. Once outside I gave him more lead and let him explore as I pondered Mark's lie, and it was clearly a lie. His body language would have tipped me off even if I hadn't already heard the truth from several sources. And then there was the argument I'd walked in on.

I'd only heard bits and pieces but based upon what I knew about the brewery finances and Mark's gambling I could make some assumptions. He'd said he was good for *it*, and Dale had said he had to find *it*, or he'd talk. Therefore *it* was most likely money, and the *talk* Dale mentioned was either to the police or a lawyer; either way, Mark's troubles were only beginning.

Other than the money issues, and the embezzlement wasn't my concern-at least I didn't think it was, ... It occurred to me that Megan had been pressuring Dale for computer files. Were they proving the embezzlement or something else?

That led me to think about Megan's computer and the files I'd copied. I wondered if she had anything on there about Mark. Connie had promised to go over the thumb drive and since I needed to order some items for decorating Thanksgiving the office would be my next stop.

The office. I snorted. How easy that popped into my mind. I couldn't quite believe Connie had put so much into motion, but the idea of owning my own business was growing on me. Now if only I could get paid for the job I'd completed ...

The Colonel tugged on his leash, demanding that we move toward the hedge of camellias that surrounded the formal garden. I let him lead and we entered the main gate. I shortened his leash so he wouldn't get into the flower beds, and we ambled along the path, pausing for a rest when we reached the central fountain.

I'd been sitting for a few minutes when footsteps alerted me that I had company.

"Hello, I didn't know you were here!"

I smiled as Glenda Timmons approached carrying a plastic dry cleaning bag. She sat beside me, laying the bag on the concrete bench. "Hey, Glenda. What brings you out here?"

Her smile was sheepish. "My costume. I changed that night and with everything going on I forgot to return it to the rental company. Since I was making a trip I thought I'd check on how the house renovations are coming along, I just hired a mason that only does heritage work! My general contractor says we are on schedule and should be able to move in by next May!" Her eyes radiated excitement and again I wondered if that was where all of Mark's money was going.

"What brings you and The Colonel out?" She bent and patted my boy on the head and dislodged the bag, sending her costume to the ground. "Shoot! Hope it didn't get any dirt on it." She retrieved her costume and gave the bag a shake. There was a clink of metal as something gold slid from the bottom of the bag.

"Hey, what's this?" I picked up a belt of fake coins hanging from a gold chain. I glanced up as she sat back down.

She was staring at my hand and her eyes were wide. For a minute she looked scared like I was holding a snake, and then she blinked and met my gaze.

"Oh, that's the belt from my costume!" Her smile was rueful. "That's gonna cost me. It must have caught on the concrete ..."

I inspected the belt and found the break. "Maybe ...," I frowned. Something about the Greek Coin belt was bugging me. I bit my lip and wracked my brain, but nothing popped up. I shook my head; it'd come to me.

I glanced at Glenda. "I doubt it just happened. It looks like it was a repair that didn't hold up because you can see tool marks on this link." I raised my hand and pointed. "See? This one has been pried closed but, whoever did it just didn't realize they'd left a small gap." I handed the belt to her, careful not to let the little Greek coins slide off. "You can fix it, just need a pair of needle nose pliers ..."

"Umm, I'll see if I can manage. Thanks for catching it. Those rental places charge a fortune if anything gets messed up." She secured the costume belt in her purse. "Now then, what did you say brought you out to the islands?"

"Oh," I shrugged. "I just stopped by to pick up the remainder of the decorating fees, but Mark said I'd have to wait. Wasted trip-well, not according to The Colonel, he loves to walk the grounds."

Her smile faded. "Mark didn't write you a check?"

"It's all right. I can wait a week." From her expression, I guessed that Glenda was puzzled over Mark's not paying me and I had to wonder if she was aware of the gambling.

Something told me she wasn't. Ordinarily, the manners Mama had pounded into me would have kept me from letting the cat out of the bag, but Dewey's freedom was on the line and, while I still felt Glenda was too nice to be a killer, Jessica's statement about the morals clause for Saint Anne's was fresh in my mind.

I shifted so I could look her full in the eye. "No, he couldn't find the checkbook and said Gail would have to write it and she won't be back in the office until next week."

Glenda's brows drew together. "But it should be ... I mean, oh, he can write a check!" She started to rise. "Come on, I know where it is-"

"Glenda." I put my hand on her arm to stop her from getting up. "Thing is, I think Mark ..." I bit my lip and searched for the right words.

She looked like an angel, big blue eyes, strawberry blonde hair; trust and innocence radiated from her. I felt like a heel, but it had to be done. "Glenda, I'm pretty sure Mark is in some financial difficulties-"

"What? Why would you think that?"

Reluctantly, I told her what I'd learned and what I suspected. "So, you see, it all makes sense."

"He's gambling." She swallowed hard and wrung her hands as she stared off into space. "Gambling and now embezzling. How could he?" She met my gaze. "Come by the house and I'll write you a check from my personal account-"

"Oh, that's not-"

"Yes, it is." She rose. "I'll be home tomorrow afternoon if that's convenient?"

"You really don't have to ..." my voice tapered off as Glenda rose and headed for the brewery. Her posture was stiff, and her expression said she wasn't quite the angel her looks implied. I jumped up and hurried after her.

"Glenda? Wait, please." The Colonel and I hobbled down the path and caught up to her just outside of the garden gate. "Look, I didn't come here to make trouble."

Her lips were pinched and there was no warmth in her eyes. "Of course, you didn't, but I thank you for telling me what I should have seen." She sighed and sadness made her eyes dim. "I've been so wrapped up in getting the Saint Anne's job and other things, I should have suspected-no matter." She shook her head and forced a smile. "My cross to bear." She patted my arm. "Come by tomorrow, okay?"

Feeling like a heel, I bit my lip and nodded. "If you insist."

"I do." She gave a little wave and started toward the brewery steps.

I was so caught up in my guilt that I almost forgot the other reason I'd come. "Hey, Glenda?"

"Yes? Something else I can do for you?"

I sucked in a breath. I'd already dropped a bombshell on the woman and propriety said leave well enough alone but I needed to know ... "Um, yes. I was wondering if you can recall where you were when the police think Megan Hearn was killed."

My words came out in one rushed sentence, but Glenda was able to decipher them. Her eyebrows rose and her face seemed to lose a bit of color. "Goodness, um ... what time was that?"

"Between 11:15 and 11:45. I'm really sorry to ask, I'm just checking everyone's-"

"Don't worry about it. Um, I can't ..." She frowned. "Maybe I was talking with Edison? I know he and I spoke at some length on the filming of his novels, but I couldn't swear to the time."

"That's okay, I appreciate your help."

"Of course, such a tragedy. I only spoke with her a few times, but Ms. Hearn was a nice girl, so full of promise."

"Mmm, yes it's a shame." I snapped the leash and waited for The Colonel to trot over to me. "Well, we're gonna head home now. I'll see you tomorrow, thanks again!"

The bulldog and I were sitting in traffic on the Goodwin bridge when a thought hit me. Glenda had half-heartedly claimed Edison as her alibi, but Edison had claimed to be speaking with Rae Ella around eleven and then there was Rae Ella's insistence that she'd spoken to Edison earlier than when he claimed ...

If I wanted to be technical about it, Edison, Glenda, and Rae Ella had questionable alibis, though Rae Ella's could be confirmed if I got up the courage to talk to her husband. But something else Glenda had said was bugging me.

She was the first person I'd met that said Megan Hearn was nice, even the radio station manager had said she could be difficult. I snorted and shoved the truck into gear as the bridge swung back into place. Glenda Timmons was either delusional or a saint.

Chapter Fourteen

Connie was visible in the display window of the craft store as I pulled into the lot. I tapped on the glass, grinned when she jumped, and then motioned I was going next door.

Once I'd settled The Colonel on his bed and put out fresh water, I pulled my tablet from my bag and sat at my desk for the first time, well the first time I'd come prepared for work. The design of Cannery Wharf's shops was interesting. Every other space faced the opposite direction, making the entire façade look more residential and welcoming than walls of glass side by side in an unbroken line.

Glitter and Garland's large picture windows faced Bay Street, perfect for drawing customers, while Coastyle Events' windows faced the wharf, perfect for soothing my harried soul. Connie had chosen a perfect color palette, walls of light gray blue, honey-colored floors, and white furniture made it seem as if the natural world hadn't stopped at the door.

After indulging in some ideas for wall art, I knuckled down and used my stylus to draw a rough sketch for the Waterfront Christmas Village. Ms. Lou Lou had emailed me the bid package and the particulars the Chamber of Commerce would be supplying.

My lips twisted into a smirk. Local kids were gonna love it, but the business association had better pray for unusually cool weather in December or the generators would be working overtime; making snow in the Lowcountry, whoever heard of such a thing?

The idea of snow did give me an idea. I'd toyed with several decorating themes for the Christmas village, but nothing had jumped out as the winner until I'd seen what activities had been planned. Along with the vendors for crafts and food, the village would have a tree lighting ceremony the first night.

The following day was the main event, with a morning of fun in the snow and a family snowman building contest. Wrapping up the evening was a bonfire, carolers, and traditional holiday goodies. The event would end with an interfaith service and a visit from Santa.

I'd be responsible for general decorations for official areas, the park gazebo, and green spaces. Whatever I created for the park, would be enforced on the participating vendors; the theme was mine to choose. Snow, bonfires, goodies, Santa, traditions ... and visions of sugarplums popped into my head.

The Night Before Christmas would be our theme! My stylus flowed as I scribbled notes and sketched my vision of Goodwin Park transformed into a Holiday market and festival. The open field on the west end of the park could be set up like a typical main street and their theme would be sugarplums, transitioning to various stages for performances. The backdrops for each area could be something traditionally associated with the holiday season. I was lost in my vision and didn't know I had company until Connie tapped my desk with her fingernails.

"Earth to Holly Daye ... calling Holly Da-"

"Funny." I shook off the cobwebs and slid my tablet toward her. "Putting together a bid for designing the Goodwin Park Holiday Market. What do you think?"

Connie pulled a chair closer and studied my notes and drawings. I rose and made us both a drink, coffee for me, tea for my friend, and then puttered around the room. Her prolonged silence encouraged my self-doubt to grow. I chewed on my bottom lip. Why had I thought ... I wasn't trained for design ... no one was going to pay me-

"This is amazing."

I jerked around to see Connie staring at me, her mouth hanging open and eyes wide. "You, uh aren't just saying that?"

"What? Oh my gosh, just stop already!" She nodded at my desk. "Those plans are incredible; I can just feel the ... the-" She frowned. "What's the word I'm looking for?" Her eyes widened and she snapped her fingers. "Coziness! That's what it evokes in me, just the ideas make me feel warm and cozy and I think of family, home, traditions ... if I get all of that from your words imagine the reaction to the real thing!"

My smile was tentative. I was happy about the praise but ..., "You sure, Connie? I mean, you're biased."

She snorted. " 'Cuz we're friends? Honey, if it was crap I'd be the first to tell you so!" She laughed and shook her head as she returned to the drawings on my tablet. "The ideas are fantastic, but you haven't quite gotten the hang of pricing so, can I help? Because you didn't charge River Rat Brewery nearly enough nor Heather Rudd. Don't be afraid to actually make a profit, your time and talent are worth it!"

Connie was right, at least about my charges. After paying Dewey and then Whopper, plus buying supplies I'd barely made gas money. I nodded. "I'd appreciate the help, though I might need to hire goons to get my money out of Mark Timmons!"

It'd been meant as a joke, but Connie's eyes widened. "He is refusing to pay you? On what grounds? Of all the ... someone being murdered at his party is no excuse for not pay-"

"No, no, Connie!" I laughed at her outrage on my behalf. "He hasn't outright refused but he's stalling. If it had occurred to him, I've no doubt he'd use Hearn's death as an excuse but so far he's just claiming he can't find the checkbook and the bookkeeper is out until next week."

"Oh, for the love of-he could at least make up a better lie!"

"To be fair, he's running out of reasons besides the truth; he's dead broke." I sat at my desk and started saving the documents on my tablet.

"Mmm, he's in a heap of trouble, at least according to Megan Hearn's notes."

That brought my head up. "You finished going over that thumb drive?"

She shook her head. "No, there are a lot of files on there," I started to protest but Connie held up her hand. "But I got through the ones she'd been working on most recently."

I wanted to ask how she knew that but didn't want to get ribbed over my lack of computer skills as I was sure she had a simple way of figuring that out. "So, what did you find on there?"

Connie sighed. "Weeell, a whole lot and not much."

"Oh, that's helpful."

She laughed. "I try. Thing is, your podcaster wasn't the most organized of souls, or else there is a method to her madness that I'm not privy to."

"Like what?"

She huffed. "For instance, there are several word files that are just random words in long sentences- hold on a second and I'll show you."

She jumped up and rushed out the door, I assumed to retrieve her laptop. I closed out the last of my files pertaining to the Christmas Market project and made a few notes on the gorgeous cream and blue note paper Connie had stocked in a basket constructed of seagrass. I was writing a list of items I'd need to order for the Rudd project when Connie came back in.

"Okay, this is what I've found so far."

This was a document with words and abbreviations spread over the page. Hearn had strung sentences together in no discernable order.

Missing teen graduation F M pirates? Beach emerald bag

The words made no sense to me. "Are they all like this?"

"No, but there are quite a few. Like this one."

Boat Charleston Tropica rigged? Owned? Crew dates captain

"Hmm, they look like notes. Seems like a stream of con-scious-just let it all flow."

Connie nodded. "Yes, and that makes it hard to know the meaning. I'm assuming these are notes on things she was planning to make shows about?"

"Agreed. But this second file? That one I think I can decipher. Tropica is the company that runs the gambling cruises that J.T. Minton suggests are the source of Mark Timmons' money troubles, so I am gonna assume that long sentence of random words was her thinking out loud about her investigation." I gestured toward the keyboard. "Are there other files like these?"

My friend laughed. "Yep. She named them in code, so I'd have to open each file to know their contents." She snorted. "That takes more time than I have at the moment so, I pulled up the ones with dates ranging from September until the time of her death. Figured that was a place to start?"

As I'd thought, my friend had devised a simple way to winnow the huge amount of information. "Good idea. I wonder if it was something about this casino business that she asked Dale to take from Mark's computer."

Connie scrunched her nose and frowned. "Maybe? Let me see something though ..." she typed a few things and then scanned a long list of file names. "Hah, I thought ... take a look at this."

My eyes widened after skimming the first paragraph. Connie had found a file with images. I perused an ariel map of Saint Mariana Island, and several places were marked with an X. The lay of that land, with yards of shoreline on the Indigo River ...

"Connie, is there any way to make this photo bigger?"

"You need a basic computer skills class." She rolled her eyes and made a few clicks. "There, anything important?"

My eyes narrowed as I studied what I realized was a plot map, a plot map of Rosedale Plantation. "Wow, I think this is what she was after from Dale and the only reason I can think of for her wanting it was in relation to her investigation of J.T. Minton's business dealings."

"Oh, not that again! Mr. Minton is just a –"

"Connie, J.T. is not just anything. He comes across as a genteel old Southern gentleman but ..." I shrugged. "There is something about him I don't trust, but regardless of my feelings, Hearn was looking into the man's business deals and this was one of them."

"How can you be sure?"

"Look at her notes." I pointed farther down the page. "She reverts back to the style of jumbled phrases but if you know what you're looking at in the image ..."

Connie still looked puzzled and unconvinced, but I was positive my assumptions were correct. The renovations of the manor house were extensive and, judging by the expert historical contractors Glenda was using, expensive. Add in that Mark was gambling, begging for money, and had even stooped to stealing from his partner the whole story became clearer.

"You know Mark is having money problems." She nodded so I continued. "He's all over the county asking for investors and was seen dining with Minton. It was assumed he was begging him to invest as well, right?"

"Not assumed, Mr. Minton admitted it. He even said he had no interest in owning a brewery."

I smirked. "Oh yes, he's clever." I ignored her pursed lips and annoyed expression. "I'm just saying! Minton has everyone believing he wants nothing to do with what Mark's offering, an investment in the Brewery, and he *doesn't* want it as an investment. He wants it belly up and sold to him for cents on the dollar so he can build a gated golf course community."

"*Really*, you got all of that from an image?"

"Nope, I got it from what she wrote below that." I nodded to the paragraph in question. "See? *Debt, Foreclose, tax auction, cards, loans* .. the more I read the clearer it becomes." I looked up and met Connie's eyes. "I think Megan Hearn was looking for a connection between Mark Timmons' sudden financial problems and J.T. Minton and his plans for a riverfront en-clave-*and*" I hurried on as Connie scowled and started to inter-ject. "And that plays into something Rae Ella said about Mark bragging about how well the brewery was doing last year." I shrugged. "He was flush last year and now he's about to lose the plantation. It's not clear if he's behind on taxes or loans, maybe both, but Hearn seemed to think Minton was waiting in the wings to scoop up the property."

Connie huffed. "So what? That's not illegal. Maybe a bit unfeeling but not-"

"What if Minton manipulated Mark so that he would get into debt?"

Her eyes about popped out of her head. "No way! That would be-that's straight out of a book, it would never happen in real life ..."

"Wouldn't it?" I pointed to Hearn's file on the Tropica. "What if Megan Hearn suspected a set-up on Timmons? She was investigating the Tropica and Minton. Perhaps she was looking for a connection between the gambling cruise line and Minton ..."

Connie's cheeks puffed up as she blew out a deep breath. "Wow, that is some high-level crime ..."

"Yep. Not saying that is what is going on, but it does make me think."

"So you're thinking Minton killed Hearn?"

I shook my head. "No. I'd say he had motive, but no opportunity and I don't think he'd act so hastily. Whoever killed Hearn didn't plan for it to happen. If Minton did the deed he'd make it look like an accident, I think."

She snorted. "You really don't like him."

I frowned. "I don't *dislike* him. I just don't trust him. If that makes sense?"

"I guess ..." she laughed. "So where does this lead in your search for the killer?"

It was my turn to heave a sigh. The thumb drive had not been the smoking gun I'd hoped for. All of the files I'd seen concerned J.T. Minton or Mark Timmons. I didn't think Minton had done it, but Mark could have. I explained my logic to Connie.

"True, he could have killed her, you said his alibi didn't check out?"

"Well, he claimed to be talking with Griff Reid and I haven't talked to him yet, but I recall that neither Mark nor Glenda was in the tent in the minutes before everyone walked to the brewery for the launch event. I remember seeing Dale acting like a good host and thinking how well he was picking up the slack."

"Okay, then it's Mark or Glenda."

"Eh ...," I grimaced.

"What? What's that look for? You don't think it was the Timmons'?"

"I don't think it *isn't* them, but the only real evidence is the debt, him lying about gambling, and his confrontation with Megan in the garden; he refused to address that point blank but if you could have seen his reaction." I laughed. "Connie, his face was purple, he was apoplectic! Then there's the alibi. My gut says he's lying about that, but I'm not jumping to conclusions until I can confirm it. Then there's Glenda. She claimed to be with Edison Marlow but she either lied or was mistaken because Edison claimed to be talking to Rae Ella and I am positive she is correct about where she was."

"Okay, I'm confused. Mark doesn't have an alibi and you think he lied, right?"

"No, he has an alibi I haven't checked out yet, but my gut is saying it's a lie. Edison doesn't have an alibi. The question with Edison is, did he lie on purpose or was he just confused?"

She cocked her head to the side. "And what do you think?"

What did I think? I thought I had no clue who had killed the podcaster and my brother was going to be tried for murder. At the end of the day, I didn't think the state had a compelling case, but I wasn't willing to risk poor Dewey's life on that assumption.

Connie cleared her throat, making me smile. "Impatient? The truth is I don't know, not one hundred percent. If I had to make a choice though ..."

"Yeah? Who is the number one pick if it's do or die time to choose?"

I cocked an eyebrow at her choice of words. "In that situation ... Edison Marlow."

Her expression fell. "Oh, do you really think so? He was so ashamed of what he did to his poor dead wife I just don't think-"

"Connie, regardless of him being pitiful, all evidence currently in my possession points to him." I raised a finger. "One. His pipe was found on the stage near the witch's circle. Two. When asked about something missing from his costume he looked jumpy and wasn't very convincing in his denial. Three."

Connie started to argue but I rolled on. "*Three*. He said he was never near the stage or those decorations, another lie because we found his pipe."

"Yeah ... but-"

"*But* there's more! Four. He lied about his alibi and, five, he argued with the victim. I'm not even touching on the phone call I overheard but he was angry, was talking about someone being dead and that's the end of it. The end of what? Who did he mean?"

Her expression grew solemn. "Okay, you've made your point. What do you do now?"

I shrugged. I was considering a response when my phone buzzed. Mama had texted that our dinner was waiting at the Country Kitchen. I packed my tablet and phone back into my bag before rousing The Colonel. "Come on, buddy. Time to go- come on, lazy butt. You want dinner?" That got him moving. I snapped on his leash and moved to the door as Connie shut off the lights.

We walked over to Glitter and Garland, and I helped her close up. We chatted about the upcoming holidays. I invited her to Myrtlewood for Thanksgiving, we tossed around options for an easy centerpiece that could work for Heather Rudd and our own table, and my bid for the Sanctuary Bay Christmas

Market. What we *didn't* discuss was what I was going to do about Edison Marlow.

Chapter Fifteen

In the early hours of Monday morning, I was treated to another nightmare as my wake-up call. This time it wasn't about the shooting, thank God, but it was just as terrifying. I'd dreamed that Mama was tied to one of the Live Oaks at Myrtlewood and a bulldozer was barreling toward her.

Covered in a cold sweat, I shook off the last vestiges of the dream and jumped into the shower. My subconscious must have latched onto my concern over the information that Minton was looking to develop on Saint Mariana. I considered the nightmare as I dried off.

Rosedale was one of a few plantations that had dotted the Sea Islands in the 1700 and 1800s. Most had been raised completely while others had disappeared as the heirs sold off the land. Finding a large tract along the river was rare, I could count on one hand how many properties fit the requirements of a development like the one Minton proposed and our ancestral home was one of them.

I'd been thinking about what to do with Myrtlewood because we were paying ever-increasing property taxes on it and most of the time it sat empty, but my thoughts had been leaning more towards leasing it out like we did the farmland or making Daddy's dream a reality and opening for living history tours. Never, in my wildest dreams, had I considered outright selling the property to anyone, much less to a developer!

I slipped on a pair of jeans and a t-shirt. I'd grabbed a cardigan and my bag, thinking I'd get an early start on the day, when my gaze landed on the little blue notebook Dr. Styles had given me. Crud monkeys, I had to do the focus therapy.

Muttering choice words and scanning the furniture for an innocuous object, I stalked across the room and flopped onto the bed, spilling my purse in the process. I was putting the detritus back when my hand fell on the flyer someone had left in my truck. I shrugged; it'd work as well as anything else.

Flat, shiny, colorful ... my breathing was slow and steady as I cataloged the flyer's properties. Several times my mind tried to revisit the issues with Myrtlewood but turning back to my focus object was getting easier, or I just wasn't that upset. The true test would come if I had another panic attack.

The timer on my phone was counting down the remaining seconds and I put one final effort into the exercise. Words, colorful, treasure chest, red writing – I cocked my head and squinted, with my glasses on, the messy handwriting was becoming clearer.

The alarm sounded. I turned it off and carried the flyer over to the window. Under natural light, I had less trouble deciphering the scrawled words above the pirate's chest.

See   and you   find

See and you find. I was pretty sure the letter after the word *see* was a K and if I had to guess, the other word I couldn't read was *will*. Either way, it was a riddle and, after learning Jessica had not found a flyer in her car, I felt confident in assuming the flyer with its almost illegible note had been meant for me.

The riddle suggested I seek something and then, presumably, I'd find something, but what and where was I supposed to do the seeking? After searching the rest of the flyer for more clues to looking up legends of buried pirate treasure in the Lowcountry, I finally decided to visit the pirate tour shop; perhaps they could shed light on the meaning.

First, I had to talk to Griff Reid and the very idea of doing that made me want to crawl back into bed and hide under the covers. The tip-tap of dog nails and yapping coming from the front porch suggested Ms. Maybelle Everette had brought Coco and her three hellion children over for a chat which meant The Colonel and I were scurrying out the back; the little Pomeranian and my bulldog got along fine but he wasn't too keen on the rambunctious pups.

I caught sight of little Cocopuff as I backed down the drive. Shortly before I'd been shot, a local dognapping ring had stolen a heavily pregnant Coco from the front yard, and I'd been assigned the task of solving the crime. Since my involvement in the case had resulted in The Colonel making his home with me I was eternally grateful for Mama and Ms. Maybelle pestering me to investigate!

Slobber jowls liked the wind in his face, so I rolled the window down and we both enjoyed the salty air. It was going to be another beautiful Fall day in the Lowcountry, and I hoped to finish my chat with Griff Reid early enough to get a start on planting the Dianthus and other bedding flowers Mama had ordered from the nursery.

The law offices of Reid, Daye, and Powell were located in a refurbished historic home situated one block north of Bay Street. The small lot was full, forcing The Colonel and I to park on the street but neither of us minded. He because the short walk afforded him opportunities to sniff unfamiliar trees and me, because I dreaded encountering my ex-husband.

All too soon we were standing in the foyer and forcing a smile as the perky young receptionist greeted me with a good morning, Mrs. Daye how may I help you?

Was it appropriate to address me as Mrs.? I hadn't changed my last name back to Barker but what was the appropriate prefix for a divorced woman? I'd have to ask Mama; she could cite Miss Manners chapter and verse.

The receptionist cleared her throat, prodding me from my rambling thoughts. I kept my smile in place and requested a few minutes of Griff Reid's time.

Her smile faltered but she nodded and scurried away, murmuring something about seeing if he was in. I commanded The Colonel to sit and stay and then wandered around the lobby stopping at a gallery wall of pictures spanning decades of the firm's outings, client victories, and other events. I smiled as my gaze landed on a picture of Brooks with Brooks Jr. at a father/son golfing tournament. The two were dressed in matching golf attire and each held one side of a trophy that was almost as big as Jr. There were several with me and Brooks; a gubernatorial inauguration, one from a New Year's Eve gala in Charleston ... I wondered how long before those were removed-

"Holly? Something I can do for you?"

I jerked around to find Brooks wearing an uneasy smile. The timid receptionist hovered a few steps behind him. I glanced at her and then focused on Brooks. Poor man, did he think I'd come to press him for more alimony? I hid my laugh in a short cough and shook my head.

"Hey, Brooks. You're receptionist misunderstood. I've come to have a few words with Griff."

His eyebrows rose. "So I was told but Griff hasn't arrived yet and I'm not sure ... do you need legal advice because I'm more than happy to, only you know we don't handle criminal work ..."

My eyes widened. He thought I'd come about Dewey. I smiled. "Uh thanks, I'm not, this isn't about Dewey, well it is but not-" I shook my head. What the heck was wrong with me? I was starting to ramble like Mama!

I swallowed and started again. "Thank you, but I just need to speak with Griff about the brewery party ..." the party made me think of something Brooks could help me with. "But if you have a minute I could use some advice ..."

His expression was solemn and not for the first time in knowing the man for over twenty-five years, I thought he needed to lighten up. Brooks put his arm out, gesturing for me to precede him into his office while he told the receptionist to hold his calls.

He chose to sit on the leather sofa that took up one wall in the paneled study. A tray of coffee sat on a low table and numerous manilla folders lay scattered on the other couch cushion making it clear Brooks had been working before my interruption.

I settled The Colonel at my feet and then sat in a club chair opposite him, waving away his offer of coffee but taking a cookie for The Colonel.

Brooks snorted. "You and that dog ..."

I ignored him; Brooks was one of the few people that didn't fawn all over my bulldog. It said more about him than it did about The Colonel. I glanced up and noticed Brooks checking his watch. "Look, you're busy, I don't want to keep you from-"

"No, no this ..." he waved a hand toward the papers beside him. "I'm just refreshing my memory for a deposition this afternoon, you're not -it's fine." He stirred cream into his cup and sat back, looking relaxed for once. "What do you need to talk to Griff about?"

I shook my head. "Nothing ..." I cocked my head and considered my words before continuing. "Brooks, back in high school.

I seem to remember you and Griff were best friends and then all of a sudden you stopped hanging out with him and then he took off ... what happened?"

His eyes narrowed. "Why?"

"Just wondering, someone mentioned it and I couldn't remember ..., what caused you to cut ties?"

He huffed. "He had family troubles and started getting into trouble ... then he ran away, and I wasn't into that, okay?"

His defensive answer made me snort which seemed to act in a similar fashion as a red flag to a bull with my ex-husband. A streak of red showed on his cheekbones. He sat up poker straight and his brown eyes darkened almost black.

"What? Wish I'd gone to Florida with Griff? Wish I'd left so we never started dating? Huh? Your life would be so much better if you'd never married me?"

I reared back and stared at him. Where had all of that hostility come from? "Deflection much, Brooks? I have never wished that!" I scoffed and shook my head as I wondered what had gotten into him. "I admit regret in not finishing college but never having-God, Brooks! We'd have never had Junior!"

He dropped his gaze to the floor as some of the rigidness left his body. I schooled my features and voice. "Look, I didn't come here looking for a fight." I snorted. "I didn't come to speak to you at all."

He glared at me. "Ah yes, you came to see Griff. What about?"

I shrugged, though I resented his demanding tone. "Nothing much, I just need to ask him where he was while Megan Hearn was being murdered-" My mouth snapped shut as Brooks choked and sputtered on his coffee. I moved to pat him on the back, but he waved me away with a scowl.

He set the cup down, wiped his mouth, and then glared at me. "What do you mean, asking something like that? No, let me guess, this is about your worthless-" He scowled. "Junior said he recommended a criminal attorney and I checked; Maxwell Bernard is more than capable so why are *you* asking questions?" He crossed his arms over his chest. "You're not the police anymore, Holly, and sticking your nose into this could hamper the investigation. And involving Griff! What are you thinking? You could wreck his election chances!"

I stared at him in shock. He never lost control. His voice had risen an octave and his face was once again florid. "Hey, first you need to calm down, you're getting riled and that's not like you." His chest rose as he drew a deep breath and for a minute I thought he'd explode with anger, but he shook himself and then sighed.

I nodded. "Good take another deep breath. Secondly, I don't need a badge to ask people questions and *third*," he started to object. I gave him a look that was part Mom and part Cop. His mouth pursed but he let me continue. "Third, someone claimed Griff as their alibi, and I wanted to check the veracity of their statement. Those are hardly career-ending inquiries."

Brooks' expression was mulish, even if he had calmed somewhat. It was stress I didn't need, even secondhand. I rose from my chair. "Look, I didn't come here to fight. I'll wait in the lobby for Griff."

I had taken a few steps when he called out.

"Holly, wait." I turned and cocked an eyebrow.

Brooks sighed and dragged a hand through his coal-black hair. I noticed it was streaked with a lot more white than had been there six months ago; Trying to keep up with a girl over half one's age would do that. I wondered if I was a terrible person for being happy about that.

"Look, I'm sorry. I've got a lot on my mi-never mind, please have a seat. You said there was something I could help you with."

He seemed calmer and definitely contrite, so I resumed my seat, but he'd gotten me so out of sorts that it took a few minutes to remember what I'd wanted to ask him and his earlier mention of Griff going to Florida wasn't helping; something about the state was teasing at memories.

We sat in silence for a few minutes as I retraced the tangled threads of conversations and thoughts we'd trampled through-oh! My business venture!

I cleared my throat and Brooks met my gaze with a cocked eyebrow. My smile was sheepish. "Sorry, took me a second to remember ..., I was wondering about ways to incorporate and which one I should choose and also is it necessary right now ..." I shrugged.

Brooks frowned even as he seemed relieved to have the conversation on a more practical footing. He never had been good at emotions or introspection, much less deviating from a routine. Poor man, I'd arrived in his office and upset his apple cart!

He shifted some papers and returned them to a folder before meeting my gaze. "Um, what do you need to incorporate?" His eyes widened. "You aren't thinking of becoming a private investigator!"

The look of horror on his face made me laugh out loud, though now that he mentioned it ... I snorted and shook my head. "No, nothing like that! Lou Lou Tomlin and Connie have pushed me into accepting more decorating jobs; Connie's even set up an office for me right next to her craft store." I tucked a strand of hair behind my ear and leaned forward, excitement building in my voice as I started telling him about my venture into business.

"I have a small job coming up and Lou Lou wants me to submit a bid for a Christmas Market in Goodwin park she's pushing the Chamber of Commerce for ... oh, and the ladies auxiliary at Osprey Point want me to call them. I think it's something to do with their annual fashion show and silent auction .. so, you see I just thought there might be legal stuff I needed to do."

Brooks' smile was wide, though whether through happiness for me or just relief that I wasn't planning a business that would embarrass him I couldn't determine. He poured a fresh cup of coffee and relaxed in his seat.

"A decorating business, wow, that's great, Holly!" His expression softened. "I'm proud of you. It's something you should have done years ago ..." The smile in his eyes dimmed for a moment and then he blinked, and the professional tone was back. "Now then, you're going to need a bank account separate from your personal-have you done that yet?"

I bit my lip. "Uh, no. Mark paid me half up front for the brewery job and I just deposited it so I could buy supplies- have I screwed up already?"

He shook his head. "No, just keep good records of what you bought, and when you meet with an accountant they can note that deposit and any expenditures but, going forward it'll be easier tax-wise to keep it all separate."

"Ok, not that I will have much to put into an account right now. I haven't charged Heather anything yet and I probably won't see the rest of the money from the brewery job ..."

Brooks frowned and leaned forward. "He's refusing to pay you? Because that woman died?"

The outrage on my behalf warmed my attitude towards Brooks. I spent a few minutes telling him about Mark's money troubles which led to a synopsis of my entire investigation and an admonishment not to get involved.

"Not that I think you'll listen to me." He rolled his eyes. "Back to your business venture. You could operate as a DBA or doing business as, but it won't protect you from liability and, after that woman died in one of your displays-"

"Hey, that was no fault of mine! She was murdered."

He held up a hand. "Don't come at me! I know you did nothing wrong but the fact that you're defensive tells me the idea of negligence has been raised?"

Reluctantly, I rolled my eyes and nodded.

"As I thought. Decorating spaces could expose you to legal risk meaning they could sue you and come after your personal assets ..."

I sucked in a breath as I considered what he was saying. My divorce settlement, savings, retirement account, co-ownership of The Oaks and Myrtlewood ... I gulped and met Brooks' gaze. "Um, perhaps I should just forget about all of this-"

"What? Don't be ridiculous," his lips twisted as he shook his head. "We're going to incorporate and I'll find you some liability insurance. You'll also need ..."

He rattled off a bunch of legal mumbo jumbo and ended by saying he was going to get the paperwork in order. He also said he wasn't charging me for his time, and he'd personally pay for the filing fees with the state and the first year of the insurance.

I protested but he waved away my concerns.

"I insist. I'd have done it while we were married if you'd ever shown an interest. I never meant for an accidental pregnancy to steal your dreams ..."

He was on a guilt trip, so I gave in; I wasn't going to turn my nose up at saving thousands of dollars! I'd just signed a limited power of something or other so he could get the filings completed when Griff knocked and stuck his head around the door of Brooks' office.

"Hey, Tiffany said you wanted to speak with me, Holly?"

I smiled at him. His blonde hair, with just a touch of gray at the temples I noticed waspishly, was tousled and he was dressed in chinos and a sweatshirt, leaving me to assume he'd just arrived from Rose Island; I'd never considered living on an island not connected to land by roads as a detriment but seeing Griff I realized commuting could be a chore.

"Yeah Griff, if you have a minute?" Since I'd already told Brooks about the investigation I didn't bother asking for a private chat. "Mark Timmons is claiming he was talking with you between around eleven and quarter 'til midnight. Can you confirm that?"

He frowned. "I did speak with Mark, Rae Ella and I both did, but it was much earlier in the evening." He looked down and licked his lip. "The more I think about it, I know where I was at about the time you mention. Rae Ella was bugging me to leave for home, and God help me, I wish I'd listened."

No doubt he did. Everyone that attended that party likely wished they had. I'd accomplished what I'd come for; Griff had an alibi and Mark didn't, but I was still curious if my gut was right, had Hearn been blackmailing Griff?

Griff's blue eyes widened. "Wh ... what kind of question is that?

My eyes narrowed as I considered his stammered non-committal reply. I'd verified his alibi and Mark's lack of one, but I was still curious. The verbal sparring Jessica had overheard between Griff and Hearn had included the words Florida and people change. Brooks had said Griff went to Florida when he ran away from home ...

"Was Hearn threatening you over something that happened in Florida when you were a teen? Was that why Rae Ella had been crying?"

I'd been thinking out loud, not really directing the question at Griff so much as working it out in my mind and letting my mouth participate in the exercise but the effect on Griff was electric. He went white as a sheet. His breaths started coming in short pants, his spine stiffened, and his eyes bulged.

I shot a concerned look at Brooks, but he was too busy glaring at me to notice. "Griff?" I stepped closer and reached out to nudge him to a chair. "You don't look so good, maybe you'd better sit-"

"Don't touch me!" He jerked away and started pacing. "How ... who told you?" Without waiting for my answer, Griff turned to scowl at Brooks. "I thought you'd taken care of him!"

Brooks threw his hands up as if to ward off Griff's anger. "I did! He won't bother you-"

"Hey, hey, hey! Don't say anything else, I may not be active duty, but I'm still a retired law enforcement officer."

My declaration brought the room to silence. Both men turned to stare at me, and their expressions suggested I had sprouted wings.

Brooks' brow furrowed. "What?" He glanced at Griff, who shrugged, and then looked back at me. "What does your being a retired deputy have to do with an old friend needing help?"

It was my turn to be confused. I rubbed at the back of my neck and thought back over what they'd said and what had made me interpret the meaning as Griff being blackmailed ... nope, I hadn't missed anything. "A friend in what? What did they need help with?" I shook my head. "And what did it have to do with Megan Hearn blackmailing Griff?"

Brooks glanced at Griff and gave a tiny shake of his head, but Griff ignored him. He looked at me as he sighed. "It's over, Brooks, she knows."

I didn't know beans, but I was smart enough to keep my mouth shut and let him tell on himself. I perched on the edge of my chair and motioned for Griff to take the one next to me.

He sat, but he was on autopilot, his eyes were distant and fixed at a spot somewhere across the room. We sat in silence for several minutes, the only sound Griff's ragged breathing. Finally, he sighed and looked down at the floor.

"You know I ran away to Florida."

It wasn't a question and I refrained from answering or even moving, lest I interrupt his flow.

"I ..., I was foolish and selfish. Brooks tried to tell me not to go but I-"

"Man, stop beating yourself up! It's done, over, nothing will ever be said about it beyond those that already know! And you,"

I jumped as Brooks pointed his finger at me and snarled. "You have no reason to dredge up ancient history. You're as bad as the old ladies; just looking for gossip."

"What? Brooks, I'm not asking so I can gossip!" I didn't bother continuing trying to convince my ex. "Griff, you don't have to tell me anything except ..., I have to know. Was she blackmailing you? Did you kill her?"

Griff's shoulders drooped. He still wouldn't raise his gaze from the floor and his voice was just above a whisper. The only acknowledgment that he'd heard me was his answer to my questions. "No, I didn't kill her, but I'm not sorry she's dead ... sh-she was," his head rose, and he made eye contact with me. "She was vile! Hounding a sick man, and for what?"

Gone was the pitiful Griff, now his blue eyes shown with the light of indignation. He startled me and The Colonel when he jumped from his seat and began to pace. His words came faster and louder as he worked himself into a righteous rage.

"He took me in, helped me, loved me..." his voice dipped back to a strangled whisper. "Hateful woman. She turned what was good and pure into something sordid and shameful ..."

Without warning, Griff walked out of the room leaving me with unanswered questions. I cleared my throat and looked at Brooks. "Hearn uncovered a relationship with a man in Florida and was trying to blackmail Griff?"

Brooks huffed. "Yes, happy? She stumbled across some racy photos from back then-Griff got into the South Beach club scene and well, he ran out of money, was living from couch to couch and a nice man took him in. He hired him to be a housekeeper/caretaker as he traveled a lot, but Hearn was implying other things. Griff was only sixteen and this man was almost forty .." Brooks met my gaze. His voice took on an earnest quality as he continued to explain. "Griff had just lost his father, he was vulnerable, hurting ... this man was good to him, and that malicious viper threatened to twist that relationship into something nasty, just in time for the election!"

I absorbed what he'd said. "So, she was blackmailing him with exposure and implying it was an underage sexual situation." Brooks nodded. "Okay, but what was she asking for?"

He snorted. "Money and influence. She hinted about wanting access once he was in office; it was never going to stop."

Blackmailers usually didn't stop, and that meant Griff had a very strong motive. I mentioned that to Brooks and got a scathing reply for my trouble. "Give us a little credit, Holly Marie!" He made a disgusted sound and rose, crossing to his desk and pulling out a stack of documents which he dropped into my lap.

"What are these?"

"Those are sworn affidavits from Mr. Ban-er, the older gentlemen, swearing that numerous claims Hearn was threatening Griff with were all bogus. There is also a video deposition from him."

I frowned. "I don't understand, how was this going to help Griff, should Hearn have followed through and released her lies?"

"It'd be out there but those papers let us sue anyone who publishes it or repeats it because it is baseless slander." He shrugged. "Best we could do on short notice."

"Okay, but what was that about taking care of him? That seemed to imply you paid the man off."

Brooks rolled his eyes. "The man is dying of cancer. His savings are depleted, he sold his condo ... he's living quietly in a retirement home." He cocked an eyebrow. "Would you let someone you love live like that if you could afford better?"

He didn't wait for my answer. "All Griff did was instruct me to buy a place on the beach and hire a full-time care nurse. He'll have the best of everything for the short time he has left. There was nothing illegal in that but, surely you can understand the desire for privacy?"

I nodded and stood up, patting my leg for The Colonel to wake up and let me attach his leash. "Thanks, Brooks. I didn't mean to pry you know, I just needed to eliminate him as a suspect and verify Mark Timmons'." I crossed to the door and looked back. "And please tell Griff I won't say a word."

Dealing with my ex and then sparring with Griff Reid had me longing for a nap but, time was running out for Dewey. It was a little shy of the lunch hour, but I decided to visit the Pirate tour kiosk before eating; a lot of the places geared toward tourists had odd hours during the off-season.

Corsair Cruises specialized in our area's pirate history. A two-hour cruise took customers around the islands and waterways while telling them the history of Sanctuary Bay; how we earned our name by being a haven and freeport for pirates, that pirates were instrumental in saving town's people during the

Indian wars, and that Anne Bonny was likely a Lowcountry local.

During the cruise, they'd take a shore excursion to one of the many uninhabited islands and follow treasure maps to uncover a buried hoard conveniently placed by the company earlier in the day. Years ago for one of Brooks Jr.'s birthdays, I'd lost my mind and taken a dozen or so kids on an adventure. It'd been fun, exhausting, but the kids had a blast.

The business occupied a small kiosk at the marina. I parked the Scout and hurried inside in case marina owner Cooter Drummond was around; he'd start jawing and I'd never get lunch.

The Colonel and I entered the store to find four men clustered around a TV, hanging from the back wall. They were all large men; tall and brawny. Two had beards hanging down to their chests, and all of them wore identical black leather jackets with a patch featuring a lone cross encompassed by a circle with the words Vassal for Christ.

Christian bikers. That made me feel a bit more comfortable approaching the counter. The guy with the long red beard turned the TV down and nodded at me. "S'up? Sorry, but we aren't running any cruises right now. We're taking reservations for the next one, which will be a special holiday tour.

"Thanks, but I'm not here for- actually, this is gonna sound silly, but someone put one of your flyers in my truck the other night, and, well I'm wondering if you might know something about this."

I pulled the glossy postcard from my bag and slid it across the wooden counter. In the blink of an eye, he'd pulled a box from beneath the counter as he informed me they'd been waiting for me.

"What? I don't understand, how would you-"

He shrugged. "I was asked to give this to whoever presented a card with writing like that."

I stared at the box, inspecting it with some of the focus I'd learned in therapy. Square, an inch deep, wrapped in plain brown paper, no identifying marks ... "What's in it?"

He shrugged and pushed it toward me. "No idea, you want it or not?"

"Yeah, yeah I'll take it but ...," he'd turned back to the television, making it clear he was finished talking. I pushed the glass door open and then paused, looking over my shoulder. "Guess you can't tell me who left this for me?"

A snort was my answer.

Chapter Sixteen

Satisfying my curiosity was my top priority and as soon as my butt hit the seat of my truck I was tearing off the paper wrapping. Unfortunately, I was met with another mystery to solve because the only thing inside the box was a small silver key with a pink plastic cover over the top half.

I turned the key every which way, held it up to the light even, but still found nothing to identify it other than the letter *B* followed by *47*. Without knowing who wanted me to have the key or what it unlocked I was stuck. With numerous other things to occupy my tired brain, I slipped the key to the unknown into my bag and set about coaxing the Scout into reverse.

Luckily, the transmission seemed to approve of backward motion, and I was soon rolling toward home. Half way to the house I remembered Glenda Timmons had insisted on paying me the remainder of the brewery job charges. A few turns and I was rerouted and on my way to Pelican Cove.

Pulling up to the gate house for the subdivision elicited no feelings in me one way or the other, which wasn't surprising as I'd never wanted to buy the house in the stuffy and restrictive golf course community in the first place; that had been all Brooks' idea. He'd wanted to keep the house, so part of our divorce settlement included him paying me for my half. I now *loved* the brick monstrosity crammed onto a tiny lot with only one shade tree!

The Timmons' home was in the newest phase of Pelican Cove. Farther away from the clubhouse amenities, and with no golf course or marsh views, it was also a less expensive area, relatively speaking. That should have been a blessing to Mark Timmons' bank account, but I suspected Glenda viewed the two-story Colonial style home as a temporary measure until Rosedale's renovations were complete.

A mid-sized car was parked in the circular driveway, just across from the front door. I couldn't recall what Glenda drove, but I was pretty sure it wasn't an older model dark green hatchback, either way, I parked behind it and hoped I wasn't intruding on a visit with friends.

The doorbell had barely finished chiming before the leaded glass door swung open to reveal Cricket Morrison juggling a laundry basket, a set of car keys, and a plastic tote holding cleaning supplies. Somewhere nearby raucous music was blaring.

"Hey, Holly, how are ya? Hold this a second, will ya? Gotta catch this phone call."

Reeling from her rapid-fire sentences, I accepted the basket thrust into my arms without protest. The music ceased as she took the call, but Cricket greeted whoever was on the other end of the line like a long-lost friend, leaving me standing on the doorstep with a load of dirty clothes.

Nudging her aside, I stepping into the foyer, closed the door, and set the basket beside a round table sitting in the middle of the black and white tiled floor. The house was quiet, aside from Cricket's exuberant discussion on the relative merits of Cluck's Bar over Harry's out by the interstate, and I was pretty sure Glenda wasn't at home.

Still, I poked my head around the entry to the living room and called for her, then walked half way up the stairs and tried again. I was heading toward the back of the house when Cricket hollered. "They ain't home, Holly!"

Thank you for stating the obvious, Cricket. I retraced my steps to find her still yakking. Hoping Glenda had mentioned I'd be coming by, I hung out and waited for Cricket to finish her call.

Killing time, The Colonel and I wandered into the formal living room. Cream silk wallpaper, accented by the wide white woodwork, framed a room furnished in shades of cream, white, and soft gold. Pops of cobalt blue in the form of stacked books, pillows, and pottery drew the eye around the room. Potted palms dotted the space, and thrived in the natural light afforded by a wall of floor length windows with French doors that opened onto the lanai and provided views of a beautifully landscaped yard.

The home was beautifully and tastefully decorated and Glenda either had great taste, or she'd hired a designer that did. Curious to see the dining room, I was crossing the foyer when The Colonel bumped into the round, Chippendale style table, knocking a clear plastic bag to the floor. It landed with a thud, making me cringe and pray the bag didn't contain something fragile or priceless.

I picked it up and sighed with relief; it was just a pair of shoes! Something about the shoes drew my attention. They were white suede, with long ties meant to lace up the calf. Along the soles were splotched stains where they'd either gotten wet, muddy or both. I frowned as something about the shoes triggered a memory. What was it I should remember-

"Those are mine; Glenda was gonna throw them out, can you believe it?" Cricket, finished with her call and car keys in her hand, was holding her hand out for the bag in mine.

Shrugging off my puzzlement, I handed them over to Cricket.

"Thanks. Look at that!" She snorted and held the bag up for me to see.

A discreet tag sewn to the back of the heel strap proved that someone had shelled out a few hundred bucks for the now ruined footwear. I shook my head and met Cricket's wide-eyed gaze.

"Imagine having the money to throw out a pair of *Bulucci's*!" She pointed to the soles and then tossed the bag on top of the dirty clothes basket. "So they're a little stained. Bit of shoe polish will blend that in and besides, who looks at your feet?"

The fact that someone paid more than a car payment for shoes, and she was giddy to receive a pair of damaged sandals, suggested at least some people did look at one's feet, but that reasoning escaped Ms. Morrison.

I refrained from giving my opinion on expensive shoes, bags, and other designer label products in favor of getting down to business, namely the business of tracking down my money.

"You said Glenda isn't home?"

She chomped on her gum a few times before replying. "Yeah, she left a few minutes ago and I was just headin' out, too. You want to leave her a message? Might be some paper in the kitchen. There's a little desk built in by the minibar-"

"Ah, no thanks. Glenda had told me to come over and pick up a check but I'll just come back-"

"Oh, hold on, she left an envelope here, said someone was comin' over for it; didn't know it was you." She pointed to the buffet in the dining room.

I retrieved the white envelope while Cricket continued to rattle on about the shoes and how she was gonna wear them when her latest man took her dancing.

"... and I only wish she'd have ruined them earlier. These things would have went great with my Halloween costume-"

My eyes widened. That was where I'd seen the shoes, Glenda's Halloween costume! I'd remarked on them earlier that evening because with the flimsy straps and flat sole she would have likely had wet feet when the dew fell.

That answered who I'd heard in the shrubs that night but what had she been doing? I thanked Cricket for her help and waved good-bye as I continued to ponder another piece in the puzzle that was who killed the pugnacious podcaster.

Mama played spades at the community center on Monday nights, so I was on my own for dinner. Not fancying take-out or Country Kitchen and feeling restless, I loaded up The Colonel and set off to find adventure, or at least something to eat.

Finding Glenda's ruined shoes, along with the mysterious key, had thrown me. I'd been set to go see Brannon and lay out my case against Edison Marlow but now ... I sighed and shoved the Scout into third gear. We rolled across the Adler Creek bridge, no destination in mind other than a full belly and a reprieve from the thoughts running through my mind on an endless loop.

My course was aimless for about thirty minutes before my stomach started protesting. I'd ended up near the interstate and had just passed the state trooper barracks when I remembered many of my former colleagues hung out at Riley's bar and grill to watch Monday night football. With nothing better to do and not fancying eating alone, I made a few course corrections and was soon pulling into the gravel lot of the local cop hangout.

John Riley, a retired trooper, had started Riley's several decades ago as a place for law enforcement to socialize and unwind. At any given time you could find a handful of officers enjoying a beer or a game of pool, but the food had never been much to write home about so the place stayed small and true to its founder's intent.

After his death, the kids had tried to keep everything the same but John's oldest had trained as a chef and, even though he had a restaurant on Belle Isle, Will Riley hadn't been able to resist spiffing up Riley's menu. As evidenced by the number of vehicles in the lot, word on the upgrade in food had gotten out.

With the change in food had come changes to the interior. Gone were the roughhewn cedar plank walls and scuffed heart pine floors, replaced by shiplap and porcelain tiles. All was not lost, however. The Colonel and I entered through the main door, waved to the harried hostess trying to seat another family in the bursting at the seams dining room, and slipped through a battered looking door marked Squad Room.

Stepping through the door was like night and day; literally, I had to stop and let my eyes adjust to the cave like lighting. Once I could see though ... here was John Riley's place. What the kids might have 'wrecked' for most of the building, they'd only enhanced in the bar. The original walls and floors remained, but because they'd taken over half of the space to create their restaurant, they'd added a screened porch, complete with a fireplace, for overflow when the bar got too full and also for those who wanted a comfortable place to talk and not have to shout over multiple televisions barking sports reports.

I had fond memories of Riley's, and the porch. I'd spent many evenings talking with Harley Goodwin, Noble County's former sheriff and mentor to me. The Colonel and I were headed to the bar when I heard my name called. I scanned the room ...

"Over here!"

My gaze went to the door leading out to the porch, where Craig Everette stood juggling a beer and a plate of food. He jerked his head in a silent invitation to join him and continued on his way. The Colonel was sniffing and snorting around on the floor looking for any crumb of food, so I hurried to place an order and dragged his greedy behind outside.

Craig had chosen a table just to the right of a roaring fire that still afforded a decent view of the big screen TV. Days in the Lowcountry were still mostly balmy mid 60s to 70s, but the nights had turned a tad chilly. The Colonel happily settled in front of the hearth as I took a seat across from my friend.

"Hey Holly, whatcha doin' out this way?"

I shrugged and sipped my iced tea. "Took a drive to clear my head and ended up here; must be fate."

Craig grinned and toasted me with his bottle of Witch's Brew. My eyes widened. "Can't believe your drinking that." I glared at the bottle. "Darn thing's birthday has caused me nothing but trouble."

He snorted and bit into his cheeseburger. I snagged a French fry as I waited for him to respond.

"It's good beer, I'll give 'em that." He took another pull and wiped his mouth. "How's the unofficial investigation going?"

I cocked an eyebrow and sighed.

Craig laughed. "That bad, huh?"

"You don't know the half of it." I leaned back as the server deposited my shrimp basket onto the table. "You heard the DA is presenting Dewey's case to the Grand Jury."

"Yeah, sorry." He shook his head. "Brannon is a fool at the best of times, but this is ignorant, even for him! I pointed out that there were witnesses to the victim scratching Dewey, but he refuses to look at any evidence that doesn't confirm his initial theory ... shoddy police work."

"So you think there is any point in me going to see him about my suspicions?"

Craig's eyes narrowed. "Who, Brannon? And, what suspicions, you got a theory of who killed her?"

"Yes to Brannon and ..." I bit my lip and debated rehashing my investigation with Craig. I'd been over it so many times I could have recited it in my sleep. I'd also talked it out with Jessica and Connie, but the snarky inner voice that lived in my head rent free chimed in that Craig was another cop. I hated agreeing with that know-it all!

I blew out a breath. "I have several suspects and one strong possibility."

"Well, let's hear it! Who do you think killed Hearn?"

I ate a few popcorn shrimp to fortify myself. "Ok, if you're sure you wanna talk shop ..." Craig nodded. "On your own head then."

I pushed my empty basket to the edge of the table, took a sip of tea, and settled back in my chair. "I'll start with Whopper, no sorry, I just learned something today so let me back up." I ignored Craig's smirk and continued. "Just before y'all arrived at the tasting pavilion I'd heard someone in the shrubs near the gate to the garden."

Craig nodded. "Yeah, I remember you told Brannon, and an officer checked it out. Found a footprint didn't they?"

"Yep, but the soaker hoses had been running and the ground was soft so whoever had been in that garden bed would have had mud caked on the soles of their shoes, and no one present fit that description." I snorted. "I didn't think much more about it because, by the time Brannon got around to looking in the hedges he'd allowed half of the guests to leave!"

"Yep, I remember." Craig shook his head and muttered, "Fool. You telling me you found the owner of the shoes?"

"Eh, let's just say I found stained shoes that were worn as part of a costume that night and I am assuming they were ruined by the wearer standing in water, dirty water."

Craig laughed. "I'm assuming you aren't naming this person for a reason?"

I nodded. "Yes, because I want to lay out the clues and see if you are thinking what I'm thinking. First, I should tell you that Connie and I whittled the list of suspects down to six guests: Dale Scruggs, Mark Timmons, Glenda Timmons, Griff Reid, Rae Ella Reid, and Edison Marlow." Craig nodded so I continued. "The first thing I consider a clue is a plastic pipe that Whopper found while helping me clean up Sunday after the party."

Craig's eyes got wide. "Wait. Did you turn that in to Brannon?"

I smirked. "I did attempt to be a good citizen but the head idiot in charge refused to listen to me. He insulted me, threatened me, and all but threw me from his office. I am under no further obligation."

"Is that a legal fact?"

"Probably not but ..." I shrugged. Brannon was the least of my concerns at the moment. His pigheadedness had placed me in the position of solving a murder, he could suffer the consequences. "I have let Dewey's attorney know, however. He had it bagged and tagged. Know idea what he plans to do with it."

"Okay, you found a plastic pipe. Do you mean like plumbing pipe? Why is that significant?"

I wasn't sure if Craig and I had attended the same costume party or if he was just less observant; though to be fair, his date's costume had shown off her best assets. Still, I'd mock him for it. "A plumbing pipe? How many beers have you had?" I laughed. "It was a pipe you smoke. The big ones with the curve in the stem; like Sherlock Holmes smoked."

"Oh! Sorry, long day." He frowned. "Sherlock Holmes, you say? Wasn't someone dressed in that get-up? I seem to remember the hat with the ear flaps and a long cape ..."

"Uh-huh, Edison Marlow, the writer. He claims not to have been anywhere near the stage and his alibi denies he was talking to her at the time he claims."

"So you think he's the killer."

I'd planned to lay out my investigation step by step and let him decide but Craig had knocked a hole in one, so I saw no point in backtracking. "He's the obvious one, but they all have motives, well kinda. Glenda and Rae Ella don't have strong ones that I can see."

Craig nodded. "Okay, if you're sure about Marlow are you gonna tell Brannon?"

I heaved a sigh. "See, that's my dilemma. He's already refused to listen once. How do I get him to do it now?"

"Take Dewey's attorney in with you? Threaten to call a press conference if he doesn't look into what you've found?"

"I guess?" I tipped my head back and stared at the shiplap ceiling, watching the shadows from the fireplace flicker. Craig had a decent idea, but I was loath to talk to Brannon again, ever. I told my friend and he laughed.

"I hear ya, I avoid him at all cost but how else to get Dewey off of the hook?"

"No idea but Sentinel Security *postponed* his interview." I sighed. "Any chance you can talk your friend into holding that position open a little bit longer?"

Craig drained his beer and set it on the table before nodding. "Yeah, I'll give Doug a call, but Holly, he can't keep it open indefinitely."

"Of course, just ..." I forced a smile and tried to project confidence. "I'm close to solving this thing, a few more days at most." My phone sent a text alert, and I noticed the time.

"Wow, it's getting late." I rose and rustled The Colonel from his comfy spot, earning several snorts and grumbles for my trouble. "Come on, I'll get the electric heater out when we get home. You can sprawl in front of that." I shook my head and met Craig's gaze. "Dog is the biggest Diva on the planet."

He chuckled and patted The Colonel on the head and then went ahead of me out the door. We ambled toward the Scout, taking our time so the dog could do his business and we could finish my conversation. "You really think I should go to Brannon with what I've found on Marlow? There's more I haven't told you like he was being blackmailed by Hearn, and a couple of conversations I overheard that are at least curious ..."

Craig shrugged. "All you can do is try." He lifted The Colonel into the truck for me. "Boy, you are heavy!"

"It's all the treats! I swear half of Sanctuary Bay has a bet to see how fat he can get."

He snorted. "I wouldn't put it past them. Now, about Dewey's case. Go to Brannon, you might even ask the Sheriff to attend a meeting. If it was Harley I'd say absolutely do that but with Felton ... that's gotta be your call." He tapped the side of the truck and waved. "Good talkin' to ya, Daye. If I don't see you before, Marla and I will be at Myrtlewood for Thanksgiving. Drive safe and watch for deer!"

The Scout went into gear like a well-oiled machine for once, letting me occupy myself with whether or not I should present my case to Brannon. Either way, Craig was right. I should request the Sheriff be present, and probably the DA and Maxwell Bernard too. Course decided, I pushed aside my worries over Dewey.

Windows down, wind whipping my hair and The Colonel's jowls, I embraced the solitude of the roadway and the brilliant night sky. I slowed to cross an intersection and was resuming cruising speed when I noticed a white SUV closing the distance in my rear-view mirror. They were gaining speed fast, the high beams blinding me.

Thinking they wanted to pass, I let off the gas, but the car dropped back with me, so I got back up to speed and forgot about it. A waning moon made the area outside of my headlights dark blobs. Approaching the salt marsh, I slowed and watched for deer.

The car behind me turned off, leaving the road to me and my faithful companion. There was something magical about the Lowcountry, night or day, but when everything was dark and quiet ... it was like being transported back in time. The tropical vegetation, massive Live Oaks dripping with Spanish moss ... seemed like a prehistoric creature could emerge from the marsh at any moment.

All too soon I was back in civilization. As I made a right onto Bay street, my headlights illuminated someone with long dark hair crossing the road about twenty feet ahead. I hit my brakes and muttered a curse at stupid people who walked at night and didn't bother to wear reflective clothing.

I continued on and was a block from home when I looked in my rearview mirror and saw another white SUV coming toward me. I frowned. Was that the same- but no, that car had turned off a mile back ... this was another one. I snorted. My nerves were shot.

The Oaks was a fenced property, with electric gates blocking the drive. I'd just passed the neighbor's house and was reaching for the gate remote when I came to the apron of my drive and found they'd been left open. I rolled my eyes and proceeded up the drive. *What was the point of having a gate if you didn't use it?*

I pulled to the back and parked in my space to the left of the garage. The Colonel was feeling frisky after his long nap by the fire, so I closed the gates and then let him roam the yard while I grabbed my bag and locked up.

Ten minutes passed and The Colonel was still frolicking somewhere in the garden. I whistled and walked toward the front yard; thanks to the presence of squirrels hunting acorns, he loved to sniff and snort around under the Live Oak.

I rounded the corner of the house, used my phone flashlight to confirm the bulldog was still wandering around under the tree, and then moved down the front walk, intending to swing on the porch until the boy was ready to call it a night.

As I walked along the path, I admired the flowers Mama and I had spent part of Sunday afternoon planting; we'd gotten through two flats but three more were waiting in the greenhouse. I was a few feet from the porch when my light bounced over something on the steps. I frowned and slowed my pace as I squinted to define it.

Mama and I had staggered pots of mums with battery-operated lanterns and various-sized pumpkins and gourds on the steps but whatever I was seeing now was in the middle, far from where the decorations we'd placed. Slowing to a crawl, I inched forward until I could angle my light onto it.

I gasped as the beam reached the fourth stair tread where a clump of uprooted dianthus sat in a pile of loose soil. A note lay on top of the dirt, pinned in place by my pointed weeding tool. Careful not to touch the tool handle, I leaned over and read the words scrawled on the paper.

Stick to digging in the dirt instead of people's business, You'll be healthier.

Chapter Seventeen

A restless night followed by an early alarm had me racing to make my physical therapy appointment. Hands free cell phone usage wasn't available in 1971, and I had no intention of installing non-factory parts in my Daddy's old truck, so calling Dewey's attorney would have to wait.

The gym parking lot was slammed, forcing me to get my cardio in early. Being at the edge of the lot also meant The

Colonel wanted to mark the new territory so I used the time to make my call.

"This is the voicemail of Maxwell Bernard, attorney at law. I'm not available to take your call right now. Please leave your name, number, and a brief message and I will return you call as soon as possible. Thank you."

Voicemail. I rolled my eyes and tried to sound coherent while also being succinct. "Hey Max, Holly Daye. Pretty sure I've found the real killer of Megan Hearn. I need to know what you want me to do with the information, thanks. Give me a call." I hit end call and persuaded The Colonel we needed to start the hike across the wasteland that was the asphalt parking area.

My mind wanted to dwell on my reluctant choice of killer and the threatening note left on my porch but Lance greeted me seconds after I stepped from the locker room, demanding I push everything aside and focus on getting well.

"Holly, great day, isn't it?"

He stretched his arms toward the ceiling and then twisted his body from side to side, his smile never wavering. I cocked an eyebrow but managed a slight smile. The man was far too chipper that early in the morning.

The Colonel settled in a nearby corner, and I got down to work, stretching, and then the recumbent bike, followed by floor exercises. I completed my final set of weighted crunches and asked for the next set of instructions. Lance, who'd been chatting with the girls at the desk, hurried over, stumbling over my bag in the process.

I tried to catch it in time, but it fell to the side, sending most of the contents to the floor.

"Oh man, sorry Holly." Lance crouched down and started scooping up the odds and ends that somehow always accumulated in a woman's bag, or at least in mine.

"Thanks, I got it .. oh, thanks." Lance handed me an ink pen and container of mints. I was pulling the zipper tab when Lance stopped me.

"Hold on! Forgot your locker key."

My wha-? I stopped. I didn't have a ... I looked up to see the key from the pirate shop dangling from his fingers. I gulped and met Lance's gaze. "Um, that's a locker key? For this gym?"

His brow furrowed and he looked at me like I'd lost my mind, and maybe I had, but I was pretty sure he'd just solve at least a tiny bit of a mystery for me.

Lance nodded. "Yeah, isn't it yours?"

I nodded and rose to my feet. "Yes. I'll be right back." Without waiting for The Colonel, I hobbled to the women's changing room. B 47 ..., I looked around, scanning the rows of cubbies until I found it. "Yes!"

My hand shook as I turned the key. What would be inside? That depended upon who had sent me on the scavenger hunt in the first place. The door swung open and ... "Empty! Of all the ..." The locker was in the second row but the lighting at that end of the room wasn't great, causing shadows, especially at the back of the cube. I stood on tiptoe and felt around. My fingers brushed against paper, and I climbed up to get a better view.

Wedged against the back wall of the locker was a picture. My fingers closed around it, and I sat down on the padded bench to see what treasure I'd found. The image had been taken on an old instant camera and the quality was degraded. It appeared to have been taken outdoors. Judging from the amount of smooth, light-colored surface in the background I would assume a beach, and the hint of scrub and sea oats in one dark corner solidified my guess.

The foreground was blurry but most of the frame focused on a woman. In profile, with most of her features in shadow, all I could really make out was the ponytail, perhaps blonde or light brown, and something green near her ear. I squinted, turned the photo every which way but loose, and still couldn't tell what the green was but, by color and position I assumed it was an earring.

I'd need a magnifying glass to know for sure and I didn't carry one around so any further investigation of the picture would have to wait. Connie had a magnifying light at the craft store for working with small items; Glitter and Garland would be my next stop.

Lance gave me another side-eye when I returned but when I offered no explanation he got back to work and put me through a few more paces. The picture kept going through my mind. I hadn't been able to see clearly but what I thought was an earring was prodding at my memory.

With the image burning a proverbial hole in my pocket, I rushed through the remainder of the workout and was soon zipping across the island. The Colonel and I arrived just as Connie was turning the sign around for lunch.

"Hey, I wasn't expecting you today- what on earth?"

I brushed by Connie with a hey, come and see this, as I made a beeline for her work table. I heard the ting of the dog bone canister and then Connie was sidling up beside me.

"What are you doing?"

I adjusted the angle of the lamp so that the magnifying glass was over the picture and cut on the light. Peering through the lens took a minute but soon I was able to get the right distance between the image and the glass. "Ah, I was right!" I stepped back and motioned for my friend to look.

"Looks like an earring, a big emerald and diamond earring." She leaned away and cocked her head. "Why is that important?"

I nibbled on my lower lip and shook my head, thinking out loud in answer to her inquiry. "Not sure. Found this in a locker at the gym-that's what the key went to ..." I'd told Connie about the flyer and then finding the key, but she still asked if that was what I was referring to. I absently replied. "Yeah, I figured it out by accident while doing therapy this morning ... something about this earring is familiar." I looked up and met her gaze. "Do you recognize it?"

She snorted. "Me? If that's real, I don't have that kind of money and, expensive or not I don't wear stuff that fancy ..."

Fancy. That was what had struck me, too. "Look at the rest of the picture. Do you think she's sitting on a beach?"

Connie followed my earlier actions of turning the photo to different angles and even using the magnifying lens. She finally met my gaze. "Yep, I'd guess a beach and if you look back here ..." she pointed to the left side of the image that had been too dark for me to see much earlier. "That's the tree line, though most of it is too dark to see, you can tell by the spiky things those are saw palmetto and ...oh! Look a little to the right and you can just make out a fallen tree laying on the sand ..." She glanced up and met my gaze. "That was taken on a beach and probably a deserted one or maybe even Hunting Island? Cuz any other beach is just dunes ..."

"You're right, but that could still be any number of places around here, the state park included." I rubbed the back of my neck and sighed. "I'm not sure the picture was even taken here, to be honest, but something about that earring is familiar. It looks real, huh?" Connie nodded. "I wonder if a jeweler could tell me more about it from this picture ...I'm gonna take this to Sea Glass and Gifts, wanna come along?"

Connie had a lunch date, and Sea Glass and Gifts had closed for lunch so The Colonel and I grabbed a chicken salad croissant and chose a shady bench in the park where I could see the minute he opened back up.

The end of the park I'd chosen was relatively vacant but farther down the waterfront the barriers were up, and people were milling around as the production company turned more of Edison Marlow or rather his wife's book into a television show. The sun was warm on my back, but the wind had changed direction and the temperature was dropping; we'd likely have strong storms later.

I finished off my lunch, giving the last piece of croissant to a patiently waiting Colonel, and rose to throw the box away. A piece of white paper laying on top of the waste reminded me of what I'd found on the front porch.

Finding the note and dianthus had been a shock but, once I'd checked the house for signs of an intruder I calmed down, replanted the flowers, and went to bed. My search of the house hadn't wakened Mama, a blessing because I had no intention of telling her what I'd found. However, I'd told Dewey just before I left for therapy.

Typical Dewey, he'd fussed and insisted I was making a mountain out of a molehill but after I'd pointed out that someone had brutally killed Megan Hearn and wouldn't hesitate to kill again to keep their secret he gulped and agreed to keep an eye on the house and grounds, make sure the gates remained closed at all times, and accompany Mama if she needed to leave.

My brother hadn't been happy about the last instruction, and I didn't blame him. Mama could run a person ragged with all of her errands and visits to under the weather friends; she was a one-person welcome wagon for Sanctuary Bay. The sooner I solved the mystery of who killed Megan Hearn the better.

Movement across the street caught my eye; Benji Archelaus was rolling the gates back on Sea Islands Glass and Gifts. I took The Colonel on a quick walk and then crossed the street.

It had only been a few minutes since the store re-opened yet when I stepped inside Benji Archelaus was ringing up a customer's purchases. I stood back and waited.

"Have a great day, and be sure to take the carriage tour before you leave!" He waved at the tourists and then smiled at me. "Hey, Holly how are you? Ooh, and hello Colonel Barker, want a treat?"

Benji reached below the counter and came back out with a small, bone-shaped cookie I recognized from the Paws and Claws pet boutique. I rolled my eyes and waited for Benji to finish fawning over my dog.

"So, what brings you in today?"

Benji's eyes widened as I pulled the photo from my bag and pointed to the earring. "Was hoping your granddad was in. Thought he might know about this earring."

He peered at the picture, holding it at eye level and turning the paper to different angles. "That's a beaut! Hard to see it well. The setting looks old, probably early 1900s, but let me get granddad."

Benji disappeared through an archway, leaving me to wander around the store. Sea Islands Glass and Gifts was a high-end gift shop and jewelry store that catered to locals and tourists. The bulk of the souvenir items they offered were things made by my local craftsman. I fingered the oyster shells mounted on a piece of driftwood in an arrangement meant to be the nativity and smiled; there were some very clever people on our islands.

A basket made from marsh grass made me pause. The Gullah traditions were alive and well in the Sea Islands. I'd grown up hearing their stories, told in a sing-song accent that bore only a slight resemblance to our Southern drawl, and had eaten plenty of their food but I'd never bought one of their creations.

I glanced at the price tag and wondered if I should treat myself to a birthday gift or give a hint to Mama. Less than two weeks from my birthday, she probably already had a gift for me ... I set the basket aside. I'd ask for Christmas.

A cough and the sound of shuffling feet brought my attention to the counter as Mr. Archelaus exited the back room.

"Holly Daye, I haven't seen you in months!" His gaze dipped to my leg and the cane I was never without. His mouth turned down at the corners for a moment before the ready smile was back in place. "How are you?"

Talk of my shooting and the aftermath was still a topic of conversation and one I never willingly encouraged so I ignored his opening to comment and launched right into my reason for visiting.

"Morning Mr. Archelaus, I'm doing well, and you look to be in fine form." I smiled and set the photo on the glass. "Was wondering if you could tell me anything about the earring in this picture."

Whatever I'd been expecting, a harshly indrawn breath and a hard stare were not among the options.

Mr. Archelaus' eyes narrowed. "Why?"

His tone made me frown. "Um, because it may have something to do with the murder of Megan Hearn? Have you seen it before?"

His expression lightened a little. He picked the photo up and pulled his jeweler's loop from his pocket. "Yes, and very recently." He glanced at me and then looked at the picture through his loop. "Yes, same earring, ..." he set the photo down and met my gaze. "Megan Hearn came in here a few weeks ago asking about this," he tapped the photo. "Only, she had the actual earrings. Mind telling me where they are?"

My eyes widened. That's why the picture was familiar, I'd noticed Hearn wearing them ... I cast my mind back and realized that was what she'd taunted Glenda with in the garden. It'd happened so quickly, and I was more interested in finishing my project, but I'd heard Glenda gasp and when I turned, Megan's hand was near her ear and she had a cruel smile on her face ... yep, it all seemed clear in hindsight, something about those earrings had upset Glenda Timmons.

I smiled at Mr. Archelaus. "I'm not sure where the earrings are now, maybe with the coroner?" I shrugged. "I just know she was wearing them the night she died."

His posture relaxed a bit. "That's all right then. I'll have Benji call over to Dr. Sawyer's office." He started to walk away.

"Mr. Archelaus?" He turned and cocked an eyebrow. "Um, why are you concerned with the location of the earrings?"

His mouth pursed and for a moment I thought he'd ignore me, but he walked back to the counter and sighed. "Those earrings are stolen, or they were reported stolen anyway." I must have looked confused because he scowled and shook his head. "I'd better start at the beginning. Ms. Hearn came in with those earrings. She said she'd found them while metal detecting on Shell Point. She thought they might be part of an old pirate's booty ..." he chuckled.

"Were you able to tell her anything about the jewelry?"

He adjusted his glasses. "Oh yes, at the time all I could confirm was that the setting looked old, I guessed 1920s by the art deco design, and that they were definitely real emeralds and diamonds. I took some photos and told her I'd get back to her in a few days." He shrugged. "She's dead now so I'm not sure it matters."

"They were pretty, a bit fancy for everyday wear I'd think."

He nodded. "By today's standards, absolutely and most women wouldn't have worn those particular stones before dinner. They were part of a set you know."

"Oh, I did not know." My brows rose as a thought occurred. "Mr. Archelaus, is there a way to trace jewelry like this? I mean if they were old and expensive ..."

He smiled. "Of course there is! That's what I've been doing." He motioned for me to follow him to the check-out counter. "I tried to call Ms. Hearn with what my research had uncovered but she never answered and then I saw that she'd been ..." He shrugged. "This file has all of the pertinent data on the earrings. You might as well take it. I called over to the Sheriff's Department thinking that detective might be interested but he said it was irrelevant to him and to keep it for whoever claimed the body."

I resisted rolling my eyes, Joe Brannon had struck again, and thanked the old man for his time. I tried to flip through the folder as The Colonel and I walked back to Cannery Wharf, but the wind was too strong, and I feared losing papers. I'd left the gift shop with more questions than answers, but I was encouraged that I was on the right track.

Clouds were building and the wind was now gusting hard enough to rock the street lights. Power outages were a definite possibility, and I didn't want to get caught out in the storm. Connie had already closed the store, so I loaded The Colonel and was headed home when my stomach protested my lack of attention.

I reversed course and soon joined the long line of customers waiting in the Chicken Hut drive-thru. I used the time to study the file Mr. Archelaus had compiled. The earrings were part of a set. My brows shot up as I read further.

In addition to the earrings, there had been a necklace, bracelet, and diadem all of which Mr. Archelaus had provided images for, saving me an internet search for just what the heck a diadem was. I'd been right, the earrings were too fancy for wearing to an outdoor Halloween party. But Megan had done so, and so had the mystery woman on the beach come to think of it.

Reading further I saw that the set had been commissioned by a man named Arthur Midford on the occasion of his marriage to Florence Reeves. Mr. Archelaus had not been able to tell if the jewelry had changed hands over the years, but he did find that the earrings had been reported lost about ten years ago, though the claim had not listed who had filed it.

The line of cars moved forward, and I was able to place my order. I read over the file again and decided to beg a favor.

"Jessica Ziggler."

"Hey, Jessica, it's Holly, you got a minute?" She'd sounded frazzled when she answered.

Jessica laughed. "That's about all I've got, rushing across the parking lot to make it to the courthouse before they close. Whatcha need?"

I quickly told her about the pirate tour key leading to the gym locker and the photo ending with Mr. Archelaus' research. "So, if you get time can you check into Arthur Midford and the woman he married, Florence Reeves. I'd like to see if that can tell us who reported them lost ..." I flipped through the file for the date. "June 2007."

She promised to look into it, and we hung up. Minutes later I was struggling to keep a voracious bulldog from devouring my bucket of chicken. I was fussing with The Colonel and not paying close attention to my driving. I went through an intersection and seconds later heard numerous car horns blaring.

Thinking I'd done something, I slowed and glanced in my rear-view mirror in time to see a white SUV had been caught halfway through the light. They were now blocking traffic. The driver crept forward, intending to take the route I had, but there were too many cars blocking the path. They took a right and I shook my head. Last night I could have sworn someone driving a white SUV was following me and then they had almost hit a pedestrian. Last week I'd also noticed an SUV behind me ... what was it about white cars and crazy drivers?

Chapter Eighteen

The next morning Mama convinced me to take her hair appointment. I must have looked *really* bad for Mama to forego her weekly shampoo and blow-out but since I'd intended to go in and let Kitty Wagner work her magic on me, I didn't argue.

Arriving promptly at the appointed time, I still had to wait more than half an hour before Kitty was free. She then convinced me to blend my grays with highlights without telling me I'd be sitting in the chair for almost 6 hours. I thanked all that was good and gracious that I'd decided to leave The Colonel at home; poor thing would have been miserable with the chemical smells not to mention no snacks.

It was past five o'clock when I left the Kut and Kurl; but I felt like a new woman, a starving new woman. I decided to treat myself to dinner at my favorite Italian restaurant. Mario's Cucina held pride of place at the corner of Bay and River Streets.

One of the few buildings located on the park side of the street, the views from the patio were second only to the food. A band was playing in one corner of the dining room, and I wasn't in the mood, so I opted to hold out for a table on the patio. That meant waiting in the bar. I'd just sat down when someone whispered in my ear.

"Hey, pretty lady can I buy you a drink?"

Despite my determination to keep our friendship on a platonic footing I couldn't help but smile as I turned to meet Tate Sawyer's gaze.

He feigned surprise. "Holly Daye! I didn't recognize you."

I rolled my eyes and motioned to the seat beside me. "Care to join me? I'm waiting on a table."

He shook his head. "If you'll consent to dine with me, my table is ready."

Fate was a funny thing. I'd avoided letting Tate take me out to dinner because I was afraid to ruin a friendship and yet I'd ended up there anyway. I surrendered graciously. "I'd be delighted, Dr. Sawyer."

He tried to be gallant and offer me his arm, but the restaurant was too crowded. I followed the hostess, and we were soon seated in a quiet corner of the patio with a view of the river and twinkling stars overhead. It was far too romantic for my comfort, but a little murder talk should hold any aspirations Tate might be harboring at bay.

Orders placed, we made small talk. We exhausted the weather as a topic, briefly discussed the upcoming elections, and he amused me with another humorous tale of the senior Doctor Sawyer's antics at the over-50 community; Tate's father was a good looking, moderately well-off widower and the things women did to get to his attention never ceased to amaze and amuse me.

Our food arrived, manicotti for Tate, seafood alfredo for me. "Oh my, this looks so good!" The server smiled and left us in peace. "I haven't been here in ages."

Tate swallowed and then directed an amused smile at me. "If you'd accepted my numerous dinner invitations ..."

I smirked and rolled my eyes at him and defaulted to changing the subject. "So, haven't heard from you all week. What have you been up to?"

A mischievous smile lit his face. "Why, did you miss me?" When I offered nothing but a small smile Tate sighed and continued. "A man can hope. But, to answer your question, we're down a man at the morgue and I've been up to my eyes in work. What's been keeping you busy?"

I polished off my alfredo before answering. "You know I'm looking into who killed Megan Hearn?"

Tate nodded. "Yes, and I have misgivings but ..." He shrugged. "With a detective like Brannon though, nothing else to do but solve it yourself. Otherwise, Dewey is going to trial and risks conviction."

"Exactly. I was reluctant to go digging-oh! Remind me to tell you about the dianthus- "I laughed as Tate grinned and pantomimed taking notes. "As I was saying, if I'd had respect for the investigator, I wouldn't have gone down this road but Tate," I laughed. "It's been so obvious!"

His eyes widened. "So, you know who killed her?"

"Not ..., it's complicated." I proceeded to tell him about Marlow and Tate agreed he was most likely the perpetrator. "Thing is, what do I make of the muddy shoes? Who put the flyer in my car and guided me to the locker key? Who is in the photo, and what is it about those earrings?"

Tate cocked his head and frowned. "Earrings? What kind?"

"Um, big, gaudy emeralds with some diamonds, oh, and they were clip on ... here, let me show you the picture."

Tate studied the photo for a few seconds and nodded. "Yep, those are the ones, well one. The victim was wearing earrings like these, but one was not on the body or anywhere near the crime scene."

"Yes, I'd seen Megan wearing them earlier that night, though I didn't realize she only had one when we found her ..." My brow furrowed as a snippet of conversation with Rae Ella came back to me. "Tate, when I was speaking with Rae Ella Reid, she mentioned that Mark Timmons and Megan Hearn were in the garden acting like guilty lovers."

I repeated what I recalled of her version of events. "Rae Ella said that she'd walked by them but heard something that made her turn around just in time to see Megan's hand near her ear and then she threw something, do you think it was one of these earrings?"

He shrugged. "Possibly, though why would she-" he snorted. "Makes about as much sense as me finding dirt under her nails and traces of Rosmarinus officinalis L. on her hands, arms, and clothing. Oh, and she was clutching a piece of gold chain that we can't explain."

"A Chain? Like a necklace?"

Tate shook his head. "Bit big to be worn around the neck but anything is possible."

Hmm. I vaguely recalled seeing something in her hand as they removed her from the cauldron. Other than that, a chain didn't stand out in my mind. However, I was remembering something about Megan's nails that I'd noticed while I was waiting for the police to arrive. She'd had long red nails, acrylic if I had to guess- "Tate, traces of what was on her hands?"

"It's the essential oil from the rosemary plant."

Tate's explanation derailed my thoughts. I blinked and focused on what he'd said. "She had rosemary oil on her body?"

"Uh huh, heaviest on her hands and forearms but we found smaller amounts on the sleeves of her blouse and on her pants. What are we having for dessert?"

Our server was waiting for a reply. The evening was winding down. I'd intended to make a quick excuse to end it before Tate could get any further ideas that this was a date but, his expression was so happy and carefree ... my lips twisted into a smile. I grabbed my bag and dug my credit card from my wallet as I tipped my head toward the patio steps that led down to the park.

"Come on, let's pay the bill and walk down to Scoops."

Tate shook his head and waved my hand away. "Yes, to ice cream, no to you paying the bill."

After a bit of arguing, I let him pay and we took the park route one block down to Scoops and Sweets. Owned by Shelby and Josh Bailey, the ice cream and candy store was a hit with both locals and tourists.

During the high season, the line would wind halfway down the block but now it was only marginally packed. Tate and I took our place in line and reminisced about the candies of our youth. Painted in bright white with accents of green, orange, and pink, Scoops and Sweets was a wonderland for children, or those who were kids at heart.

Shelby ran the ice cream side, concocting seasonal flavors and dreaming up new add-ins for sundaes and shakes while Josh was the candy master. The obligatory pralines and fudge were made on the premises, but Josh came from a long line of hard candy makers and gave demonstrations on making ribbon candy.

Along the walls were glass shelves filled with the shop's signature sweets as well as various confections that brought back memories of dime stores and freeze tag until the streetlights called us home. A large glass canister filled with wax lips made me grin and remember chasing the boys with threats of kisses.

Tate laughed. "I'm perfectly willing to be indulgent if you want to relive that segment of your childhood ..." He cocked an eyebrow and licked his lips.

I laughed and slapped his arm. "Stop it." I nudged him to move and ignored his protest that I couldn't blame a guy for trying.

Scoops offered hard or soft ice cream. I loved a good chocolate and vanilla twist in a waffle cone but the multitude of flavors on offer in the display case drew my eye. Coffee? No, only in my cup. Pistachio? Pretty color but I wasn't a fan of hard bits in my treat. I passed over the brightly colored sherbets, the Superman and Birthday Cake meant to attract the kids, and homed in on the *gourmet* varieties. Salted Caramel swirl, Almond Biscotti, Bourbon Brown Sugar ...

"Holly?" I followed Tate's gaze and realized it was time to order. "Oooh, decisions, decisions. Um, let me have a single scoop of- "

"Uh huh, two scoops Ms. Daye, we are celebrating tonight."

Sensing Tate's celebration had something to do with our impromptu dining arrangement I steered clear of any discussion and went for two scoops. "Ok, let me have Salted Caramel and ..., oh I don't know, eh, just let me have peanut butter and chocolate."

Tate's eyes widened at my hodgepodge choices but placed his order and, to my surprise let me pay. We wrapped our cones in paper napkins and exited on the Bay Street side of the shop.

"Oh man ..."

"Mmm, decadent."

"Yes, but ...," I wiped my mouth. "I feel so guilty." Tate cast me a questioning glance and I explained. "The Colonel loves to visit Shelby; she developed a special pup cup in honor of him." I sighed. "He's gonna pout."

We laughed and continued chatting as we strolled back to my truck. We'd just crossed Pine Street and had taken no more than a dozen steps when someone called my name. Tate and I swung around to find Edison Marlow twenty feet or so behind us on the opposite side of Bay Street.

He raised a hand in a wave and stepped off the curb. "Holly, hold up!"

The light changed and he started across. He was in the middle of the lane when an engine revved, tires squealed and, in a flash of white, an SUV struck Edison Marlow, sending his body up and over the roof to land with a bone-crushing thud on the pavement.

The vehicle never slowed. We raced to Edison, Tate assessing injuries and calling emergency services while I tried to get information on the vehicle. Several people milled around talking about what they'd seen. I asked them to stop and wait for an officer to take their statements and then returned to Edison and Tate.

The author was as still as a corpse. Tate was applying pressure to a deep gash on his leg so I crouched by his head, offering what comfort I could. His face was as white as my shirt and his breaths were barely noticeable.

The ground is hard, something is poking in my lower back, but I can't seem to make my legs work-Stop it, you've been over this before!

I shook my head and tried to focus but, oh ..., a red stain was spreading across the bottom of my blouse and my lap felt warm and wet ...

I'm cold. Cold and thirsty and the sky is getting darker. It's quiet I'm all alone, except who is that laying across the road-I gulped, and my fingers trembled as images of me in a similar position started to crowd my mind.

The sirens were drawing near. I blocked everything from my mind and forced myself to categorize like Doctor Styles had shown me but everything I saw had an emotional impact. Oh God, I was going to be sick, where were the EMTs? I needed to get up-

Edison's eyes opened and he gasped. I brushed the hair off his forehead. "Don't talk, help is coming." His eyes were glazed and unfocused and he continued to try and speak.

I bit my lip, fighting to hold off a panic attack but I was losing the battle. My teeth chattered; I wasn't going to last much longer. *Focus, Holly!*

I met Tate's gaze for a moment and tried to get him to help me, but my body had a will of its own. My heart was racing, I was panting so hard that Edison's head was jiggling.

Tate called my name, but it sounded so far away, and Edison was laying in my lap still trying to speak ... I leaned closer, putting my ear near his mouth. "Sh ..., sh..., she ...," he stuttered out the word and went limp in my arms.

No! Someone screamed. I flinched and looked away but, too late. Blood gushed from Edison's leg; Tate's hands were covered. The ambulance screeched to a stop, doors slamming, voices yelling commands ... my whole body trembled; bile rose in my throat.

Move. Get up. I kept commanding my body, but it had gone on strike. The red and blue emergency lights cast garish shadows over the crowd. My heart felt like it was going to leap from my chest and sweat dotted my upper lip.

Again, I tried to focus but there was so much commotion, I could find nothing to ground myself. Darkness was creeping in from the sides of my eyes, everything I looked at was getting farther away.

Tate moved to my side as the EMTs took over. I turned to meet his eyes. He was speaking, but I couldn't hear ...

Chapter Nineteen

Waking up was like coming up from a dive to the bottom of the ocean. My mouth was as dry as cotton. Where was – I relaxed as the familiar blue walls of my room came into focus, but I groaned as a simple stretch revealed every muscle in my body ached.

A rustling drew my attention toward the window. My eyes widened as Tate jolted upright, rubbed his eyes and dragged a hand through his thick dark hair ... My eyelids drifted closed. Pretty hair, pretty eyes, too ...

"I'm flattered."

I'd said that part out loud! The bed dipped and my eyes sprang open to find Tate leaning over me. "Tate," I shrunk back against the pillow, and he sat up straighter, putting distance between us. "What-uh, what's going on?"

He laughed and took my hand, his finger resting on my pulse. He looked at his watch as he murmured. "Nothing like what you're imagining, to my ever-lovin' regret, but glad you're awake!" He released my wrist and peered at me with a detached, professional gaze that set me at ease, or to a semblance anyway. "Feeling better?"

I swallowed but my mouth was too dry. "Um, fine. Head aches a bit but ... nothing caffeine won't cure uh ..." I bit my lip and wondered how to end the awkward, at least for me, situation. "You, uh, want to meet me in the kitchen and tell me what happened last night and why you're here?"

Tate's smirk was sinful, and I braced to not react to whatever flirty and provocative thing popped out of his mouth but, to my surprise and a smidgen of disappointment I refused to address, he merely nodded and rose, closing the door behind him.

Pressing needs in the bathroom were my first priority, followed by ice water splashed on my face. Clean teeth, combed hair, and comfy clothes later, The Colonel and I trudged down the stairs and entered the kitchen to find Tate seated at the kitchen table with Mama chirping a mile a minute while flitting around trying to offer him all manner of breakfast foods.

"Well, I was gonna treat you to breakfast- "

"No need. Tate is gonna sit right here and let me thank him for saving my child."

"Hardly think I was in danger, Mama." I set a bowl of kibble in front of The Colonel.

"Humph." She nudged me toward a chair. "You didn't see your face when he carried you in here."

And that was a can of worms I had no desire to open. I dug into the plate of hashbrowns, and eggs Mama had set before me and glanced at Tate. "Am I imagining things or did Edison wake up and speak to me?"

Tate nodded. "He did, though I didn't catch what he said." He looked down at his plate, muttering. "Too busy taking care of you."

My memories of the night were sketchy. I could remember Edison calling my name, us stopping to wait as he crossed the street, and -my fingers began to tremble and the fork tumbled onto my plate with a clatter.

A warm hand enclosed mine and his thumb started rubbing lazy circles. I met Tate's gaze and gulped. Images of a broken and bleeding Edison Marlow were shoved aside as I saw the emotion swimming in Tate's eyes. My stomach dropped. Crud monkeys, this was going down a road I wasn't prepared-

"Hey," Tate gave my hand a squeeze and then returned to eating. "Stop thinking."

I laughed. "About what?"

"Anything, everything, just ..." He shrugged and graced me with a lopsided grin that made his dimple wink. "Go with the flow, Holly."

I snorted. Easy for him to say, he wasn't the one with a racing heart and a stomach full of butterflies -okay, that's enough of that! I gulped my coffee and drew a deep breath. *Focus Holly. Forget that a handsome man is seated at your breakfast table. What did Edison say?*

I gave myself a mental shake and let my mind go back to Edison trying to talk to me. His eyes opened, he was staring into space, my hands were shaking-nope, don't go there, what did he say? "Tate, I think Edison said, *she.*"

Tate blinked and cocked his head. "Uh, okay. Why would he say that?"

I shrugged and continued eating. "Dunno. Was the driver a woman?"

Tate shook his head. "Maybe, I haven't heard if anyone even saw the driver well enough to confirm that. I've been here all night."

"And we can't thank you enough, can we Holly Marie?" Mama took Tate's and my plate to the sink and started talking as she washed the dishes. "In my day, the doctor would make house calls but ..."

I tuned Mama out and continued to press Tate for answers. "Did anyone get a plate? I tried but only saw the first two letters were R and T."

Tate shrugged. "Gonna have to ask Craig or another friend on the force."

I nodded and rushed on before he could remind me that he'd spent the night in my room. "I'll do that. I checked my voice mail before I came downstairs. Maxwell is meeting with Brannon and the DA this afternoon, though now that the likely killer is dead ..., poor man, murderer or not he didn't deserve to die in the street."

"Oh!" Tate shook his head. "He's not dead, at least he wasn't as of two this morning when I called County Gen to check on him."

My brows rose. "He's alive? Can he talk? Has he said anything about who-"

"No, nothing like that. He's not talking and I'm not sure he ever will; has a skull fracture and is in a coma."

On that sober thought, we finished our coffee and said goodbye to Mama. The Colonel and I hitched a ride back to town with Tate. He'd just started his car when a funny look came over his face.

He stared at the front porch for a second and then looked at me. "I forgot to remind you about the flowers?"

I frowned and then remembered. "Oh, it was nothing just, I pulled in the night before last, Dewey had left the gates open, and I found a clump of the Dianthus Mama and I had just planted were uprooted and sitting on the front steps with a note."

Tate finished backing out before glancing at me. "A note with flowers? How unusual ..."

I smirked. "Well, it is when the flowers still have their roots, and the note tells you it'd be healthier if you stuck to digging in the garden instead of people's business."

Tate pulled over and looked at me. "What did you say?"

Tate's expression had flipped from lazy teasing to intense concern. I frowned. "Basically, keep my nose out of what doesn't concern me." I shrugged. "Nothing to worry about. Probably one of the-"

"Just gonna blow it off then? You're not concerned that someone threatened you? Not taking any precautions even though you're looking for a murderer?" Tate huffed and set the car in motion. "Help me understand that cavalier attitude, Holly, because I can't-"

"Blowing it off?" I rolled my eyes. "Tate, I'm not dismissing the note. Yes, it was threatening, but if or until they take further action there is nothing to be done. I'm a police officer-"

"No, you aren't!" He shook his head. "Not anymore. Tell them about the threat."

Having no intention of starting my day out angry, I turned my head and looked out the window. Tate didn't understand. Regardless of carrying a badge, I was and always would be an officer of the law. I was trained to assess risk and take appropriate action and that is what I'd done when I found the note.

After photographing the evidence in situ, I'd slipped it into a plastic storage bag taking care not to deposit my fingerprints. I'd then texted Craig the images with a brief explanation and he'd responded with a suggestion to take the same precautions I'd already implemented.

In a perfect world, I'd have felt confident in alerting the detective actively working the case, but the reality was I'd been rebuffed by Brannon already and there was no point in trying again. Which meant I needed to secure my home and person at all times.

Everyone in my family had been instructed to keep the gates locked at all times, to be aware of who might be lurking before opening them, and as a final precaution, I'd told Mama about my new office and business endeavor before changing all package deliveries to the cannery wharf address. Aside from that, for the foreseeable future, Mama would not go out alone.

Tate visibly relaxed as I explained my precautions in light of the threat. "You see, everything that can be done has been. I mean, aside from carrying a weapon, and with my continued PTSD symptoms manifesting at unpredictable times I'm not comfortable taking that route."

"We agree on that point." He stopped for a red light and turned to meet my gaze. "I don't mind admitting you scared the hell out of me last night." His eyes narrowed. "Are the attacks always that bad?"

I fidgeted with the strap of my bag as I answered. "Depends on what you mean by bad." I glanced up and shrugged. "I've never passed out before, but then I always have The Colonel with me."

His mouth pressed into a thin line, he refrained from comment until he'd parked beside my Scout and loaded The

Colonel into the passenger seat. I got behind the wheel and rolled the window down. Tate leaned on the sill.

"If the episodes aren't as severe when The Colonel is present then I think you'd better make sure the boy goes everywhere with you. Your heart rate was elevated, you were panting, and just before you lost consciousness, you weren't responding to outside stimuli. Had you been alone-"

"I know!" I huffed and tapped my fingers on the wheel. "Trust me, I am aware of how much I need the bulldog, but it wasn't good for him to sit in the beauty salon yesterday ..." I clenched my hands into fists and growled. "I hate being so weak, I should be over this by now!"

He reached in and covered my hand with his, squeezing gently until I relaxed. "That's better." His gaze searched my face. "Don't be so hard on yourself, you've experienced major trauma. The shooting was life-altering and you have to be patient as your body and mind adjust to a new reality, physically and mentally."

Everything he'd said made perfect sense but I wasn't prepared to admit it. When I didn't respond, Tate sighed. "Look, continue the physical therapy and your leg will get stronger and don't skip your visits with Dr. Styles; it'll help you, just give it time."

My gaze fell to my lap as I absorbed what he was saying and more so, the feelings and emotions driving the advice. I forced a chipper tone and bright smile as I met his gaze. I'd started to make a joke when Tate interrupted.

"Not today, Holly, okay?"

His blue eyes were clouded with concern? Sadness? Frustration? I couldn't determine the emotions, but he could just join the club because I was feeling all of those things and then some! "What? I don't-"

"I'm not up to playing your game today." His eyebrows rose and his gaze was direct. "I care too much to make light of what happened last night."

Before I could respond to that loaded bunch of sentences Tate pulled my hand through the window, planted a soft kiss on the palm, and folded my fingers over the kiss."

He released me and tapped the car door. "You be safe today and call if you need me."

Before I could pick my jaw up off of the floor Tate had returned to his car and pulled away with a toot of the horn. I stared after him, at a loss for words or coherent thought.

I looked over at The Colonel. "Well dang, what do ya make of that?"

Chapter Twenty

Feeling out of sorts both from the events with Marlow and then dealing with Tate, I scrapped my plan to go to the office. I pulled into the driveway, taking a nap my first and only priority when I caught a glimpse of Mama pulling her gardening buggy full of Dianthus and Snapdragons to the front yard.

Making sure the gates were closed, I set The Colonel free and went inside to change; looked like gardening was on my agenda. I'd barely set foot on the front porch when Dewey waylaid me.

"And then Max said the DA ain't budging." He stomped his foot. "It's all for nuthin', Holly! They're gonna put me on trial-"

"Not necessarily, Dewey." I trotted down the steps, fairly impressed to find my leg was able to bare more weight than usual; Tate had been right about the PT working, not that I'd admit it. "Mama, get up from there and let me do that! You'll have your back protesting-"

"I'm perfectly capable, thank you." She stood up and stretched. "But now that you're here ..." She handed me the trowel and headed for the front door. "I'll make some lunch."

"Oh, let's all worry about a full belly. Not like I'm facing twenty to life!"

Dewey paced and ranted as I knelt on the path and finished mounding soil around a plant Mama had just set. When he'd run out of steam I offered what comfort I could. "Don't borrow trouble, Dewey. I'm pretty sure Marlow is the killer, but there are a few loose ends to chase down ..." My gaze was drawn to a couple of young guys walking up the neighbor's drive.

Long-haired men carrying Bibles wasn't a common sight in the Bayview neighborhood but that wasn't what held my attention. One of the men turned his back toward me and I noticed his black leather jacket. "Dewey, is that a cross on the back of that coat?"

"Huh? What are you-them over there?" He pointed next door. "I guess so, why? What's that got to do with-"

"Put this stuff back in the greenhouse, okay?" I got to my feet and brushed soil from my pants.

"What? Why? Where are you goin'? Mama wanted these planted ..."

I ignored Dewey and called for The Colonel. Door-to-door ministry, black leather jackets, long hair ... I had a pretty good idea where I could tie up another loose end.

A quick internet search yielded an address and within twenty minutes, The Colonel and I were striding through the door of a former retail space in a rundown strip mall located on the edge of Noble County.

The windows were covered with a mural depicting a motorcycle in front of a dark depiction of the road to Calvary. Inside it resembled a colorless shopping space. Tan walls, commercial flooring, rows of folding chairs, a rectangular table with flowers, and a podium. Behind and to the left of the makeshift alter were instruments for a three-piece band.

The assembly area ended at a wall with two doors. One marked restrooms and the other denoted the office. I'd taken a few steps toward the office door when my eyes widened; the black-haired lady that had stared at me in the Country Kitchen waltzed through the door, followed by a burly guy with long brown hair and a beard to match.

"Hello-oh, what are you ..." the woman's mouth snapped shut. She looked at the man beside her and muttered. "What do we do?"

"Do? For starters you can tell me why you were so interested in me and," my eyes narrowed as things started clicking into place. "and which one of you stuck that flyer on the seat of my truck?"

My guess had hit the target. Both of them looked flustered and the woman started to stammer convoluted explanations. The man heaved a sigh and shook his head.

"It's all right, Jan, she knows." The woman, Jan apparently, gulped and wrung her hands. "I'm so sorry, Duke! I was careful! I never meant-"

"It's okay." He patted her on the shoulder and then gestured toward the front row of chairs. "Have a seat, Deputy Daye."

"Holly. I'm not with the force any longer." I told The Colonel to sit and then made myself comfortable on the cold, hard, metal chair. Once we were all seated I met his gaze. "We haven't been introduced."

He grinned. "Sorry, I'm Pastor Duke Mobley and this is Jan Busby."

"Nice to meet you. Now, wanna tell me why you're interested in me?"

Pastor Duke glanced at Jan. Her head ducked in a quick affirmative motion. He sighed and smiled at me. "I guess I should start by telling you I was helping Megan Hearn investigate a cold case."

Of all the things he could have said ..., I sat up straight and stared at him. "What case?"

Again, he glanced at Jan and waited for her approval before answering. "The death of Jan's daughter." He met my gaze. "She was listed as a missing person until her body was discovered at Shell Point last month and Megan-"

"Shell Point! You mean the remains they found when the hurricane destroyed that old hunting cabin?"

Duke nodded. "Yeah, that was Jan's daughter, only I didn't know that until Megan tracked her down! If I'd known," his face showed grief as he turned to Jan. "I'd never have let you suffer all these years not knowing. I can't imagine-"

"Ssh, it's okay, Duke, you didn't know." Jan nodded at me. "May 27, 2005. Noble County High School graduation ceremony was the last time I saw my daughter." She sighed and wiped at her eyes. "She went out to celebrate with friends and never came home."

"I'm so sorry." A high school senior out celebrating ... why was that ringing bells? A million questions were running through my head, all being swamped by the grief and sorrow emanating from Jan.

My brow furrowed as I tried to recall what little I knew about the remains found on Shell Point. Jessica had said-"Jan, the authorities aren't releasing the name of the body until her next of kin has been notified. If the poor girl found out there is your daughter you need to contact the Sheriff's department ..."

Jan started shaking her head. Her eyes were wide and fearful as she looked between me and Duke. "I can't, I can't go back there ... please don't-"

"It's okay, Jan. No one is going to hurt you and Ms. Daye won't tell ... will you?"

Since I didn't know what I wasn't supposed to tell I shrugged. Duke took that as a yes and continued to calm Jan. Once she had herself under control he sent her for coffee and then smiled at me.

"Sorry about that, Jan is uh," he glanced over his shoulder and lowered his voice. "She was an addict, lived on the streets a while, has been in and out of mental hospitals ..., she won't go to the police."

"Are their warrants outstanding? Because I can't let her –"

"She's not a criminal!" Duke held out a hand, pleading with me to understand. "She might have some warrants from when she was doing drugs, but you know how it is, she didn't hurt anyone, I promise! My ministry is helping her get back on her feet. She has a job and we're finding her a place to live ..., please don't take that from her."

Mentally deciding to have Craig run her name through the system, I agreed to leave her in Duke's hands. "But if she has any outstanding warrants for violence or theft ..."

"I understand, of course. But she doesn't, just vagrancy, trespassing, panhandling ... we can help her more than prison can."

I had to agree. Very few people were helped via the corrections system. Speaking of which, I had to keep my brother out of that system. "I'm trying to find the killer of Megan Hearn. What does any of this have to do with her death?"

Duke stroked his beard and stared off into the distance. He was quiet for so long that I jumped when his gravelly voice rang out.

"First, what I'm gonna tell you ..." Once again he wore an imploring expression. I don't want anyone to know it's me tellin' ya, okay?" His gaze roamed the room. "All of this? Me and a couple of buddies started this ministry seven years ago and we do a lot of good ...," he cleared his throat and stared at me.

"I understand. If I can, your name will be left out of it." I frowned. "But what is *it*? How did Jan's daughter end up dead and buried on Shell Point?"

"For me, it starts with the FMP. I was young and-"

"Wait, FMP?" That had been in some of the notes that Connie found on Megan's computer along with some other words that were rushing back to me. "Full Metal Pirates, the biker gang. Megan had notes, something about a party ..." My eyes widened. "And emeralds! What is the deal with those earrings?"

Duke winced at my tone. "I'll get to that, but I need to start at the beginning." I nodded and he continued. "So I was running with the Full Metal Pirates, you gotta remember I wasn't even twenty-one, okay?"

"You were young, I understand. Please finish the story." Everything in me wanted to scream at him. My gut was telling me this was why Hearn had been killed, only I wasn't sure how every piece fit.

"The gang wasn't into nothin' heavy, okay? Like, a little dealin' but mostly just guys lookin' to party and act tough. The leader, Pyro, he was datin' some rich chick from the Sea Islands. She had just graduated and was gonna party out on Shell Point with her friends. Pyro, convinced a bunch of us to go out there and surprise her." He shrugged. "Someone borrowed a boat and about seven of us rode out to Shell Point."

His voice had steadily gotten softer as he told the tale until I had to lean in to catch the words. He paused, staring at nothing for several minutes. "What happened when you got to Shell Point, Duke?"

Prodded, Duke sat up straighter and met my gaze. "Pyro's girlfriend was happy to see us but her two friends didn't look pleased. When we brought out the beer and weed, Jan's daughter was ready to go, only they'd all come on the other girl's boat, and she refused to leave or take her friend home." He gulped and looked down at the floor. "The guys started ribbing her, you know?" He glanced at me, and I nodded. "Teasing her, goading her into partying, only she wouldn't."

A terrible sense of foreboding crept over me as Duke again got lost in thought. "What did they do?"

His sigh was ragged. "She sat down on the edge of the fire circle with the boy that had come out with them-"

"Boy? What was his name?"

Duke shook his head. "No idea. Never got any of their names. That's why I went to Megan with the story. She researched and figured out who the three were. Only name she told me was Jan's daughter, Sheila Peavey. All I know about the boy was that he was a scrawny kid, brown hair, wire-rimmed glasses, real egg head type, kept talking about books."

Damn storm, she's dead ..., Oh! The last thing Edison said was *she*! I'd thought he meant the driver was female but what if he had been trying to say *Sheila*? If so, the parts of Edison Marlow's phone conversation made more sense. I had nothing but a hunch, but he'd be the right age. Trouble was, I still didn't know who he'd been talking to. If I had to guess though, I'd put money on it being the girlfriend of Pyro the bike gang leader.

"Was Pyro's girlfriend responsible for her friend's death? Did she kill her?"

Duke shook his head. "No, it ... it was kind of an accident."

My expression didn't hide my skepticism. Duke grimaced and looked away.

"What I mean is, no one meant for her to die. It was more of a joke ..."

"What was, Duke? What did they do to Jan's daughter?"

He swallowed hard and stared at the floor. "Some of the guys were grumblin' that Sheila thought she was better than everyone else cuz she wasn't partyin' and a couple had tried to hit on her, you know how it is."

I did know, and I braced to hear what had happened to Sheila Peavey. I didn't have to wait long. Duke twisted his beard between his thumb and index finger. "She wasn't a total stuck-up, Sheila I mean. The three of them had brought a couple of bottles of wine and she was drinking some in a plastic cup." He shuddered. "One of the guys dropped some pills in her drink when she went into the woods to use the bathroom."

My eyes widened. "I had expected you to say they uh, that a violent assault occurred."

He nodded. "Well, they were intending to get her high and then ... but she drank half the glass and started to slur her words. Everyone was laughing, telling her to just ride the high, but she struggled to her feet and came over to her friend ... oh man, she begged to leave, and then she fell to the sand and started flopping like a fish out of water. White foam was coming out of her mouth, everyone started screaming and hollerin' and that geeky guy rolled her on her side and started shouting for help, but it was too late. Sheila went stiff as a board and then she was layin' on the sand limp as a dish rag."

Tears were running down his face as he met my gaze. "She didn't have a pulse, no breathing ... the guys panicked and were gonna bail but Pyro said we had to hide her body ... and they did. Under the floorboards of the old hunting cabin." He sniffed. "I didn't kill her, had told them not to drug her and gotten punched for my trouble, but I *did* know where she was buried and I let her mom suffer until I found God and ... well, that's my shame to live with."

There was nothing I could say to counter that; he seemed to be making amends by changing his life and helping others, judgement wasn't up to me. Lost in our own thoughts, we both jumped when Jan came back pushing a cart containing cookies and coffee.

Small talk filled the silence as we made our coffee and ate some of the best chocolate chip cookies I'd ever had. After picking away the chocolate to give The Colonel a bite, I finally had my head wrapped around what I'd heard and had slotted it into what I knew about Megan Hearn.

"Duke, if you didn't know the names of the high school kids, how did Megan find Jan?"

His eyes went round. "Oh, I didn't ..., sorry I forgot." He glanced at Jan. "You want to hear this?"

"It's okay, Duke. I know you didn't- I mean, I forgive you."

What parts of his face not covered by hair flushed scarlet and I couldn't help but wonder if a tragedy would help two people find companionship. Duke coughed, derailing that line of thought.

"After they uh, buried Sheila everyone was cleaning up the party site so we could leave. Pyro wanted it to look like nobody had been out there. Anyway, we were loading up in the boats when I noticed Sheila's bag laying by the log she'd been sittin' on." He shrugged. "I saw it, so I was told to bury it ... and I did."

Megan's pirate booty! At Shell Point! "You told Megan, and she went out and found the bag."

Duke nodded. "Yeah, when the hurricane hit and they found Sheila's ... well I had to do something and if I went to the police I feared it'd wreck the ministry ...," he shrugged. "And leaving it to Megan worked out. She dug up the bag. Lots of stuff was junk, but the driver's license was legible enough to find Jan. Oh, and them earrings were in there."

Ah yes, the earrings and the picture. "I get that you were trying to remain anonymous, but what was I to do with the picture you left in the locker? What's so special about those earrings?"

Duke shook his head. "Wish I knew. Jan said they weren't Sheila's. Megan thought they belonged to the other girl, the one dating Pyro but she never said if she found out who that was ..., sorry."

I thanked them both and left with a few answers but more questions. Namely, was the discovery of Sheila Peavey what got Megan Hearn killed? If so, and I was inclined to at least rank it as high of a motive as the accusations of plagiarism, then I was looking for someone that owned or had been in possession of a pair of art deco emerald earrings.

343

Chapter Twenty-One

I got home too late to finish gardening but was up bright and early the next morning but, with an overflowing laundry basket and an inch of dust on the dresser, cleaning my bedroom became my priority. After walking The Colonel I headed to my room for what I thought would be a solitary task, but Mama followed me up the stairs, chatting ninety miles an hour about so many topics my head was spinning.

"And did you know that the Williams girl is pregnant? Barely out of high school ..., don't suppose they'll marry."

"No Mama, probably not." *Her parents won't shame them into a bad marriage to avoid public embarrassment.*

I tuned my mother out and stripped the bed sheets, before grabbing the dust cloth and attacking all exposed surfaces. I tossed the dirty sheets down the stairs and returned to find Mama running the vacuum. It wasn't worth arguing with her, so I started sorting my dirty clothes.

Colors, delicates, denim and darks over there ... I worked my way down to the bottom of the basket and scooped up the largest load to start.

"Make sure you check the pockets of those jeans, Holly Marie!"

I sighed and turned around, dumping the clothes onto the bed. I'd sorted half of the pile when Mama finished sweeping and plopped down on the bed to help.

"You know, this would be much easier if you'd get into the habit of emptying your pockets when you take off your-hmmm, what's this?"

I looked over to see a small gold circle in the palm of her hand. Her other hand held the brown corduroy pants I'd worn for the masquerade party. "Let me see that ...," my eyes narrowed. What Mama had found was thin metal painted gold. An image of a Greek God was on one side, with a crown of bay leaves on the other. I couldn't explain why the fake coin was in my pocket until I noticed the teeth marks. "The Colonel!" The bearer of the sobriquet thumped his tail and snorted in his sleep.

"What about the dog?"

I glanced at Mama and absentmindedly explained how my boy had been chewing on the coin after the party, but my mind was preoccupied with the origin of the item. Where had I seen it before? Round, shiny, thin metal, meant to look like Greek coins ... "Oh. Glenda Timmons was dressed as a Greek Goddess and-"

"What does it matter what she came to the party as? You need to focus on who killed that woman, so my baby boy doesn't end up in –"

"Yes ma'am, that's what I'm working on. Give me a second, Mama. I'm trying to think." My mother flounced out in high dudgeon, but I got my peace and quiet.

Glenda's costume. Thinking about it brought to mind the day I'd gone to the brewery in search of a check. She'd been taking the costume back and it slid from the garment bag. That's where I'd seen the coin and dozens of them had been attached to the belt, a gold, chain-length belt. Was a piece of that belt what Tate had found clutched in Megan Hearn's fist?

My mind continued to ponder the costume pieces as I started to plant Mama's Dianthus and Snapdragons. The Colonel had found the coin near the cauldron, I'd swear to that. Couple that with a piece of gold chain in Hearn's hand and what did I have? Had she killed Megan? It was possible, but why? She and Rae Ella Reid had the least reason of anyone to want Megan silenced.

I worked my way down the sidewalk, planting Dianthus in front and the Snapdragons directly behind them and in between the shrubs. An hour and a half later all of the flowers were in the ground. Now to water them in. Dewey had left the hose laying in the bed across from the porch and, when I returned from cutting the water on the ground and sidewalk were a muddy mess.

Shaking my head, I found a semi-clean spot to stand and proceeded to water the new plantings. What, if anything, did the costume belt have to do with the murder of Megan Hearn and, was any of that connected to what had occurred on Shell Point all those years ago?

The earrings. The picture of the girl on the beach wearing the earrings. It couldn't have been Sheila Peavey. Her mother would have recognized her. That meant it had to have been the friend whose biker boyfriend had brought drugs and thugs to a graduation party and caused the death of Sheila.

Who was that girl? Had Megan figured it out? I moved down and started watering the baskets of mums sitting on the steps. I only had two female suspects on my list. If the earrings were a clue and the death of Sheila Peavey was the reason Megan had been killed then either Rae Ella Reid or Glenda Timmons had to be the killer.

Evidence to make a case against Rae Ella was lacking but Glenda ... her costume belt was found with the victim but was that enough? The case against Edison Marlow was still much stronger, unless ..."Mama, careful where you walk,"

Mama came around the side of the house, yakking on her phone and paying no attention to where she was stepping. I shut off the hose and waved for her to stop. "You'll get your white tennis shoes all muddy-" mud. Muddy white shoes ... "Glenda's shoes!"

She'd been in the shrubs. It was her footprint they'd found in the camellia hedge but why had she been in there? I packed my garden tools into the buggy and walked toward the greenhouse as I ran everything I knew through my beleaguered brain.

Edison Marlow, pipe, blackmail, lying about the alibi, his conversation with Megan and on the phone ... and Dale Scruggs. Hearn had blackmailed him for information on Mark Timmons. I snorted. Mark Timmons. The man was broke, indebted to J.T. Minton, and he'd fought with Megan ... my brow furrowed. What had Rae Ella said?

Mark and Megan were in the garden. Rae Ella had said Megan had thrown something. *Girl had a good arm on her. Whatever she threw arced in the air and landed a good ways away.*

An image of Rae Ella demonstrating Hearn's actions popped into my mind. Arm bent at the elbow, hand near her ear ... I gasped. Could Megan have thrown an earring?

I closed up the greenhouse and entered the house through the back door. Tate had said only one earring had been found on the body, along with the chain clutched in her hand and, oh my I'd been so blind! I grabbed my bag and scrambled out the door. "Colonel? Come on boy, hurry, hurry!"

The Colonel lumbered around the corner of the house, Mama right behind him. "Where are you off to, it's almost dark! I thought we could try that new restaurant out on Belle Isle -"

"Sorry Mama, something's come up." I hefted The Colonel into the Scout and started the engine before Mama could pester me with more questions. With a bit of percussive maintenance and a few choice curses, the Scout slid into gear, and The Colonel and I headed to Rosedale Plantation for a late-night treasure hunt.

Chapter Twenty-Two

The drive out to Saint Mariana Island was hampered by road congestion. People dressed to impress were mingling on the sidewalk outside of the Morris Theater and I remembered that a traveling theater group was performing. The crawl down Bay Street afforded me more opportunity to consider everything I'd learned and what bearing it had on the murder of Megan Hearn.

If she had been killed because of her investigation into the death of Sheila Peavey the question became, which of my suspects had been present that night? One was a male, the other female; and the girl had been wearing the emerald and diamond earrings ... why would a girl that age have such expensive earrings, much less wear them on the beach?

Traffic was at a standstill, so I pulled out my phone and called Jessica.

"Hey, Holly, what's up?"

I snorted. "How much time do you have?" I proceeded to give Jessica a synopsis of my meeting with Pastor Duke and Jan.

"Wait, so you think Megan Hearn was killed because of her investigation into this Sheila Peavey's death?"

"Yes, it makes sense, though I don't know who was wearing those earrings in the photo. I'm pretty sure the boy was Edison Marlow, however."

"Aside from the little bit you think you overheard while he was talking on the phone ... I mean, it could be someone else."

I huffed and set the phone to speaker as traffic started to move. "Like whom? Of the men on the suspect list, Edison is the only one the right age to have graduated in '05 ..."

"And Mark Timmons. He graduated from Saint Ambrose a year late because he missed so much the year before." She chuckled. "He caught Mono."

"How on earth do you know that?" Jessica was six years younger than Timmons and the rest.

"I interviewed him for a business spotlight last year. Hey, where are you headed? I was about to get a bite at Mario's-"

"Sorry, I'm headed out to Rosedale. Did you ever find anything on the original owners of the earrings?"

"No, I'm waiting on an email from a friend at the Noble Country Historical Society. Why are you going out to the brewery? It's pitch dark! Wait until morning and I'll go with you-"

"For what?" I laughed. "I'm just gonna look in the shrubs. It's not like anyone will-"

"Holly, someone ran Marlow over! What if they did that to keep him from talking? What was it you overheard him say? Something about *he'd talk*?"

"Yeah, and he also said *damn storm and she's dead*! That's why I think he killed Megan, it makes sense. The hit and run was probably someone drunk or driving with no license - Look, I gotta go. I need two hands to shift."

I hung up and considered what my friend had said. I'd been convinced that Edison was the boy on the beach, but could it have been Mark Timmons? Was that why he'd been arguing with Megan? I shook my head.

Marlow's pipe had been found near the crime scene. He'd lied numerous times; Megan had been blackmailing him ... I'd been right the first time. Marlow had killed Hearn to keep her from exposing his role in the death of Sheila Peavey and, he could have done it because of the plagiarism allegation. Either way, he was in a coma and Jessica was being silly. I had nothing to fear.

Away from the lights of Sanctuary Bay, millions of stars were visible against a blue-black sky. An offshore breeze drove the clouds, causing smoky streaks across the horizon and leaving a chill that would manifest as a light frost by morning.

The Colonel was curled in the front seat, his nose tucked under his paws and his body quivering every few minutes. I cranked the heat and directed the vents on him, but he still grumbled and sighed.

"I'm sorry, Buddy. Gonna have to buy you a sweater if they make 'em big enough for your tubby self!" The Colonel responded with a baleful eye before he repositioned himself to face away from me. I snorted. *Diva.* I'd need to add a blanket to the truck for the winter.

Rosedale Plantation sat at the end of a long, winding, private road but the gates had long since rusted on their hinges, making after-hours access a snap. I slowed and watched for deer as I drove through the woods and fields that comprised the bulk of Rosedale's land. It made me sick to think Minton or any other developer would get their hands on such a beautiful place.

The Scout's headlights illuminated the manor house, revealing scaffolding next to the chimney, piles of bricks, and a cement mixer. Other than the repairs to the fireplaces I saw no evidence of projects in the works and again wondered if Mark Timmons' money problems originated in the massive restoration he'd attempted.

The house fell back into darkness as I took the right fork to the brewery. The road wound away and then curved back toward the manor and, as I rounded a curve a flicker of light in an upstairs window drew my attention. I stopped and waited but when it never reappeared I drove on and was soon pulling into the gravel parking area designated for the brewery.

I slowed and was about to park in the nearest spot to the walkway when it occurred to me that I'd need more than a flashlight to examine the hedge row. Plus, it was cold, and my leg protested more in inclement weather. It'd be better all-around if I parked closer to the brewery. The fact that the coroner's van had driven down to the tasting pavilion settled my decision.

Shoving the Scout into gear took more than the usual amount of effort but I managed to get it moving. Estimating the best angle for the headlights to illuminate the shrubs, I settled on a short rise that led down to the pavilion and set the emergency brake.

The Colonel started to rise as I opened my door. "No Buddy, I'll just be a minute." I patted his head and slid from my seat. "You stay here where it's warm." I reached over him and opened the glove box because, even with the headlights, a flashlight would be helpful. As my hand closed around the light, my gaze skidded over the pistol I always carried. Jessica's concerns rising in my mind, I debated a moment but dismissed the concern; there was no one around and it was too cold for gators or snakes to be moving.

The hill was slippery from the dew, but I made it down unscathed and was soon peering into and around the waxy leaves of the camellia hedge without success. The snap and crackle of underbrush made me pause but, when I heard nothing further I dismissed it as deer and continued my examination of the formal garden.

Rae Ella had said Megan threw something, that I now believed to be an earring, and it had arced and went farther into the garden. I frowned. What if the arc were high enough to clear the six-foot hedge? Where would that put the potential landing? I exited through the gate and started looking at the shrubs that lined the main sidewalk, taking care to watch for loose soil; I didn't relish slipping into the rosemary-huh.

What had Tate said? I worried at my lower lip and cast my mind back to our impromptu dinner at Mario's. Hearn *had dirt under her nails and traces of Rosmarinus officinalis L. on her hands, arms, and clothing.* My gaze dropped to the pruned rosemary hedge. I'd slipped on loose soil right around ... I took about six steps and started looking in and around the rosemary. Several feet from where I started, I hit pay dirt.

"Ah hah!" I stretched out, half laying on the sidewalk with my arm extended under the thick, fragrant bushes until my fingers closed around the earring. "Now to get to my feet ..."

Grunts growls, and a few curse words later I was again upright. I squinted against the glare of the headlights and raised the earring to eye level. Dirt was encrusted in the setting, but it was definitely the same jewelry worn in the picture. Now to figure out who the old jewels belonged to-

I caught my breath as the sound of a gun being racked blended with the ticking of the Scout's engine.

"I really wish you hadn't found that."

The hair on the back of my neck rose as a woman's voice sounded. The headlights were blinding, I could see nothing but the outline of my truck and a halo of yellowish light but that voice, and more importantly, that gun had been close enough to clearly hear them above the hum of the Scout's motor.

My mouth went dry, and a tremor started to work itself along my limbs. Rae Ella or Glenda? I hadn't been able to tell by the voice, but logic said it was one of the two. Either way, keeping them talking and distracted was my only way out.

"Hey, who's there?" I shaded my eyes and schooled my voice to sound friendly and unconcerned. "You scared the beejeebus out of me, I was just-"

"I know what you were doing, Holly, cut the pretense." Glenda stepped in front of the Scout, splitting the beams of light and allowing me to see her face; her expression was hard, uncompromising, and composed. A woman on a mission and I was standing in the way.

With Glenda blocking some of the glare, I could clearly see The Colonel inside the Scout. He'd somehow managed to lean on the dash with his front legs and his face was squished against the windshield. When he saw me, he barked, and then, when I didn't respond, he dropped back onto the seat, disappearing from view. Occasionally, I'd hear a bark or whimper.

There were so many questions I'd like to have asked but the glaring lights and gun pointed at my chest ..., I'd been there before, and my body remembered with much better detail than my brain.

"You just couldn't leave it alone." Glenda huffed, though the gun never wavered. The woman was rock solid in her stance; she knew her way around a pistol.

My legs trembled, knees knocking as I braced myself on my cane and fought off the rising panic. *Focus, Holly*! God, I'd tried that the other night with Edison and gotten nowhere-deep breaths, in and out .., what was she saying?

"I've been looking for that earring. It's the only thing linking me to Sheila. Toss it over."

I squinted and tried to process her command but the ringing in my ears was rising to a fever pitch. From a distance, I heard The Colonel's frantic barking. "It's okay, Buddy ..." I managed to mutter through chattering teeth. "We'll go for a walk in a minute ..." I swayed and stumbled into the hedges.

Glenda laughed. "You won't be walking anywhere. Give me the earring."

The pungent scent of the rosemary, along with Glenda's menacing statement acted like smelling salts, grounding me long enough to get back to my feet. I drew a ragged breath and braced on my cane as I tried to meet her eyes against the glare of the lights.

"I know about Sheila. One of the bikers told-"

"Oh yes, he found God and had to make amends." She snorted. "Give me a break. It was an accident, but that fool went and told that pernicious podcaster ... she was blackmailing me!"

I jumped as Glenda's voice rose. The Colonel was now barking nonstop, and the Scout was rocking as he bounced from window to window looking for a way out. My heart was pounding, I had to force air into my lungs ... *keep her talking*! I repeated the command until my mouth could form words.

"It was an O.D., Glenda. A prank gone wrong. Involuntary manslaughter ..." I swallowed past the lump in my throat. "You could have gone to the police and thwarted Hearn. You didn't have to kill her-"

"Hah, I couldn't go to the police! My career was on the line, Holly."

My brow furrowed and I tried to make sense of what she was saying. Her career …, "Oh! The morals clause at Saint Anne's."

"Yes, the *morals* clause." Her snide tone, filled with arrogant disdain, made me grit my teeth, even as images of the shooting flashed in and out of my mind, I despised people who thought themselves better and more important than the rest of us.

Acid churned in my stomach, I needed- my eyelids drooped … oh God, stay awake! I jolted awake and bit my lip until it bled. "You let Jan Busby suffer for years. Even an anonymous letter would have-"

"Oh, shut up." She rolled her eyes. "I was not ruining my future because her daughter couldn't handle partying with the adults."

She snorted and motioned with the gun for me to walk toward the river. "Let's go."

I was losing control, over the conversation, but more importantly, of my body. My teeth were chattering so hard I thought they'd shatter. I struggled to breathe, my chest rising and falling in short, sharp bursts. I stared at Glenda, frowning as my vision blurred around the edges, and what I saw wavered between one crazy woman with a gun and two.

"Stop stalling, no one is going to save you this time …"

I stared past her at my truck. The Colonel was in a frenzy. His barking was like one long howl, and he jumped from the passenger seat to the driver's seat and back in a flurry of motion. What was that creaking noise underneath the hum of the engine?

My gaze landed on the gun and bile rose in my throat. I gagged and swallowed reflexively.

"Fine, I'll do it here ..." She stepped closer, her finger wrapping around the trigger.

"Glenda wait. I can't- I'm going to-" Darkness narrowed my vision, I swayed as I stared down the barrel of the gun ...

A grinding of metal on metal. I blinked and shook my head. What was that? My eyes widened and my mouth fell open. I raised a shaky hand and tried to scream a warning as I threw myself out of the way.

Glenda scowled and twirled around. "What are you-Ah!"

Glenda's screams as she fell beneath the wheels of the Scout were the last thing I heard before the wave of panic I'd been riding pulled me under.

Chapter Twenty-Three

Thanksgiving at Myrtlewood had been all that a gathering of thankful family and friends could ask for. Ham, deep-fried turkey, cornbread dressing, sweet potato soufflé, and collards fresh from the garden. I'd eaten until I almost popped.

After setting the kitchen and dining room to rights, the guests migrated to various areas of the huge house. Some to watch football, while others played with the kids or caught up on the latest news over coffee and dessert.

Since I'd played a major role in the breaking news, I chose to avoid prying questions by making my way out to the back lawn where Dewey and some of the other men had constructed a roaring bonfire.

The Colonel and I shuffled our way through the damp grass and gladly accepted the comfy chair Tate had secured for me; well, me and the Diva. At the best of times, The Colonel didn't believe dogs were meant to sleep on the floor but, since saving my bacon a second time he'd become insufferable.

"Come on, you spoiled brat." I patted the end of the lounge chair. The Colonel put his chubby paws up on the cushion and half-heartedly tried to pull himself up before sitting down and looking pitiful.

"Really? You have managed to get up before-Tate, he's already so rotten he stinks!"

Everyone chuckled as Tate rose and boosted the bulldog onto the chaise, going so far as to drape the end of my lap blanket over him.

"Talk about entitled!" Jessica giggled and patted his chubby head.

"Rotten is what he is, and soon he'll be putting off noxious fumes." My friend tried to pull an innocent face. I snorted and shook my finger at her. "Don't even try. I saw you slipping this pampered pooch table scraps."

She grinned. "But he deserves it!" She looked down her nose at me. "After all, he saved your butt."

"Yes, he does." Tate reached across my legs and scratched behind The Colonel's ears. "You're a good boy, saving the day after your mistress did a reckless thing like going to the middle of nowhere at night to hunt for a killer without even telling-"

"Oh please, I told Jessica." I knew he was joking but I'd been castigated for two weeks over the incident with Glenda. To my mind, if they weren't going to let it go then I should be getting pats on the back; after all, I'd found the killer and, by default solved the mystery of the remains on Shell Point.

"Uh-huh, and if you hadn't, you'd have been laying out there for two days until the brewery reopened." Tate cocked an eyebrow daring me to contradict him.

My response was an unladylike snort. Though he was only semi-right. The stars had aligned in my favor because Jessica had received an email from her historical society contact telling her that the original owner of the jewelry was Glenda Timmons' maternal great-grandmother.

She had then seen Mark Timmons in the restaurant and via casual conversation found out that Glenda was not with him because she was checking on renovations at Rosedale. The rest was history.

Truly, the hero of the hour was my Daddy's old International Scout and my procrastination in getting the transmission fixed. In The Colonel's frantic bouncing from seat-to-seat quest to get out, he'd managed to bump the emergency brake, leaving the truck to remain in Park only by the strength of it being in gear and with the state of those gears ...

I shuddered as an image of Glenda popped into my mind. My panic had caused me to faint, but I'd regained consciousness a few minutes later to find Glenda under the idling jeep, the gun laying a few feet from her lifeless hand.

I was in the process of getting the Scout into reverse when two sheriff's deputies rolled up. I'd told them the story and let them take over. The Colonel and I had watched from the sidelines until Tate arrived with Jessica.

When he'd learned about my panic attack and loss of consciousness he'd insisted on checking me over and then driving me home; I didn't complain overly much since the Scout had busted something in the collision but, ever since that night I'd had to deal with Tate and Mama hovering over me and acting like I was made of glass. The only reason Mama wasn't currently fussing was because she had a plantation full of guests and I'd had the good sense to hide.

"What I don't understand is why that woman was so desperate to get that earring. I mean, how did that prove she'd killed anyone?"

I smiled at Marla Cassidy and waved away Craig's attempts to shush her. "It's all right Craig, I don't mind talking about it." I met Marla's gaze. "The earrings had been reported stolen by Glenda right after the party at Shell Point. She had no idea where she'd lost them, though."

"It was only when Megan found the remnants of Sheila Peavey's purse that Glenda realized she'd put her earrings in the bag for safe keeping and now Megan had the means to blackmail her." I shrugged. "At least that's what Edison Marlow has said."

Connie frowned. "So he's able to talk?"

"Some, enough to give a statement." Craig snorted. "Poor guy was catching it at both ends by women. Megan Hearn was blackmailing him about stealing credit for his wife's book and then Glenda started threatening him over what occurred on Shell Point."

"Who ran him over? Was that Glenda?"

I nodded. "Oh yes, she also followed me several times and left a threatening note on my porch steps. It will be interesting to see if she walks back that confession when she goes to trial."

"Interesting she says." Connie rolled her eyes. "I'm just glad that deranged lunatic is locked up. Now you can get back to important things like building your business."

The mention of my decorating endeavors turned the conversation to the upcoming Christmas Market which I'd just won the bid to design. I had a pretty solid plan in place but, with it being the first event of its kind, everyone wanted to chime in. I let their ideas roll over me as I watched the flames flicker.

The heat along with the crackle and pop of burning wood lulled me and my head started to droop. Tate's murmur in my ear roused me before I could drop off completely.

"Time for bed?"

I shook off my drowsiness and sat up straighter before meeting his concerned gaze. This was why I'd resisted allowing our friendship to move beyond casually friendly. I didn't need a nursemaid or a nanny and that's what I'd had since Edison Marlow was run over and I'd had a panic attack.

I forced a smile I was far from feeling. "I'm fine; all that turkey."

His expression remained solemn. "More like your body is still dealing with the effects of your-"

"Tate." I sighed and searched for words. "Can you uh, just ... This lecturing me like a child is not-it's um, well it's tiring." He stiffened and sat back in his chair. "And now I've offended you." My brow furrowed as I tried to explain. "I don't mean to-that is, oh for the love of ..." I muttered under my breath.

"Just spit it out, Holly. You want me to leave you alone? Stay out of your life? You're not interested in me that way? Isn't that how women break it to us stupid men?"

He'd kept his voice low, but Jessica must have suspected something because she frowned and gave me a questioning look. I shook my head in response to her concern and turned back to Tate. He was slumped in his chair, arms folded across his chest and face like a thundercloud.

I wanted to unload on him and demand he grow up and stop acting like a baby, but I also didn't want to lose a friend. If I were honest, I didn't want to lose a potentially more than a friend, either. Tate scowled as I relayed those thoughts to him.

"So you do want more than friendship? Because I'm confused. You blow hot and cold and I'm never sure-"

"Tate, is there a fire somewhere I'm not aware of? A ticking bomb? An end-of-the-world event coming soon?"

His eyes narrowed. "What?"

A genuine smile stretched my lips as I chuckled. "What's the rush? You keep pushing me for something I'm not ready to give." I shook my head and stared at the fire as the words tumbled from my mouth. "I like you, a lot. We have great conversations and share similar interests-"

"Then what's the problem?"

My shoulders dropped as his tone again became pugnacious. I met his gaze. "The problem is I don't want to be in a relationship right now. I don't want to concern myself with the hourly welfare of another human being. I already have to worry about Dewey and Mama, and my own state of mental and physical health isn't all that great! I just want to go with the flow, isn't that what you suggested I do a few weeks ago? What's changed?"

A sheepish expression came over him and he looked down at his lap. "You went and confronted a killer and I ...," He met my gaze and smiled. "I've been annoying, huh?"

I grinned and held my fingers up, leaving a space of about an inch between my thumb and index. "Just a smidge. No biggie. We're all entitled to a moment of jackassery-"

"Hey now, I wasn't that bad ... was I?"

His worried expression made me laugh. "Not as far as you know!" I lifted my leg over the sleeping bulldog and sat up so that I could lean closer to Tate. I took his hand. "Can we just be friends right now? Supportive friends, that care for each other and sometimes indulge in Italian food and ice cream?"

Tate smiled. "But minus the whole hit-and-run victim and panic attacks, right?"

"Most definitely!"

Tate's gaze moved to the house, and he sighed. "I gotta go, Dad's on the back porch probably ready to go home." His gaze drifted over my face for a minute before meeting mine. He squeezed my hand and rose then before I could blink, he dropped a light kiss on my forehead before waltzing off, whistling a cheery tune.

"What was that all about?"

I groaned as Connie took the seat Tate had just vacated. I looked around and frowned. Craig, Marla, and Jessica were gone.

"Craig and Marla are headed back to Osprey Point. You seemed to be in an intense chat with Tate, so they didn't want to interrupt," she wagged her eyebrows, drawing a huff from me, which just made her laugh. "And Jessica got a phone call; she's walking around over there."

Jessica was pacing on the patio. I looked past her to the windows that led into the great room. Second helpings seemed to be on offer as people milled around with plates in their hands. I looked at Connie.

"We should get some dessert, someone brought Chocolate Éclair Cake and it isn't Thanksgiving if I don't have a piece of Mama's Chess Pie."

Connie agreed and we made our way indoors. She made us each a plate while I served The Colonel a half portion of his supper. "Go ahead and give me the death glare, buddy. I'm still not feeding you anymore. You ate enough for three dogs today!"

I dragged Connie back to the fire before she could fall for The Colonel's pitiful puppy act. We chatted about the election results, Griff Reid was now Congressman Reid and speculated on whether Dewey could manage to keep the job Craig had persuaded his friend to give him.

"Dewey as a security guard." I chuckled and rolled my eyes. "Can you imagine?"

Connie grinned and set her empty plate aside. "Yes actually, I can!" She leaned forward and lowered her voice in case Dewey overheard. "Though, I'm emptying my account if they assign him to guard the bank!"

I laughed and looked over at my brother. Connie needn't have worried about insulting Dewey. He and Whopper had been into the hard cider for hours. I'd lectured him about drowning his sorrows in booze and he'd taken it to heart. This was the first time I'd seen him indulge since he'd received the news that the DA had dropped his case.

That had been a celebration even Mama could get behind, though she'd merely had a small sherry. Shortly after the court proceedings had been dismissed, Dewey had gotten an interview with Sentinel Security and to my surprise, they'd hired him on the spot. Craig had sworn it was no doing of his but I was still skeptical that someone had thought my brother was competent on his own merits.

I'd mentioned my suspicions to Tate and got scolded for my trouble. He'd irritated me at the time but, after thinking about it I had to reluctantly agree with the good doctor's assessment of my brother. Dewey was the baby of the family, Mama had lost a child in between me and my brother so, when he came along she was extra protective but that didn't mean Dewey wasn't capable.

No matter what Daddy had said, Mama kept Dewey tied to her apron strings long past a healthy age. In fact, it'd taken a rare fight between my parents before Mama had relented and allowed Dewey to play sports and almost an act of Congress before she'd relented and let Daddy take him hunting.

His close call with prison had scared Dewey straight; at least it appeared that way. He'd started going to bed at an early hour, was up and to work on time, and even took care of his uniform. It was a nice change but whether it lasted remained to be seen.

Connie rose and took our plates to the trash can, interrupting my musings. I smiled as she sat back down and huddled under her blanket. "We can go in, you know."

She shook her head and stared at the fire. "No way, I love this." She tipped her head back. "A sky full of stars, a roaring fire, and great friends ... perfect ending to a perfect day."

"I agree."

Connie looked over at me and smiled. "The Rudd's house looks fantastic, by the way. I love the fan palms flanking the front door. And where did you get those gorgeous baskets lining the steps?"

"The Gullah market down the road from here. I commissioned them."

Her eyes widened. "You have to take me there. I'd love to carry them in my shop."

"Sure, wait until the holidays are over though. Ms. Ada will be too busy before then."

Connie nodded. "Sounds good. I chatted with Ms. Lou Lou yesterday when she stopped by the store. She's excited about the Holiday Market. When will you start putting it all together?"

The Market would run for seven days, the second week of December. The council had loved my Night Before Christmas theme which was great, but now I was rushing to create some of the decorative items I'd dreamed up.

"I can't start assembling things until the Friday before, but two days to get it all done isn't enough so, along with hiring some help, I'm also doing as much as I can ahead of time. I'll be working at the shop every day next week and probably the week after."

She nodded. "I can help some, but only if the college girl I hired works out. Glitter and Garland has been super busy lately. I barely finished the Thanksgiving centerpiece orders in time!"

"I know. Just shows how much people were clamoring for a floral and craft store in Sanctuary Bay." I shrugged. "All business is good business?"

Connie laughed. "Yes, I'm not complaining. I'm just glad you solved the murder so we can concentrate on the fun things that make us money!"

I tipped my head in a salute. "Cheers to that! For a while there I thought Dewey was headed to the big house."

"I know, I was so worried. Every night I combed through the thumb drive you gave me."

I cocked my head. "Why? I thought you'd found everything relevant."

"Eh, at first I wanted to make sure I hadn't missed anything but then ..."

I stilled as Connie's gaze dropped. I cleared my throat. "Then what?"

My internal alarm started to ring as she continued to avoid my gaze and started fidgeting with the fringe on her blanket. "Connie? What's wrong?"

She sighed and glanced at me then over at the fire. "Nothing, per se it's just." She bit her lip. "I found another one of those files Hearn kept, the ones with all the random words-what did you call it?"

"Stream of conscious. What did the file say?"

She shook her head. "It's probably nothing ..."

"Then there's no problem in telling me."

Connie huffed and pursed her lips. "Okay, just promise me you won't ... I don't know, worry about it? Just, you know what? Forget about it. She was-"

"Connie! Tell me or I'll look through every file on that drive myself!"

"Okay, okay," she held up her hand. "Just calm down. See? This is why I shouldn't have, Tate told me-"

"You told Tate? Before me?" My voice raised along with my outrage. "Tate is a friend, nothing more. I'd appreciate it if you'd refrain from telling him my business-"

"Oh, now you're mad. Just ..., I only mentioned that I was worried you weren't well enough-" She rolled her eyes. "I didn't go talking behind your back to Tate or anyone else, I'd never do that!" Her blue eyes pleaded with me. "It's just, you were pretty stressed after the double whammy of seeing Edison run down and then the whole thing with Glenda ..."

I rolled my eyes and fought for calm. She meant well. Heck, they all did but no one seemed to realize how much more stressful it was to have everyone figuratively wrapping me up in cotton. I said as much, and Connie winced.

"I'm sorry, you're right. We've all been doing that it's just," She shrugged. "We love you."

I smiled. "Thanks, I love y'all too. But please, just tell me what you found on Megan Hearn's computer."

Connie nodded. "Okay, but again, I think I might have over-reacted ... okay, okay, I'm getting to it!" She rushed on as I made a face. "It was one of those streams of conscious jumbles that caught my eye because ..." Connie paused and then nodded. "Here's what I found. It was one paragraph containing the words old money, attorney, boat wreck, hunting camp, civil suit, and deputy."

I replayed the words in my head. *Old Money, Attorney, Deputy, Hunting Camp,* ...My heart skipped a beat and my stomach cramped. I stared at Connie as I acknowledged the obvious: Megan Hearn had been planning a podcast on the events surrounding the shooting that had resulted in the death of Shawn Dupree and left me fighting for my life.

The End

Did you enjoy spending time with Holly and The Colonel? Why not leave a review and help others discover Holly and her friends?

Want to wander through Sanctuary Bay's Holiday Market as Holly tracks a killer? Keep reading for a sneak peek of book 2, **Carolers and Corpses!**

Available for purchase on Amazon or FREE in Kindle Unlimited! Also available at bookstores: ask them to order you a copy!

Carolers and Corpses

Rachel Lynne

All Rights Reserved

Chapter One

Darkness fell over Goodwin Park as Mayor Lou Lou Tomlin climbed the steps to the stage. She waited until all the lights in the middle section of the park were extinguished before cuing the band. A hush fell over the crowd as the drumroll began. The mayor started the count, and everyone joined in. "Five, four, three, two, ..."

The opening chords of "Joy to the World" washed over us as millions of twinkling lights draped around a thirty-foot Christmas tree sprang to life and illuminated the night. Everyone cheered and started to mingle as the Noble County High School band continued to play carols.

Mama was sitting in the historical society booth with her friends and my date had been called to the scene of an accident, leaving my bulldog and me free to roam. Date. Was that what we'd been on before duty called Tate away? I was sure he'd thought so but, as usual, my thoughts concerning the amorous coroner for Noble County were hazy at best.

We'd been friends for years, though nothing closer than 'hey, how are ya" acquaintances until my shooting and subsequent divorce. Tate had been a godsend; supportive, knowledgeable, kind. He was still all those things, but now he also wanted to be more than friends.

Skirting around a rowdy group of teens, I sighed and considered my complicated relationship with the good doctor. Mama was all for it as were my best friends Connie and Jessica. My former boss and childhood friend, Craig Everette, was staying noncommittal, though when pressed he'd say that Tate was a great guy.

Great guy. I rolled my eyes and guided my always-hungry-for-people-food bulldog away from a food truck. I wasn't disputing the goodness of Tate Sawyer, in fact, I'd go so far as to admit I found him attractive. But, regardless of his winning ways and physical attributes, the fact remained that, less than a year ago, I had suffered a nearly fatal shooting and been left with mobility issues and PTSD.

Piling onto my problems, three months into my convalescence, my husband of thirty years decided to leave me and, adding insult to injury, the other woman was a girl two years younger than our son!

Speaking of my son. I'd run into him just before the tree lighting and he'd barely spoken three words and those were only monosyllable answers to my questions. He'd helped me find an attorney for my brother after he was accused of murdering a local podcaster while helping me decorate back in October but, aside from that, Junior had avoided me like the plague.

Discounting those handful of phone calls concerning Dewey, Junior had not willingly spoken to me since the argument we had at the family celebration for July fourth. That he'd come to Mama's at all was a testament to his love for his grandmother, but he'd been cool to me. I lost my temper and delivered a few home truths about his father.

Brooks Daye had always been immature and selfish, and it was time Junior accepted it, though I should have refrained from calling his dad a filthy old pervert.

The relationship with my son had to be mended but a community event wasn't the time or place. I pushed aside my frustration over the issue and forced myself to focus on the job at hand; namely, inspecting the various activities and elements of the holiday market so that I could go home and rest.

Tents housing local organizations and charities were lined along the route leading to the far end of the park. I tried to get lost in the crowd, but Kay Emory, chairwoman of the Gray's Island Causeway Coalition, managed to spot me, or more likely The Colonel. The sad sack eyes and floppy jowls of my best buddy drew people like a magnet. I sighed and worked my way over to the booth.

"Holly!" Kay leaned over and scratched The Colonel behind the ear. "Hello you little potato." She met my gaze and smiled. "Everything looks wonderful and there's such a great turnout!"

"Thanks, Kay."

She rummaged in the bag attached to her wheelchair, pulling out a silver thermos and pouring liquid into a cup. My nose twitched as the sharp scent of mulled wine filled the air. She caught my eye and raised her glass. "Want some?"

"No thanks, smells good though." I tipped my head toward the large wooden box prominently placed on a table at the front of the tent. "How are the donations coming? Getting a good amount?"

Kay's brown eyes glowed with excitement. "People are being so generous! If they keep this up, we'll make our goal of five thousand by the end of the week!"

"That's great, Kay. It's a worthy cause, I'm sure people will continue to support it."

"I hope so, time is running out. If we don't secure our share of the funding in time, we'll lose the matching state funds and have to start the whole petitioning process again next year."

"I hope that doesn't happen." The Gray's Island Causeway had been built in the mid-1900s on unstable ground. As a result, the causeway flooded with heavy downpours and seasonal high tides, making it both a nuisance and a danger.

Kay Emory was leading the charge to get the road rebuilt. For her it was personal; traveling across the causeway during a torrential rainstorm, her car had rolled and landed in the marsh, killing her son, and leaving Kay bound to a wheelchair.

"Nor do I." A scowl darkened her face. "If only Clayton Ross hadn't died ... as chairman of the island council he was guiding the project through the proper channels, well, up until he remarried." She rolled her eyes. "God forgive me, but what was the man thinking, getting involved with that woman!"

I frowned. "What woman?"

"Brianna Bellamy, oh sorry, it's Bellamy Ross now."

My eyes widened at Kay's tone; she'd almost growled the woman's name. Never having met her, I knew little about Brianna Bellamy Ross except that she'd married Clayton Ross, a retired businessman and widower, a little over a year ago. He'd collapsed and died from a sudden heart attack not long after, leaving a devastated daughter and, according to the rumor mill, a merry widow.

I shook my head. "What does him marrying her have to do with his death?"

Kay rolled her eyes. "Oh, come on Holly, he was sixty-one and that woman can't be more than thirty!" Kay shook her head. "A man that age cavorting around like a young buck in heat! No wonder his heart gave out." Kay shuddered. "Poor Madison, imagine your father marrying a woman not much older than you!"

Since my ex-husband was dating one younger than our son I didn't have to imagine, not that I pointed that out to Kay; avoiding public speculation and gossip concerning Brooks was a point of pride with me.

I tuned back in as Kay continued to fume.

"Always prancing around in her skimpy clothes reminding people that she was a star. You know how she really got famous, don't you?"

My leg was starting to protest, it always did when I stood in one place too long. Even if it wasn't, my tolerance for gossip had been reached; if I ever found myself pining for the latest tidbit on the neighbors Mama could oblige.

Wanting to avoid any further discussion, I chose a white lie. "Yes, I believe so. I'm gonna have to—"

"Then you know she isn't any better than she ought to be! Why, I was talking with Valentina DeMarco yesterday and she said the Bellamy woman does yoga every morning on her dock!"

I'd backed away from the tent, hoping to make my escape, but curiosity got the better of me. I frowned at Kay. "What's wrong with doing yoga on the dock?"

Kay's eyes widened. "She does it naked!"

My mouth dropped open. "Ooooh! I bet her neighbors love that!" I bit my lip to keep from laughing. Really, naked yoga on the dock ... no wonder the ladies were all up in arms.

Kay scowled. "Felicity Simms lives next door and is fit to be tied." Kay leaned forward and lowered her voice. "She claims it's her teenaged grandson she's concerned about but it's probably that husband of hers. Give him a couple of drinks and Eugene always was a bit of a lech."

"Hmm, you might be right." I backed away. "I gotta run Kay, nice talking to you!"

"Okay, take care, Holly! Come out to the house and—"

The sound of her voice was lost in the chatter of the crowd. The Bellamy woman making waves in Gray's Island society was amusing but I had work to do and a hot tub calling my name.

Despite my aversion to gossip, I couldn't help but think about what Kay had said concerning Clayton and the Bellamy woman. As May/December romances went, it was one heck of an age gap!

Brianna was only seven years older than Ross's daughter. That he'd married the woman was brow raising, though surely water under the bridge now that he'd passed. Even though she was my assistant, I'd yet to speak to Madison on the subject and hoped I wouldn't have to; it was none of my affair.

The market had a huge turnout and most of the people seemed to be heading to the same area I needed to go. The Colonel was happy to be slowed to a crawl, more time for him to sniff out dropped food, but I was chomping at the bit.

Several minutes later a break in the throng let me squeeze by the meandering visitors. I increased my pace and was about to round a corner when I heard my name called.

I turned to find Gary Walston striding toward me.

"Hey, Gary."

He smiled and patted The Colonel. "Evenin' Holly, congratulations on the market. Looks to be a huge hit."

"Thanks, everyone does seem to be enjoying themselves." I motioned behind me. "I was just checking on the decorations."

Gary nodded while digging in his pocket. "I won't keep you. Felicity Simms wanted me to ask if we can stay late tonight."

I frowned. "Stay ... you mean here at the park? What for?"

"Yeah," He paused to unwrap a piece of gum. A few seconds later a smell I associated with the holidays reached my nose. I was trying to place it when Gary started talking again. "Sorry about that." He chewed his gum a few times and then flashed a rueful smile. "Using the gum to kick the smoking habit. Anyway, our choir needs to rehearse for tomorrow's performance, and we haven't been able to get everyone together but they're all here for the tree lighting, so we thought ..."

"Ah, I see." Of all the volunteers that had helped make the holiday market a success, Gary Walston deserved a medal. I'd requested temporary poles be placed around the park so we could run market lighting. It'd been approved and the public works department had been slated to install the necessary equipment but, two days before they were to begin work, the department fell into chaos.

The ex-wife of assistant director Preston Spruill had called for a welfare check after her former spouse failed to pick up their son for a birthday celebration. From what little had been reported, it was hard to form an opinion on what had happened to the man, but the responding officers had found remnants of dinner on the kitchen table and the television blaring. That seemed suspicious to me, though Sheriff Felton had dismissed the reporter's probing questions as fear mongering.

One of the area's largest general contractors, Gary, had offered his company's services and saved the day. One good turn deserved another. I smiled. "Of course. I'll add you guys to security's list."

I'd taken a few steps toward my next inspection stop when something occurred to me. "Gary? How long do you think you'll be?"

"Maybe an hour? We'll start a little after ten when the park closes."

"Ok, that'll work. We have a company coming in tonight to replenish the fake snow, but they start at the back of the park and work their way to the entrance."

His brow furrowed. "Oh, we don't want to get in the way. We can try to do it early tomorrow. "

"Nah, it's fine. We aren't putting the stuff in the high traffic areas." I waved my hand in dismissal. "Y'all go on and use the stage but the gates will be locked so you'll need to find security to let you out."

Gary thanked me again and I continued my mission. Smiling at acquaintances and waving at neighbors, I worked my way through the crowds and headed for the eastern end of the park. I'd do a final walk through starting at the back and work my way to the parking lot. Barring mishap or mayhem, I could complete my inspection and be soaking my aching leg in the hot tub in an hour.

The hour I'd estimated for completing my inspection turned into two and counting. It seemed every section I passed contained someone looking for me to solve their problems.

The dull ache in my leg had morphed into a constant throb that left me questioning the efficacy of the physical therapy I'd been faithfully attending since the beginning of November. While there was massive improvement in my mobility, my leg was still nowhere near functioning at the levels it had before I'd been shot.

Reminders of my physical limitations only served to annoy me, and an increase in aggravation was the last thing I needed at the moment. I shoved thoughts and feelings surrounding the shooting to the back of my mind and concentrated on inspecting the bonfire area.

Goodwin Park had been divided into sections with the town Christmas tree in the middle, the bonfire and other activities at the far end, and a holiday hamlet of vendor booths located nearest the entrance.

The market ran from Sunday through the following Saturday, with several special events planned. The lighting of the tree had been the featured activity for Sunday. Monday through Friday would be concerts and Christmas carol sing-alongs, story time and photo ops with Santa, and a theatrical reading of A Christmas Carol accompanied by live orchestration courtesy of the Noble County Chamber Ensemble.

To turn the temperate region of Sanctuary Bay, South Carolina into a winter wonderland, I'd hired a company that specialized in movie special effects. Each night after the market closed, workers would replenish a special polymer-based snow by spraying a light dusting over the shrubs and trees, but I'd also brought in a machine that produced real snow.

Frosty's Kingdom was a fenced off area located in the Reindeer Games section of the market. All week long, kids who might never have seen snow could frolic in the wet stuff, and Friday night would see the families of Sanctuary Bay pitted against one another in a snowman building contest.

Along with the snow machine, I'd rented an ice-skating rink, bouncy castle, and children's train. Judging by the lines The Colonel and I walked past on our way to the bonfire; Reindeer Games was the most popular attraction.

At the farthest end of the park, I'd assembled a fire pit and on the final evening, a roaring bonfire would light the night. Pastor Duke Mobley and his biker congregation would have a booth selling smores kits and hotdogs on a stick. Our theater group would lead charades, and Name That Tune would be played with a local musician.

Until Saturday, the area was fenced off. I glanced around. Everything was as we'd left it, so The Colonel and I strolled over to the cluster of tents I'd named Santa's Workshop. My best friend Connie had helped me finalize the décor for the market, but the holidays were a busy time for her craft store, and she hadn't been able to assist me in setting up the event.

For my last job, I'd hired my brother Dewey, but after being cleared of murder, he'd managed to get a job as a watchman with Sentinel Security. I was happy to see him gainfully employed but it'd left me in a bind until college let out for the holidays, and Madison Ross had been looking for a project to keep her from dwelling on the death of her father.

Setting up the event had been a logistical nightmare; coordinating with rental companies, volunteers, vendors, and city officials as well as placing decorations. Madison had taken responsibility for the Reindeer Games and Santa's Workshop areas while I focused on the holiday hamlet and the town square. The bonfire had been assembled by the fire department.

Looking around Santa's Workshop was firsthand proof that I'd been right to hire Madison. I'd known her since she worked as a barista at the Split Bean; we'd bonded over a mutual love of dogs and her desire to become a cop, but I'd given her the job because of her no-nonsense management style and ability to keep the wheels on the proverbial bus. Sympathy was also a factor in my decision; I knew what it was like to lose a father without warning.

Madison was also active in a local sewing guild and had convinced them to participate in the market. That club had brought others, and now Santa's Workshop had craft booths selling handcrafted items along with offering free tutorials and projects for kids of all ages. Its appeal rivaled the Reindeer Games.

Everything looked to be running smoothly. My eyes widened as I caught sight of Valentina DeMarco assisting at one of the craft tables run by the Saint Cecelia's by the Sea church. Her black leggings, knee high boots, and blue and gold Christmas sweater were a far cry from the Italian suits she usually wore, and her long black hair was pulled into a low ponytail instead of a chignon. I'd never seen the elegant CFO of the DeMarco Canning Company so animated or relaxed.

Valentina was manning the children's face painting table and she'd gotten into the spirit of the event by transforming her own. Cobalt blue makeup covered her, neck to jawline. The same shade of blue had been applied around both eyes, ending in a point on either side of her nose. Swaths of teal were blended with the cobalt to form a mask, and the medallion shapes of peacock feathers were drawn on her forehead in the same shades of teal, cobalt, and gold. With her dark eyes and olive skin the effect was stunning.

A small, chubby-cheeked boy pulled himself into the chair and pointed to the image he wanted painted onto his face. Valentina smiled and teased as she quickly transformed the little boy into a tiger. Her artistic talent was obvious, and I couldn't help but wonder what she'd have become if she hadn't been born a DeMarco; the calm, cool, and collected financial officer of a multimillion-dollar company was at odds with the whimsical woman I was watching.

The Colonel and I hung out a few minutes longer, observing the various tutorials on offer and doing a bit of window shopping when I could get close enough to a table. My bulldog drew attention, particularly that of children, and the main thoroughfare was jam packed with short humans, making me reluctant to go further into workshop. "C'mon, buddy, let's go around."

Intent on charming ice cream from a toddler, it took me three tries before The Colonel acquiesced. We walked around behind the tents and exited at the end of the workshop, next to the Sew Creative craft table.

I needn't have bothered taking the longer way around, the crowd of families and kids I'd intended to avoid were all crowded around my assistant's booth and, judging by the off-colored language and semi-hysterical shrieks, I was guessing a sudden interest in sewing wasn't the draw.

I winced as some particularly rough words floated on the breeze. The ages of the kids made the shouting fest doubly unacceptable. Intending to shut down whatever was transpiring, I pushed my way through the rubberneckers but gasped as my gaze fell upon the participants.

Clutching a piece of plaid fabric in one hand and punctuating her rant by waving a pair of silver scissors, my highly competent and imminently professional assistant was red faced and almost frothing at the mouth.

Eyes wide in a pale face and curly brown hair standing up at odd angles, Madison leaned across the folding table and shouted at a tall blonde wearing a skintight sweater dress.

"Liar! You were only with Daddy for his money, and you tricked him into marriage!" Madison snorted. "He only changed his will because of your lies!"

The heavily made-up woman smirked and ran her hand down her side, resting it on her thrust out hip. "Your father adored me, and he was lonely." She arched a perfectly drawn brow. "I made Clay's last days pleasurable, why shouldn't I be compensated?"

"Look at her, she's no better than she ought to be."

I frowned and glanced over to find Gary Walston and Kay Emory beside me. "Who is she?"

Gary's jaw was working overtime as he aggressively chomped on his gum. His eyes were hard as he glared at the scene unfolding in front of us, but Kay steered her electric chair a bit closer to me and tipped her head toward the tent. "That's Brianna Bellamy Ross."

Kay glared in the blonde's direction. "A cheap floozy. I don't blame Madison for yelling at her; I'd do more than yell if she seduced my father and turned him against me."

"What?" My eyes widened. "Are you telling me Clayton and Madison weren't speaking?"

Kay's chin went up and she gave a sharp nod.

I shook my head and tried to reconcile that with what I knew of the Ross family. Emma Ross had died of cancer when Madison was in middle school. Clayton had stepped up and been both mother and father.

Madison had worshipped her dad, and Clayton thought the sun rose and set with his daughter. They were a loving family, and I couldn't believe one woman had been able to come between them. I said as much, and Kay smirked.

"Morals of an alley cat but there is no denying she's beautiful, if you like the cheap, plastic, bimbo look."

Dressed in a short, body-con dress of kelly green, the new Mrs. Ross was endowed with curves in all the right places. From Kay's insinuations, I assumed her large and semi-exposed attributes were fake.

A glance at the long blonde tresses made me wonder if they were also not standard issue. I murmured my suspicions and was rewarded with more details of the bombshell's behaviors and beauty secrets than I ever wished to know.

"I can't believe you don't know her!" Kay rolled her eyes. "Do you watch any television?" She didn't wait for my reply. "I thought everyone had heard of Brianna Bellamy and her infamous sex tape! It rocketed her back into the spotlight when her singing career fizzled. Then she got that reality TV show … nothing? Not ringing any bells?"

I chuckled. "Nope, sorry. I'm at least twenty years out of date music wise and we don't have cable. The only shows I watch are over a decade old." I shrugged. "No interest in the exploitive stuff that passes for television now."

"Unbelievable." She shrugged. "But in this case, you didn't miss anything. She went off to Hollywood and there was talk that she would be starring in that big blockbuster action-hero movie." She snorted. "All of a sudden it was announced that another actress got the part. Right after that Brianna moved into the house on Pineview Way and within a month she had her claws into Clayton Ross."

Kay's gossip went in one ear and out the other, I was too busy watching my assistant. Madison had a white-knuckled grip on the edge of the table and her expression said she was close to the end of her tether.

Brianna Bellamy Ross's face was set in a bland mask of haughty disdain, though the way she fidgeted with the gold scarf draped around her neck gave away her agitation.

Madison's face paled and her lower lip trembled. Her voice was strangled from suppressed emotions. "You caused hard feelings between me and my dad—"

"Oh please, that's on you." Brianna tossed the end of her scarf over her shoulder and pointed at Madison with a perfectly shaped red and white striped fingernail. "What did you expect your father to do when you lied about his wife?"

"Some wife." Madison hissed and her eyes narrowed to slits. "I saw you with Caleb!"

Brianna pouted. "A girl's got to a have a little fun."

Madison's eyes bulged and her mouth opened and closed like a fish out of water. She swallowed convulsively. "First my father and then my fiancée! You, you gold-digging whor—"

"Darling," Brianna quirked a brow. "Is that anyway to talk to your stepmother?" Her painted lips quirked into a smirk. "Relax, you can have the fiancée back,"—her nose wrinkled as she gave a mock shudder— "but maybe buy him an instruction manual before your wedding night."

A vein in Madison's forehead throbbed, and I worried she'd have a stroke. Her stepmother blithely carried on her verbal abuse.

"And, as for money, your college is paid for and, according to your father's will, you get everything when I die." She turned to walk away and then looked back over her shoulder, waving her ring finger so that all eyes were drawn to the large diamond nestled there. She smiled and mocked. "If there's anything left …"

"You hateful witch!" Madison ran around the table and grabbed Brianna's arm. "That ring belonged to my mother!"

"And now it's mine." Brianna laughed and shook off Madison's hold. Her heavily made-up eyes gleamed with malice as she flashed a cold smile. "Didn't you ever wonder why your father left everything to me?"

"You tricked him! Daddy would never have—"

"Tricked? Poor, deluded Madison." Brianna's lips turned down in a fake moue of sympathy as she shook her head. "Your father often told me what a burden it'd been to raise you."

"Liar! My father never said—"

"Oh, but he did!" She turned and started to walk away, "He also resented your mother—ah!"

A collective gasp rose above the din as Madison leapt at Brianna's back and grabbed the ends of her dangling scarf. "Shut up, you filthy—"

"Help! She's strangling me ... someone call the police!"

"Right, that's enough!" I handed The Colonel's leash to Gary and pushed my way through the crowd. "Madison! Have you lost your mind?"

Prying her fingers from the scarf, I dragged my assistant away as she and Brianna continued to hurl invectives.

"She assaulted me! You're all witnesses! Did someone video it? I'll see you in court, you crazy bitc—"

"Keep running your mouth you filthy tramp! Give me half a chance and I'll shut you up permanently and—"

"Madison!" Panting like she'd run a mile; her eyes were wild and not quite focused. I shook the younger woman until her mouth snapped closed and she met my gaze. "Take a deep breath."

Half turning, I hollered. "Ms. Ross, you need to leave." Brianna Bellamy Ross tossed her head and sneered but another hard look from me and she stalked off.

Turning back to Madison, I waited to speak until her breathing had evened out. "Madison, I know you're hurting but what you just did is assault! You'll be lucky if she doesn't file charges. You can't be a police officer with a conviction." My usually levelheaded assistant made no comment, merely glaring at the spot where Brianna had been and muttering under her breath.

I managed to catch the words "daddy" and "money" before I gave up and nudged her toward the exit. "You need to calm down. If you think that woman somehow connived her way into inheriting from your father then get a lawyer, but you can't go around choking people."

Posture rigid and lips pressed into a firm line, it was clear she hadn't heard a word I said. I sighed. "Go home, Maddie."

"I don't have a home, Holly!"

I blinked as Madison turned blazing eyes on me. "That vile woman stole it and I hope she dies!" She stomped off toward the bonfire area.

"Madison, you can't get through that way!" I yelled at her retreating back. "The gates to the parking area are locked. You'll have to go around—"

"I have a key." She hollered over her shoulder, never breaking stride.

Once she disappeared into the shadows, I returned to the workshop booths. Kay Emory rolled up accompanied by Gary. He handed me The Colonel's leash as I was contemplating going after Madison; something told me she shouldn't be left alone.

"I hope she's just going to cool off ..."

Deep in thought, I frowned down at Kay. "Huh? She needs to go home and sleep it off. She could have hurt Brianna!"

Kay shrugged. "She deserved it."

"Kay!"

"Well, she does! Everyone hates her, Holly."

I glanced at Gary and found him nodding his head in agreement. My brows rose, the woman really hadn't ingratiated herself with the islanders!

"Well, that may be but Maddie's better off away from here tonight. "

Gary cleared his throat. "Madison is on the causeway committee ..."

Kay gasped. "That's right! We need her to take a turn in the booth!" She dug into her bag and pulled out a cell phone. "I'll just call and remind her."

"Better if you replace her, Kay."

"But Holly, it'll mess up the rotation! "

My leg was protesting in earnest and if The Colonel pawing at Kay's festive holiday leggings was any indication, he was getting anxious. It was time to head home. I waved, ignoring her continued arguments. "Have a good night, Kay."

She huffed and spun her chair around, yammering at Gary as they walked back toward Santa's Workshop. Turning to leave, I noticed Valentina DeMarco and a woman dressed as an elf that I thought was Felicity Simms enter into a heated discussion with Gary and Kay.

The way that they pointed toward the sewing booth left no doubt they were rehashing the scene we'd just witnessed and, being Sanctuary Bay, no doubt tongues would be wagging all over town before morning.

The crowd thinned out as we approached the Christmas tree. We were strolling along when The Colonel picked up the scent of something, probably food, and jerked me into a trot.

"Hey, boy, heel!" I tightened my grip on his lead and gave a sharp tug, but a bulldog on the trail was a tough beast to dissuade. Pulled through the field, I struggled to keep his pace and avoid running into other visitors.

I tried once again to rein in The Colonel but that broke my concentration and in short order, I'd walked into someone's back.

"Oh my gosh, I'm so sorry! Are you hurt?"

"Hello Deputy Daye."

I gulped and stumbled backwards as Roland Dupree, father of the young man I'd shot and killed while serving in the Noble County Sheriff's Department, turned to face me. He held my gaze but said nothing.

Uncomfortable, I looked down, absently noting he was wearing a pair of dirty tennis shoes and workout pants. Desperate to chase away thoughts of the shooting, my mind latched on to the oddity of his appearance.

Our paths had crossed over the years, whether at charity functions or various dinners and parties my husband had dragged me to. As a personal injury attorney, Roland Dupree was famous throughout the Lowcountry, and he'd always looked like he stepped from the pages of a gentlemen's magazine.

Custom suits, gold watches, and monogrammed cufflinks; he'd oozed wealth and power, but he was a shell of that man now. I glanced at his face and stifled a gasp. Aside from the ratty clothing, his complexion was ashen, and a day's growth of hair dotted his cheeks and chin.

Stunned as I was by his unkempt appearance, it was the hollow, vacant look in his brown eyes that put a lump in my throat. My palms started to sweat. I struggled for words. "I ... er, Roland I ..."

The social niceties drummed into me by Mama kept running through my head but, throat drier than the Sahara, I couldn't make a sound. Besides, I'm sorry for your loss. I'm sorry I killed your son; What was the appropriate platitude in such a situation? Shawn Dupree was dead by my hand ...

Without warning a vision of that fateful night at the hunting camp rose in my mind.

The lights are blinding, I shade my eyes and try to figure out what is lying in the road. A deer? No ... the hair on the back of my neck stands on end, I raise my gun hand above the car door, finger inching toward the trigger—

Roland touched my arm and cleared his throat, pulling me back from the abyss of my memories. My stomach rolled as our gazes collided.

He opened his mouth to speak, and my heart kicked into overdrive. Civilized discourse dictated I should express some remorse for killing his son, only I realized with a start that I felt no guilt or shame; in fact, I felt nothing. Bile rose in my throat and my heartbeat pounded in my ears ... I needed-Oh, God, I couldn't—

Without thought, I pivoted around Dupree and started to hobble away as fast as my bum leg could manage, dragging The Colonel toward the parking lot like the hounds of hell were nipping at my heels.

Order your copy of Carolers and Corpses
Available on Amazon and Other Major Retailers. Ask your
favorite book store to order your copy today!

Welcome to Sanctuary Bay!

If you're new to the area, Holly and her friends have had several adventures!

Back when Holly was still a Noble County Sheriff's Deputy, she tracked a ring of thieves and met The Colonel.

See how Holly's little buddy got his name by reading the prequel, **Hounds and Heists!**

Visit www.rachellynneauthor.com to read this snippet of Holly's past as a FREE eBook or find it in paperback on Amazon.

Holly has moved on from her law enforcement days and started *CoaStyle,* but decorating for events has certainly not led to a slow and safe lifestyle!

Following her debut as a decorator in **Masquerades and Murder**, Holly went on to create a Christmas market for the town in **Carolers and Corpses** and then tracked a killer to Sandpoint Abbey in **Priests and Poison**.

You'd think our reluctant sleuth could catch a break by decorating for a wedding in **Plantations and Allegations** but ... as The Colonel says, the *Lady that Pays the Bills* finds trouble wherever she goes.

Lucky for Holly, her bulldog is always on the case!

After surviving the events surrounding the *wedding of the year,* Holly took a much needed vacation and celebrated the cooler temperatures by organizing a fall festival but,

with a corn maze full of **Scarecrows and Scandals** she's sure to find herself in the thick of things!

There will be 12 books in the Holly Daye Series as our decorator friend fills her calendar with clients every month and slowly unravels the secrets behind the shooting that ended her law enforcement career.

Stay tuned, it promises to be a wild ride!

Since you've finished my book, it'd be redundant to tell you that I'm a writer. But I'm also a mom, a grandma, a housewife, and a former grocery worker; all titles I proudly hold!

I wrote my first book, Ring of Lies in 2011, got the idea for Broken Chords and wrote a few chapters and then promptly let life get in the way. I did volunteer work while I homeschooled my daughter and helped my husband start a business but, when she decided to attend high school, I decided to find work outside the home.

I was managing a department in a grocery store, (which I loved doing) and I'd find myself writing stories while I put away stock; there is something about muscle memory work that lets the subconscious play. I started carrying a sharpie in my pocket along with my box cutter and, when I'd get an idea, a snippet of conversation between characters, or a creative way to axe someone I'd scribble it on a piece of cardboard!

As much as I loved my job, I realized I had some pretty good ideas on those scraps of empty boxes and that is when I quit and started writing full time. To date, I have 8 books published with many more to come: there's no stopping me now!

All of my books take place in and around the Lowcountry of South Carolina and Georgia because that is where I call home and I am in awe of this region's natural beauty and its history.

Join my newsletter, The Cozy Crew Club, and you'll hear more than you probably ever wanted to know about the Lowcountry and its unique culture.

Follow me on Facebook and Instagram. You'll see my crazy menagerie of animals, the day trips my husband I take, recipes, chapter readings, and more!

Hope to meet you soon!

Rachel

To be a part of Rachel Lynne's Cozy Crew Club go to www.rachellynneauthor.com

You can also find Rachel active on Facebook and Instagram under Rachel Lynne, Author and links are provided on her website.

www.ingramcontent.com/pod-product-compliance
Lightning Source LLC
Chambersburg PA
CBHW060610300726
48975CB00005B/1521